楊佳瑜◎著

iBT 學術
新托福字彙
「勝」經

必背精華版

Must Words for TOEFL iBT

最新具指標性的iBT新托福單字書

只需要 **2000⁺** 必背學術英單 ＋ 延伸同、反義關鍵字彙

輕鬆應戰 iBT 新托福 必背、必備！

◎ **最詳實擬真！**
iBT新托福分類式學術閱讀：
→ **字彙量＋閱讀能力＋聽力** 同步快速提升
突破iBT 110⁺！

MP3

作者序

　　文字是最有力的軟實力，懂的單字越多，就越能精準的表達自己。托福不只測試考生的單字量，更挑戰對單字的敏感度，因此，就算是碰到不懂的字，也要練習從上下文推測意思。英文就和中文一樣，可以非常有彈性的調整用詞，因此，學習單字不能只是死背，更要靈活的練習用不同的方式「換句話說」。

　　本書的特色在於用文章引出單字，讓讀者在閱讀的同時，非常自然的消化單字。文章的選題廣泛，囊括歷史、文化、科技、科學、商學、自然、地理、人文科學、藝術等範疇。每一章有四到五個單元，每個單元有兩篇文章，第一篇大多是該主題的概論介紹，第二篇是趣事探討。為了刺激讀者的批判性思考能力，筆者刻意在某些單元中安排前後兩篇文章分別討論同一主題的正反論點，甚至涉獵種族歧視、性別平等、氣候變遷、廢核等議題。

　　語言的學習沒有最好，只有更好。除了幫助準備托福考試之外，更希望本書可以啟發讀者學習的興趣，讓讀者觸類旁通，從多元議題延伸學習，這樣考過托福順利出國後，才能用更寬大的心胸與世界接軌。學會了單字，要刺激思考，這樣才能靈活運用，內化成自己的「單字庫」！

楊佳瑜

編者序

　　為了能幫助考生更有效率準備 iBT 新托福考試，本書因而誕生。有效記憶 iBT 新托福字彙於聽、說、讀、寫四大項目上的成績都能有顯著提升。於選錄 iBT 字彙上，作者精心規劃 iBT 新托福一定會碰上的學術類文章，從歷史、文化、科學科技、行銷商業、自然地理到人文藝術 7 大類型，並於每大類文章中整理出常見的 iBT 字彙、相關同反義字、延伸字彙；藉由書裡擬真的學術文章，讀者便可熟悉各種閱讀文類，於吸收新知的同時，還能有系統地建立自己的字彙量。累積單字，不再雜亂無章且有效率！

　　不過，字彙的累積最終仍舊要回歸到閱讀，從閱讀找到字彙的意義和「位置」，如此字彙才會在腦海裡留下深刻的印象，也才能記下更多相關的單字。為了能讓讀者慢慢找回閱讀的樂趣，每個單元皆收錄兩篇文章，一篇程度較難；另一篇則減少一些沉甸甸的專業知識，程度較為簡單，讓考生準備考試的空檔，也能稍稍思考、彙整一下。另外記憶單字的技巧在於多聽，跟著本書的 MP3，邊聽外師錄製的學術短文，磨練英語聽力，iBT 新托福單字、聽力、閱讀能力藉此一次提升，勝利達成 110 分以上！

編輯部

目次
Contents

Part 1 　歷史篇 History

Part 2　文化篇 Culture

Part 3　科學科技篇
Science and Technology

Part 4

行銷商業篇
Marketing and Commerce

Part 5

自然地理篇
Nature and Geography

Part 6 人文篇 Humanities

Part 7 　藝術篇 Art

Unit **01**

—————————— 1.1 —————————— Track 01

The Cradle of Civilization

Far before the Western world became the **dominant** mainstream culture, there were already the Four **Cradles** of **Civilization** – Egypt, **Mesopotamia**, **Indus Valley** and China.

The Egyptian civilization **flourished** in the **Nile Valley** between 3200 BC and 340 BC. The predictable flooding and **irrigation** of the Nile Valley produced **fertile** ground for agriculture, supporting their rich culture of Egyptian civilization. The Egyptians were ruled by their absolute monarch, the **pharaohs**, whose pyramids have been guarded by the great **Sphinx** even today.

The Mesopotamia civilization occurred in roughly the **territory** of today's Iraq. The mass population grew in the area between the Tigris and Euphrates Rivers. The three main groups of the residents were the **Sumerian**, the **Babylonians**, and the **Assyrians**. The Sumerians invented **Cuneiform** around 5000 BC which was the first written language of human civilization.

The Indus Valley civilization, also known as the Harappan

Part 1

Part 2

Part 3

Part 4

Part 5

Part 6

Part 7

civilization, was located at today's **Pakistan**. The first site was excavated in the 1920s with lots of **vessels**, accessories, and ancient coins discovered. So far, the Harappan civilization remains the most mysterious ancient civilization as the linguists are still in the process of figuring out the Harappan words.

The civilization of China, can be traced back to more than a thousand years ago, originated from the Yellow River Valley. Throughout the history, there were more than twenty **dynasties** with different cultures and languages. The last dynasty, Qing, ended in 1911. One of the biggest legacies, the **Great Wall**, still stands miles across the North of China today.

中文翻譯

文明的搖籃

在西方世界佔據主流文化之位前,早有四大古文明的存在,也就是埃及、**美索不達米亞**、**印度河流域**以及中國古文明。

埃及文明在大約西元前 3200 到西元前 340 年間,於尼羅河域**蓬勃**發展。可預測掌握的河水氾濫和**灌溉**,培養出利於農業發展的**肥沃**土地,並支持其豐富的文化發展。**法老王**以完全君主制統治埃及人,其金字塔如今仍由**人面獅身像**保衛著。

美索不達米亞文化起源於大約如今的伊朗**地區**。大量的人口成長於底格拉斯河與幼發拉底河的兩河流域之間,當時的三個主要族群為**蘇美人**、巴比倫人與亞述人。其中，蘇美人於大約西元前五千年發明楔形文字，是人類文明發展出的第一種書寫文字。

印度河流域古文明又稱為哈拉帕文明，位在今天的巴基斯坦。其第一座古蹟於 1920 年發掘，找出許多器皿、首飾配件和古錢幣。由於語言學家仍在解讀哈拉帕文字，目前這仍然是最多謎團的古文明。

中國文明可被追溯遠至超過1500年前。觀其歷史，有超過二十個朝代發展出不同的文化和語言。最後的朝代清朝，結束於 1911 年。最大的古蹟之一，萬里長城，如今仍屹立橫跨中國北方。

 重點字彙

1.　世界四大古文明：

- **Egypt** 埃及古文明
- **Mesopotamia** 美索不達米亞古文明
- **Indus Valley** 印度河流域古文明
- **China** 中國古文明

2.　**dominant**（*adj.*）佔優勢的、支配的、統治的；（遺傳基因）顯性的；**dominate**（*v.*）支配、統治、控制

① He stands at a dominant position behind the president.
　他在總統的背後具有統治權力。

② The kingdom was dominated by that single family for centuries.
　這個王國被單一家族統治數百年。

Part 1
Part 2
Part 3
Part 4
Part 5
Part 6
Part 7

3. **civil**（*adj.*）民用的、公民的；（法律）民事的；文明；
civilized（*adj.*）文明的、開化的；**civilization**（*n.*）文明

Please, gentlemen, can we solve this problem in a more civilized way?
各位先生們，我們能不能用文明一點的方式解決問題？

4. **cradle**（*n.*）搖籃；發源地；撫育

① The parents lean against the cradle watching their baby falling asleep.
這對父母靠在搖籃前，看著寶寶入睡。

② Jerusalem is the holy site that cradled Judaism, Christianity, and Islam.
耶路撒冷是孕育出猶太教、基督教和伊斯蘭教的聖地。

5. **flourish**（*v.*）茂盛、繁榮；炫耀

After struggling for the first six months, their business finally started to flourish.
熬過了頭六個月之後，他們的生意總算開始旺了起來。

6. **Nile Valley**（*n.*）尼羅河流域

The flooding of Nile River is a blessing that brings fertile soil.
尼羅河的氾濫是帶來肥沃土壤的好運。

相關字彙

● **Pharaoh** 法老王；**sphinx** 人面獅身像；**pyramid** 金字塔

Despite the Pharaoh's curse, the grave robbers still walked through the Sphinx to explore the treasures under the pyramid.

儘管有法老王的詛咒，盜墓者仍從人面獅身像面前走過，探索金字塔底下的寶藏。

7. **irrigate**（*v.*）灌溉

The whole county relies on the reservoir to irrigate the land.

整個縣都靠這個水庫灌溉土地

8. **fertile**（*adj.*）肥沃的；多產的；**fertility**（*n.*）生育能力

① Their farm occupies the most fertile land in this area.

他們的農場占了這個地區最肥沃的土地。

② In the past, women's only value was their fertility of producing male heirs.

在過去，女人唯一的價值就是生出男性繼承人的能力。

9. **territory**（*n.*）區域；領域、領土

The dog barks at the postman as he steps in the territory of its master's house.

郵差一踏進主人房子的領地範圍內，狗就開始對他狂吠。

10. 世界四大古文明居民

● **Sumerian** 蘇美人;**Babylonian** 巴比倫人;**Assyrian** 亞述人

The Sumerians, the Babylonians and, the Assyrians lived in different parts of the Mesopotamia area.

蘇美人、巴比倫人和亞述人居住在兩河流域的不同地區。

11. **cuneiform**（*n.*）楔形文字

The archaeologist found a stone tablet inscribed in cuneiform.

考古學家找到了一個刻有楔形文字的石板。

12. **Pakistan**（*n.*）巴基斯坦;**Palestine**（*n.*）巴勒斯坦

The conflict between Israel and Palestine has made Gaza a living hell.

以色列和巴基斯坦之間的衝突,讓加薩走廊變成人間煉獄。

13. **vessel**（*n.*）容器、器皿;血管

同義字 container

① Carrying heavy vessels on their heads is just a piece of cake for Ghanaian women.

用頭頂沉甸甸的容器,對迦納婦女來說只是小事一樁。

② Her skin is so pale that you can almost see the vessels beneath.

她的皮膚白到你幾乎看的到底下的血管。

——————— 1.2 ———————   **Track 02**

Archaeology

Archaeology is the study of human activities in the past. It is often associated with humanity, **social science**, and **anthropology**. Archaeology work process starts from **surveying**, **excavation** and then finally to the analysis of the data left from the past.

Although a load of lab work including historical researches and paper works such as reports, publications or administration works need to be done, **field work** is still the most exciting part of being an archaeologist. An archaeology project requires lots of digging so that mysterious site can be revealed. On-site archaeology field workers should be able to analyze the **stratigraphy** of the site. This is particularly important when a site was occupied by more than one culture and had been built layers and layers of which the relatively recent ones lie above the ancient ones. **Sampling** is very crucial for the work. For instance, sampling the soil or stone can help date the eras and locate the source of the material. Sampling the hair or teeth of the body found can also be used to identify the person by using DNA technology and even help understand the health and medical conditions in the past.

中文翻譯

考古學

考古學專門研究過去的人類活動，通常與人文、**社會科學**和**人類學**習習相關。考古工作流程先**考察**、**發掘**，最後再就過去留下的資料進行分析。

雖然也是有許多實驗室工作、歷史研究、諸如報告、出版發表或行政等文書工作要做，**現場實地探勘**仍然是考古學家工作中，最興奮的一環。考古計畫需要大量挖土才能讓神秘的古蹟重現天日。現場工作人員必須有能力分析現場的**地質分層**，這對曾有不只一個文化站駐過的地點尤其重要，因為地底會有一層一層的建物，年份越近的越上面，年代久遠的則在底下。**抽樣**也是非常重要的工作，舉例說，對土壤和石頭抽樣，可以幫助追溯年代以及推論建材的出產地，對出土的遺體抽樣其頭髮或牙齒，也可以利用 DNA 技術比對身分，甚至幫助了解過去的健康醫療情況。

 重點字彙

1. **archaeology**（*adj.*）考古學；**archaeologist**（*n.*）考古學

Due to his poor health, the archaeologist left the field to work in the lab.

因為體力不支，這位考古學家離開挖掘現場，改到實驗室工作。

2. **social science**（*n.*）社會科學；**sociology**（*n.*）社會學；**sociologist**（*n.*）社會學家

Social science is the study of societies and the relationship among individuals within. Sociology is a branch of social science that study social behavior.

社會科學是研究社會及其內部人們之間的關係的學科，社會學則是社會科學的一個分支，研究社會行為。

3. **anthropology**（*n.*）人類學；**anthropologist**（*n.*）人類學家

The anthropological understanding of human origins might be challenged by the new excavation.

最新的挖掘出土，可能挑戰目前人類學對於人類起源的認知。

4. **survey**（*n.*）調查、測量、考察；民意調查

① The marketing team took an in depth survey on consumers' preferences on online shopping platforms.

行銷團隊針對消費者的線上購物平台喜好，做了非常深入的調查。

② The two candidates received very close numbers in the latest survey.

兩位候選人在最新的民意調查中數字相當接近。

5. **excavate**（*v.*）挖掘、開鑿；（古物）發掘

The channel was excavated for the pope to escape to a safe shelter.

地道是為了確保教宗逃到安全住所所鑿的。

6. **field work**（*v.*）野外工事、野外探勘；現場訪問

Compared with the boring paper work, she enjoys meeting with people on the site much more.

比起無聊的紙本作業來說，她更喜歡去到現場工作認識別人。

7. **stratigraphy**（*n.*）地層成層情況

By analyzing the stratigraphy of the Ice Cap, researchers figured the pattern of climate changes.

藉由分析冰帽的成層情況，研究員描繪出氣候變遷的模式。

8. **sample**（*n.*）採樣；樣本

The beauty company gives out samples of their new product in the launch event.

美妝公司在發表會上發送新產品的樣本試用品。

iBT 新托福字彙閱讀應試技巧

Question 1: Which of the following combination is not correct?

(A) Egyptian Civilization and Nile River

(B) Mesopotamia Civilization and Tigris River

(C) Euphrates Civilization and Indus River

(D) China Civilization and Yellow River

解析 本題意在測驗古文明及其重要河流的關係，(A) 尼羅河孕育出埃及古文明；(B) 美索不達米亞位在底格拉斯河與幼發拉底河的兩河流域之間；(D) 中國文明起源自黃河流域，但 (C) 印度河流域發展出的應是哈拉帕文明，幼發拉底為兩河流域之一的河流，故錯誤的組合為選項 (C)。

Question 2: Who invented the first written language in human civilization?

(A) Egyptians

(B) Chinese

(C) Babylonians

(D) Sumerians

解析 蘇美人於西元前五千年發明的楔形文字，是人類文明的第一種書寫語言，因此正確答案為 (D)。

Question 3: There are four graduates applying for the position in the new archaeology project. Who is the least likely to get the job?

(A) Sue struggles to remember the exact number of the years. But she never messed up with the order of eras.

(B) Jimmy cannot work long hours in the field due to his injury but he knows how to use all the equipment in the laboratory.

(C) Pierre graduated with the highest score but his supervisor noted in a report that he lost an ash urn excavated from an ancient tomb.

(D) Celine doesn't have much experience in the field but her in depth historical research have been selected to publish in several world class publications.

解析　(A) 蘇雖然常常忘記確切年份，但從不弄錯各年代的順序，這在有多種文化駐留過的地區非常重要。(B) 吉米有傷不能在挖掘現場長時間工作，但他會操作所有儀器，可以在實驗室工作。(D) 席琳沒什麼實地經驗，但她精闢的歷史研究被多個世界級出版單位選中出版，本計畫可藉她的長才撰寫出版報告。然而，(C) 皮耶雖然高分畢業，但指導教授卻註明他曾在一個古墓挖掘工程中遺失一個骨灰罈，這會讓考古工作無法從骨灰中取樣研究，因此，答案為 (C)，皮耶較不適合這份工作。

Unit 02

—————————————— 2.1 ——————————————   Track 03

The Colonial History

The Colonization History originated during the **Age of Discovery** started by Portugal and Spain. The Portuguese established the first global **empire** in history. This practice was followed by England, France, and the Netherlands to set up colonies in America, Africa, Asia and the Pacifics. The European countries benefitted from trading the goods from the colonies, including spices, tea, coca, sugar, gold, etc.

By the year of 1922, the British Empire had become the largest global power and ruled up to one-fifth of the world's population and almost a quarter of global land area.

Despite the fact that some of the colonial authorities introduced modern development to their colonies such as railway, education system and medical care, colonization is still a **brutal** history. Forces, or even **massacre** were used to **suppress** those who **disobeyed**. The colonized people were **stripped of** with their language, religions and cultures. Colonizers **exploited** natural resources for their interests, leaving **permanent** damage to the land. After most of the

previously colonized areas gained independence, some of them still used the colonizers' languages as the official languages as they've already lost the mother tongues. Even until now, most of the previously colonized areas still suffer from global globalization whilst the European countries continue enjoying the privileges established by their colonizer **ancestors**.

中文翻譯

殖民史

殖民史始於由葡萄牙和西班牙掀起的**大航海時代**，葡萄牙人建起了史上第一個全球性的**帝國**。這個範例引起英國、法國和荷蘭跟進，紛紛在美洲、非洲、亞洲和大洋洲建起殖民地。這些歐洲國家利用從殖民地奪取的商品，進行貿易並從中獲利，包括香料、糖、黃金等等。到了 1922 年，大英帝國統治全球五分之一的人口，遍部將近四分之一的陸地面積，成為當時全球最大的勢力。

儘管有些殖民當局在殖民地引進了一些現代發展，例如鐵路、教育系統和醫療技術，殖民仍然是一部**血淋淋的**歷史。**拒絕服從**的人被武力**鎮壓**，甚至遭到**大屠殺**。殖民地人民的語言、宗教和文化都**被剝奪**。殖民者**剝削**自然資源以中飽私囊，讓土地留下**永久性的**傷害。即便在大部分的前殖民地獨立之後，有些國家仍使用前殖民者的語言作為官方語言，因為他們早已失去自己的母語。直至今日，大部分的前殖民地仍然在全球經濟中屈居劣勢，而歐洲國家仍然享受他們殖民者**祖先**所立下的優勢。

重點字彙

1. privilege（*n.*）優勢

Born in a highly privileged family, he never suffered from hunger yet felt for the poor.

他出身極佳，從沒挨過餓，卻對窮人感同身受。

2. Age of Discovery（*n.*）大航海時代

Tea was a luxury in the spice trade during the Age of Discovery.

在大航海時代下的香料貿易裡，茶葉是昂貴的奢侈品。

3. empire（*n.*）帝國；大企業

Who would believe that his business empire started from a small rice vendor?

誰會相信他如今的大企業當初是從小小的米販起家的呢？

4. brutal（*n.*）殘忍的、殘暴的、嚴苛的

Tens of thousands of refugees left their homeland to escape from the brutal civil war.

數以萬計的難民為了逃離殘酷的內戰，而離開家園。

5. **massacre**（*n.*）大屠殺

It's hard to imagine there was a massacre taking place here before as fear kept people silent for decades.

很難想像這裡以前發生過大屠殺事件，恐懼讓人們幾十年來都保持沉默。

6. **suppress**（*n.*）鎮壓

The government is condemned for sending armed police to suppress such a peaceful protest.

政府因為派武裝警察鎮壓和平抗議而備受譴責。

與 condemn 相關的 延伸字彙

同義字 blame, castigate

反義字 acclaim, applaud, commend, extol

7. **obey**（*v.*）服從

延伸字彙

- **obedient／obedience**（*adj.／n.*）順從（的）；**disobedient／disobedience**（*adj.／n.*）不服從（的）
- **compliant, in compliance with, acquiescent, submissive, yielding**
- ① Unlike her obedient mother, she grew up as an independent woman.

  不像他個性順從的母親，他長大後成為一個獨立自主的女性。

② Montgomery Bus Boycott Movement, started by an African American woman being arrested for refusing to give a seat to a white man, was one of the first practices of civil disobedience.

從一位非裔美國女性拒絕讓座給白人男性開始的蒙哥馬利公車抵制運動，是最早的公民抗命表率之一。

③ The students are too submissive to the teacher's orders and are incapable to make decisions themselves.

這群學生對老師的命令太過順從，無法自己做決定。

④ All construction work must be carried out in compliance with safety regulations.

所有的營建工程都必須依照安全法規施行。

8. **strip**（v.）剝奪；**deprive sb of sth**（ph.）剝奪

① The heavy house work occupied all her time and even the very last bit of freedom was tripped off.

繁忙的家事佔據了她所有時間，甚至連最後一點自由都被剝奪了。

② The orphan has been deprived of his childhood and has to work as a child labor since the age of 5.

這個孤兒被剝奪了童年，從五歲起就成為童工開始工作。

9. **exploit**（*v.*）剝削

This company is notorious for exploiting employees.

這間公司是惡名昭彰的剝削勞工。

10. **permanent**（*adj.*）永久性的；固定的

同義字　lasting, durable, enduring

反義字　temporary

① After years of working as contractors, he finally found a permanent teaching position at the University.

在接了多年的短期聘僱約之後，他終於在大學找到一個固定教職。

② After the typhoon, the whole village replaced the roofs with a more durable material.

颱風過後，整個村子都用更耐用的建材把屋頂換了。

③ The refugees are sent to a temporary shelter not knowing when they can really settle down.

難民被送到一間臨時庇護中心，不知道何時才能安頓下來。

Part 1
Part 2
Part 3
Part 4
Part 5
Part 6
Part 7

2.2

Windrush

After World War II, the United Kingdom encouraged immigration from the **Commonwealth** countries to fill in the labor shortage. This included many **adventurous** men and women from Jamaica, Trinidad and other West Indian countries to find promising **prosperity** and employment in the UK.

The Empire Windrush was a passenger **liner** and **cruise** ship. She sailed forth and back from the West Indies taking passengers to the UK. These African-Caribbean migrants, despite working hard in their professional fields mostly as nurses and engineers, experienced racial **discrimination** in white people's society because of their dark skin. Most of the Windrush people didn't intend to stay long at first. When they finally decided to stay, the Chinese and Indians already opened shops and started their business. They were too late.

Nowadays, the descendants of the Windrush Generation threw big **Carnivals** in the streets of London years after years. They returned to the streets where their ancestors suffered violent attacks. They sang for the beauty of life. However hard it is, as long as there is life, there is hope. Whether they stay or not, they are just leaves in the wind, lone boats in the ocean.

中文翻譯

Windrush

二次世界大戰過後，英國鼓勵**聯邦國家**人民移民英國，藉此填補國內的人力短缺。這批移民包括牙美加、千里達以及其他西印度群島國家的男女**雄心勃勃**的前往英國，尋找心目中的繁榮與工作。

The Empire Windrush是一艘**客輪兼巡邏**的船艦。她從西印度群島將一船又一船的乘客送到英國，這群非洲裔加勒比海移民，多數為護士和工程師，即便努力在專業範圍工作，黝黑皮膚依然在白人的社會中備受歧視。當時這一批大風吹來的人，大多無意久留，直到下定決心要定居時，才發現華人和印度移民已經搶先一步，開了館子做起生意，而他們，則已經遲了。

如今，Windrush的後代子孫，在倫敦街頭年復一年的重現**嘉年華**，他們回到前人曾被暴力攻擊的大街上，高聲歌唱生命的美好。不管再怎麼苦，活著，就是希望。不論是留或走，他們只是大風吹中的一片葉子，汪洋中的一艘船。

Part 1
Part 2
Part 3
Part 4
Part 5
Part 6
Part 7

重點字彙

1. **Commonwealth**（*n.*）聯邦；協會界；全體公民

Among the 53 countries of the UK Commonwealth, Canada is the largest and India is the most populous.

在英國的五十三個聯邦國家中，加拿大是面積最大的，而印度則人口最多。

與 common 相關的　延伸字彙

同義字　pervasive, prevalent

反義字　rare, scarce, uncommon, unprecedented

2. **adventure**（*n.*）冒險、冒險精神；**adventurous**（*adj.*）熱愛冒險、大膽的

反義字　careful, cautious, prudent, wary

① The parents proudly sent their daughter to her new adventure.

女孩的父母驕傲地送她出去新冒險。

② The CEO is known for adventurous ideas, especially in developing new markets.

執行長以大膽的想法聞名，尤其反映在發展新市場上。

③ Compared with the ambitious director, the project manager is always cautious with the cost.

比起那野心勃勃的主管，這位專案經理總是對成本比較小心謹慎。

3. **prosperous**（*adj.*）興旺的、繁榮的；**prosperity**（*n.*）興旺、繁榮、成功

① Congratulations on the new shop! Wish you a very prosperous future!

恭喜新店開張！祝您生意興隆！

② After years of suffering from the war, prosperity is nowhere to be seen in the city.

經歷多年戰亂，城市的繁華已經不在。

Part 2

4. **liner**（*n.*）客輪；**cruise**（*n.*）船艦；客輪

The new weds booked a cruise holiday for their honey moon.

這對新婚夫妻訂了遊輪蜜月假期。

5. **discrimination**（*n.*）歧視

After years of staying at home taking care of the family, she decided to return to the workplace but received rejections with age discrimination.

在多年在家照顧家庭後，她決定重返職場，但卻遭到年齡歧視被拒絕多次。

6. **carnival**（*n.*）嘉年華會

She won the Queen Costume Competition in the Carnival last year.

她贏得了去年嘉年華會的最佳服裝后冠。

iBT 新托福字彙閱讀應試技巧

Question 1: Which of the following goods was least likely to be products of the colonized areas?

(A) Cinnamon
(B) Yorkshire tea
(C) Chocolate
(D) Wool

解析 文中提到歐洲殖民者從殖民地取得香料、茶、可可、糖和黃金，因此 (A) 肉桂、(B) 約克夏茶和 (C) 巧克力都屬於其中，答案為 (D) 羊毛，歐洲許多國家皆有生產羊毛製品。請注意答案 (B) 的約克夏茶雖以英國地名為名，但茶葉依然是從斯里蘭卡、肯亞、印度阿薩姆等地出產的。

Part
1

Part
2

Part
3

Part
4

Part
5

Part
6

Part
7

Question 2: Why did the West Indian British celebrate Carnivals in the UK?

(A) To show white people how to sing

(B) To celebrate the beauty of life

(C) To mourn for their ancestors

(D) To leave the history behind

解析 西印度群島裔英國人是為了歡慶生命的美好而辦嘉年華會，因此答案為 (B)，他們並非要以此 (D) 把歷史拋諸腦後，也不是 (C) 哀悼前人，更不是為了 (A) 要對白種人示範如何唱歌。

Unit 03

3.1

 Track 05

Chinese Immigration to the United States

Chinatowns represent the strength of Chinese immigrants around the world. After the tough history of immigration, ethnic Chinese now have more than 3 million population in the United States, approximately **surpassed Latino** immigration.

There were three waves of Chinese immigration to the USA in the history of America. The first wave happened in the early 19th century when they worked as cheap laborers of the **transcontinental** railroads and the **mining** industry. They had to endure racial discrimination and were called the "yellow peril." During the economy crisis in the 1870s, white Americans blamed the Chinese cheap laborers for taking their jobs. Anti-Chinese movements forced Chinese people to become **refugees** finding the chance of escape and **shelter** in Chinatowns. The hostile opposition made the **Congress** passed the Chinese **Exclusion** Act in 1882 which **prohibited** the Chinese immigration for a decade since then.

The alliance between the United States and China during WWII

Unit 03

Part
1

Part
2

Part
3

Part
4

Part
5

Part
6

Part
7

allowed Chinese immigration to the America again since 1943. Most of Chinese immigrants did manual work in restaurants and laundry shops, which were commonly done by people of lower social status. The third wave began in the 1980s when Chinese people migrated to the states as students and professionals.

中文翻譯

華人移民潮

中國城代表著華人移民在世界各地堅強韌性。經過一段艱難的移民史，華裔人士現在在美國有超過三百萬人口，幾乎就要超過**拉丁裔西語系**移民。

美國史上共有三次華人移民潮，第一次起於十九世紀前葉，他們大多在**橫貫大陸**鐵路工程以及**礦業**當廉價勞工。他們必須忍受種族歧視，甚至被稱為「黃禍」。在 1870 年間的經濟危機期間，白種美國人怪罪中國廉價勞工搶走他們的工作，種種的排華運動逼迫華人**逃**到中國城尋求**庇護**。強烈的反對聲浪讓美國**國會**於 1882 年通過**排華條款**，從此禁止中國移民長達十年。

美國與中國在二次世界大戰期間的結盟，讓華人從 1943 年起再次得以移民美國，大部分的華人移民從事社會階層較低的勞力工作，如餐館或洗衣店。第三波移民潮從 1980 年代開始，華人移民到美國就學或擔任專業人士。

重點字彙

1. **continent**（*n.*）大陸、陸地、洲；歐洲；
   transcontinental（*adj.*）跨大陸的

   ① Continental breakfast mostly contains cold dishes.
   歐陸式的早餐通常都是冷食。
   ② The transcontinental flight from Boston to New York takes six hours.
   這個跨陸航班需六小時從波士頓飛到舊金山。

2. **mine**（*n.*）礦；寶庫；地雷、水雷

   The closure of mine pits during Margaret Thatcher's rule led to a series of strikes from fuming miners.
   柴契爾夫人任內關閉許多礦坑，讓怒氣沸騰的礦工發起一系列罷工。

3. **undocumented**（*adj.*）無證的

   She struggled with an undocumented situation after her purse got stolen during a holiday abroad.
   在皮包被偷後，她陷入異鄉度假的無證困境。

4. **surpass**（*v.*）勝過、多餘、大於

   ① For the first time since the company was founded, the number of women employees surpassed that of men employee.

打從公司成立以來，女性員工的人數第一次超越男性員工。

② The artist made the record of best-seller of the year and people look forward to seeing her to surpass herself in the next album.

她打出本年度最佳銷售的好成績，人們期待她在下張專輯繼續超越自我。

5. **Latin**（*n.*）拉丁語；**Latino**（*n. / adj.*）拉丁美洲人、拉丁美洲的；**Latina**（*n.*）拉丁美洲女性

6. **congress**（*n.*）代表大會；立法機關；國會；人群

① Scholars and doctors from all around the world came to attend this congress on mental health.

世界各地的學者和醫師都前來參加這個精神健康會議。

② The media revealed a huge scandal of corruption in the Congress.

媒體揭露了國會裡的重大貪腐醜聞。

7. **exclude**（*v.*）排斥、排除；**include**（*v.*）包含、包括

① The first round of the interview excluded candidates who cannot speak fluent English.

第一輪面試刷掉了無法說流利英文的候選人。

② This dish requires many different spices, including cumin, paprika and saffron.

這道菜要用很多種香料，包括小茴香、辣椒粉和番紅花。

8. **prohibit**（*v.*）禁止；阻礙

① Smoking is prohibited in the train station.

車站裡禁止吸菸。

② The high cost of the new device prohibits its popularity in the market.

新裝置高昂的費用讓它沒辦法在市面上受到歡迎。

9. **refugee**（*n.*）難民；流亡者

The founder of the international company is the son of a refugee.

這間國際公司的創辦人是難民之子。

10. **shelter**（*n.*）遮蓋物；躲避處；避難所

Being evicted by the landlord, the single mother and her children found shelter in a temple.

被房東趕出門後，單親媽媽帶著孩子在一間廟裡稍作棲身。

3.2 ──────── Track 06

Chinese Food Invented in America

Chinese people traveling abroad often found the food in Chinatown disappointing as it tastes different from how it "should be" in Asia. In fact, some of the dishes there don't even exist in China!

One of the most common ways for early Chinese immigration to make a living was opening restaurants. To get into the market, they made **adjustments** on the dishes so that the food tastes **exotic** yet acceptable for the Americans. Soy sauce and **MSG** are extensively used in the food. The sauces are **blander**, thicker, and sweeter. Broccolis, onions, and potatoes are used to replace other leafy vegetable. Some restaurants serve English menus and Chinese menus separately. The former contains pictures of the food and the latter provides more options, such as liver, intestines, chicken feet, or other things that American customers cannot imagine eating.

For instance, the sweet and spicy fried chicken – General Zo's Chicken – started globally prevalent from New York. Sweet and sour sauce is traditionally used on fish or seafood but in Chinatown you can find sweet and sour pork. Fried rice is common in China, too, but the **presentation** as well as the taste is very different from that in America. American Chinese fried rice is often cooked with lots of soy sauce giving the rice a very dark brown color. Last but not least, crispy cookies with words of fortune inside – Fortune Cookies – you will never find it in China.

中文翻譯

華人在美發明的美食

華人出國旅行時，常會對中國城的餐點感到失望，因為那些菜跟在亞洲吃起來「應該」要有的味道就是不太一樣。其實，有些餐點在中國根本不存在呢！

早期華人移民謀生的方法之一就是開餐館。為了打進市場，他們在菜餚上做了許多**調整**，讓味道保有**異國**料理但仍能被美國人接受。他們大量使用醬油和**味精**，醬料的味道變得比較**平淡**、濃稠而且甜度較高。花椰菜、洋蔥和馬鈴薯取代其他葉菜類蔬菜。有些餐廳把英文菜單和中文菜單分開，前者有很多食物的照片，後者則提供肝類、腸子、雞爪等美國顧客難以想像的食物。

舉例來說，味道又甜又辣的炸雞——左宗棠雞——是在紐約開始世界有名的。酸甜醬傳統上是用在魚或海鮮料理，但你會在中國城發現酸甜里肌。炒飯在中國也很常見，但美國的炒飯**外觀**和味道都很不一樣。美國的中式炒飯通常都加很多醬油，飯看起來都變成深咖啡色。當然不能不提，包著吉祥話的餅乾——幸運籤餅——也是你絕不會在中國吃到的東西。

重點字彙

1. **adjust**（*v.*）適應；**adjustment**（*n.*）調整、使適合

   ① The country girl adapted her accent to fit in the workplace in town.

   鄉下姑娘調整口音以融入城裡的工作環境。

   ② The restaurant made some adaption on the spiciness for the customers' preferences.

   餐廳為了客人喜好，在辣度上做了些調整。

2. **exotic**（*adj.*）富異國情調的

   The Arabic restaurant is known for exotic belly dance performances.

   這間阿拉伯餐廳以充滿異國情調的肚皮舞表演著名。

3. **MSG**　（*n.*）味精

   My mother never cooks with MSG.

   我母親從不用味精煮飯。

4. **bland**（*adj.*）平淡無味的、無刺激性的；和藹的、溫和的

   Bland food is suggested for patients recovering from chemotherapy.

   做完化療的病患最好吃清淡的飲食。

5. **broccolis**（*n.*）花椰菜；**cauliflower**（*n.*）白花椰菜

   ① It takes longer to cook broccolis than that for mushrooms.
   煮花椰菜比煮蘑菇費時間。

   ② Cauliflower cheese is the heartiest vegetable dish!
   焗烤起司白花椰菜是最豐盛的素菜了！

6. **present**（*v.*）呈現；當下、在場；
   presentation（*n.*）贈予、呈現、介紹；外觀

   ① Living at the present is more important than thinking too far ahead.
   活在當下比看得太遠來的重要。

   ② The dish tastes good but looks too messy in presentation.
   這道菜味道很好，但擺盤過於凌亂。

   ③ She impressed everyone with an inspiring presentation.
   她充滿啟發性的簡報讓所有人都印象深刻。

iBT 新托福字彙閱讀應試技巧

Part
1

Part
2

Part
3

Part
4

Part
5

Part
6

Part
7

Question 1: Annie is an American born Chinese. Her grandfather was the first generation living in the States. Which of the following occupations should be least likely for him to take then?

(A) Railway worker   (B) Waiting staff

(C) Blacksmith   (D) Chef

解析　早期的華人在美國大多只能做社會底層的粗工，例如 (A) 鐵路工或礦工，或者到中國城裡的餐館和洗衣店打工，文中並沒有提到 (C) 鐵匠這個職業選項，因此答案為選項 (C) 鐵匠。

Question 2: Which of the following ingredients may not appear on the English menus in Chinese restaurants in USA?

(A) Onions   (B) Potatoes

(C) Carrots   (D) Edible tree fungus

解析　美國的中國餐廳通常會將英文菜餐呈現的較容易受西方客人接受，食材如 (A) 洋蔥、(B) 馬鈴薯、(C) 紅蘿蔔都是西方當地常用的食材，但木耳在西方較少見，因此答案為選項 (D)。

Unit **04**

4.1 Track 07

Indigenous Peoples - the Stolen Generations

Indigenous peoples are ethnic groups that were indigenous to a territory prior to being incorporated into a national state. They are often excluded from the majority of ethnic groups of the state culturally and politically. The Australian **Aboriginals** had a particularly bitter history, the Stolen Generations.

The Australian Federal forcibly and brutally took Aboriginal children from their parents since 1905, claiming to do so for their integration into Modern Society. Children were placed in religious, charitable institutions or adopted by White families. They were given new names and banned from speaking their native languages. Most of the boys were trained to be agricultural laborers and girls were to be domestic servants. The child removal policy lasted seven decades.

Many people of the Stolen Generations experienced **psychological, physical** or sexual **abuses** from state care or the adoptive families. **Depression, anxiety, post-traumatic stress** and

Part
1

Part
2

Part
3

Part
4

Part
5

Part
6

Part
7

suicide were prevalent among the Stolen Generations. The loss of their children put parents into a deep grief that would never be recovered. On top of that, a lot of cultural assets in the Indigenous Communities were lost during the Generations, including oral languages.

The Australia Government **launched** an inquiry into the Stolen Generations in 1995 and gave the official report named *Bring Them Home* in 1997. The Stolen Generations eventually received a formal apology from the Australian Government in 2008.

中文翻譯

原住民 —— 被偷的世代

原住民是指在合併為國家之前就已原生居住於當地的民族,他們通常在文化或政治等方面都被排除在國家的多數民族之外。澳洲的**原住民**有段特別苦澀的歷史,被偷走的世代。

澳大利亞聯邦從 1905 年開始把原住民小孩從家人身邊粗暴的強制帶走,宣稱這麼做是為了讓牠們更好融入現代社會。孩子們被安置於宗教、慈善機構或由白人家庭領養。他們被取了新名字,而且禁止說母語。大部分的男孩被訓練為農業勞工,而女孩則是家庭幫傭。這個政策延續了七十年。

很多被偷走世代的人都曾在國家看管或領養家庭中遭受**身心虐待**甚至性虐待。**憂鬱症、焦慮症、創傷後焦慮症**和**自殺**在被偷走的世代相當普遍，失去孩子讓家長陷入永遠無法平復的悲傷，最重要的是，原住民社會在這些世代間遺失了許多文化資產，包括口說語言。

澳洲政府在 1995 年起針對被偷走的世代**開始**一項調查，並於 1997 年交出名為「帶他們回家」的官方報告。被偷走的世代最後終於在 2008 年得到澳洲政府的正式道歉。

 重點字彙

1. **indigenous**（*adj.*）土產的、土生的；
   aboriginal（*adj.*）最早就出現的、土著的、原始的

   ① There are more than ten different tribes among Taiwanese Aboriginal community.
      台灣原住民社會中有至少十個不同的部族。
   ② The institution aims to preserve the Indigenous languages on the island.
      這所機構致力於保存島上的土生語言。

2. **psychological**（*adj.*）心理的、精神的；心理學的

   同義字 mental 精神的、心理的

   ① The director's demanding attitude is like a psychological torture to the team.
   這位主管苛刻的態度對整個團隊來說簡直是心理上的折磨。

   ② She suffered from severe mental disorder after the traumatic accident.
   她在那場痛苦的意外後罹患了嚴重的精神失常。

3. **physical**（*adj.*）身體的、肉體的；物理的；物質的

   ① The director is charged with requesting physical relationship with actresses in exchange for their roles in the movies.
   導演被指控以演出電影裡的角色為交換條件，要求女演員與其發生關係。

   ② The melting of ice is a type of physical change.
   冰塊融化是一種物理變化。

   ③ The talents employed are just as important as the physical assets for a company.
   對一間公司來說，雇用的人才和物質資產是一樣重要的。

4. **abuse**（*v.*）虐待、傷害；濫用

   ① Drug abuse has become a serious issue among all levels in society.

   藥物濫用已經成為存在社會各階層的嚴重問題。

   ② Being a social worker, a very risky job, has to work closely with abusive families.

   社工是個高風險的工作，必須與有虐待問題的家庭密切合作。

5. **depression**（*n.*）憂鬱症；意志消沉；經濟蕭條

   同義字 ▶ recession

   反義字 ▶ boom, prosperity

   The public was shocked that the funny and positive comedian committed a suicide out of depression.

   民眾對於那位逗趣又正面的喜劇演員居然因憂鬱症自殺，感到十分震驚。

6. **anxiety**（*n.*）焦慮、掛念；**anxious**（*adj.*）焦慮的、掛念的

   ① The parents are really anxious that they haven't heard from the daughter for a week.

   女兒已經一周沒有消息了，父母感到非常焦慮。

   ② The intense, work caused her great anxiety.

   緊張的工作讓她產生極度的焦躁感。

同義字 concern 擔心

Please let me share your pain. I am very concerned about you.
請讓我幫你分擔傷痛，我很擔心你。

與 intense 相關的 延伸字彙

同義字 acute, bitter, excessive

反義字 gentle, bland

7. **trauma**（*n.*）（外傷）傷口；（情感）創傷；**Post-traumatic Stress Disorder**（*n.*）創傷後神經失調症

Many soldiers returned home with Post-traumatic Stress Disorders such as Shell Shock.
許多軍人在返鄉後都有震嚇癡呆症等創傷後神經失調症。

與 disorder 相關的 延伸字彙

同義字 disarrange, disorganize
The books on the shelf were disarranged.
書架上的書散亂擺放著。

反義字 accommodate, alter, adapt, adjust,
You have to accommodate yourselves to the ever changing market.
你必須適應瞬息萬變的市場。

8. **suicide**（*n.*）自殺

Psychological delusions not only gave the artist continuous inspirations but also eventually led him to commit suicide.

心理妄想症讓這位藝術家總有源源不絕的靈感，但最終也讓他走向自殺。

反義字 homicide, murder 他殺、謀殺

The court declared that he is guilty for committing the homicide.

法庭宣告他犯下謀殺有罪。

9. **launch**（*v.*）發射；發動（戰爭或其他活動）；發起、出版

① Celebrities show up in the occasion of the launch of winter fashion collection.

大批明星出現在冬季系列時尚新品的發表會上。

② The whole world watched the first rocket launch into the sky.

全世界都看著第一架火箭發射升空。

延伸字彙

同義字 constitute, establish, inaugurate, initiate, innovate, institute, pioneer

反義字 halt, phase out, shut (up)

The operation of this project had been phased out.

此計劃遭暫停執行。

4.2

 Track 08

Part
1

Part
2

Part
3

Part
4

Part
5

Part
6

Part
7

The Dance of War – Haka

Māori people are the indigenous people of New Zealand. They make up 14% of total population in the country. Their language and traditions mold New Zealand's central identity. The most **representative** part of their culture is their dance of war – Haka.

Haka is an ancient Māori dance used on **battlefields**. The violent foot-stamping, **aggressive** tongue **protrusions**, loud **chant** and the **rhythm** of body **slapping** display the tribe's pride, strength and unity. Used as a way to proclaiming their strength so that they could have the upper hand in the battle, Haka was originally performed by warriors. The dance is also used for various purposes, including welcoming important guests, giving recognition to great **achievements** and occasions, ceremonies, such as funerals.

Nowadays, not only does Haka remain its unique role in Māori ceremonies, it's also became the Kiwi Style challenge in the sports field. Since it was first performed in 2011 Rugby World Cup, the dance gradually became a tradition before **rugby**, football, basketball and other games. So if you're playing with the Kiwis, be prepared for their war cry.

哈卡戰舞

　　毛利人是紐西蘭的原住民，他們佔全國總人口的 14%。他們的語言和傳統塑造出了紐西蘭的中心文化，最有**代表性的**莫過於他們的戰舞——哈卡舞。

　　哈卡舞是一種用於**戰場**上的古老毛利舞。猛烈的踏腳、**挑釁的吐**舌、大聲的**吟唱**加上**拍打**身體的**節拍**，展現出部落的尊嚴、力量和團結。哈卡舞傳統上是戰士在開戰前表演，宣告他們的力量以在戰鬥中搶得上位。這種舞也用於其他用途，包括歡迎重要賓客、肯定偉大**成就**，以及葬禮等場合、儀式。

　　直至今日，哈卡舞不只仍在毛利典禮保有其獨特角色，更在體育場上成為紐西蘭式的戰帖。從英式橄欖球2011 年世界盃哈卡舞第一次表演之後，這就逐漸成為英式**橄欖球**、足球、籃球等運動的賽前傳統。如果你等一下要跟紐西蘭人比賽，最好先做好面對他們戰場嘶吼的心理準備。

重點字彙

Part 1

Part 2

Part 3

Part 4

Part 5

Part 6

Part 7

1. **representative**（*n*/*adj.*）代表；具代表性的

The Cathedral is the most representative building of Gothic architectures.

這棟大教堂是最具代表性的哥德式建築。

2. **warrior**（*n.*）戰士

The warriors lined up, drank the wine, and smashed the glasses to show their determination.

戰士們列隊、喝下酒並把酒杯砸碎以示決心。

3. **battle**（*n.*）戰役；**battlefield**（*n.*）戰場

Duke of Wellington defeated Napoleon at the Battle of Waterloo.

威靈頓公爵在滑鐵盧之役打敗了拿破崙。

4. **aggressive**（*adj.*）侵略的；挑釁的；富有進取心的

The footballer's aggressive behavior triggered a violent conflict between two teams.

那個足球員的挑釁行為引發兩隊之間的暴力衝突。

延伸字彙

● **progressive** 進步的；先進的

Though small, the country has some of the most progressive policies in the world.

雖然小，這個國家有著許多領先全球的先進政策。

● **regressive** 後退的；退步的；回歸的

The country has a very powerful economy but regressive social regulations.

這個國家有著強勢經濟，但相當退步的社會規範。

5. **protrude**（*v.*）伸出、突出；**protrusion**（*n.*）突出物、推出物

① Make sure there are no nails protruding the surface of the furniture.

要確保家具表面沒有釘子突出。

② The church is decorated with delicate protrusions on the ceiling.

教堂的天花板裝飾許多精緻的突出設計。

與 decorate 相關的 延伸字彙

同義字 adorn, decorate, beautify, embellish

反義字 disfigure, spoil, deform

6. **chant**（*n.*）吟唱、詠唱；歌、曲；詩歌

The chorus chant in beautiful harmony.

合唱團詠唱出優美的和諧。

7. **rhythm**（*n.*）節奏、韻律

The drummer is the soul of the band that brings out the rhythm.

鼓手帶出節奏，是樂團的靈魂角色。

8. **slap**（*v.*）掌摑；責難

Caught him red-handing with the mistress, the wife slapped the husband out of rage.

妻子當場抓到丈夫和情婦在一起，盛怒之下賞了他一巴掌。

9. **achieve**（*v.*）達成；**achievement**（*v.*）成就

Never believe it when people say you cannot achieve your dreams.

當人們說你達不到夢想時，不要輕信他們。

iBT 新托福字彙閱讀應試技巧

Question 1: Jarrah was taken away from his parents with his sister, which of the following could be the life waiting for him? (Multiple options)

(A) He was sent to a boarding school where his parents could visit him once a month.

(B) He started to learn Bible under supervision of a Sister.

(C) The teacher hit him on his hands for speaking with his sister in the language of their tribe.

(D) He and his sister discussed their career options and decided to be a farmer and a maid respectively.

(E) After he grew up, he tried to find his sister but could not find her name in any record.

解析　被偷走的世代中，有些兒童被送到宗教機構，因此他的確有可能 (B) 在修女的監管下修讀聖經，(C) 使用母語的確會被屬罰，而 (E) 名字在任何紀錄上都找不到，有可能是因為妹妹被改了新名字，因此選項 (B)、(C)、(E) 都有可能符合當時情境，為正確答案。小孩是不被允許和父母見面的，因此選項 (A) 不可能；兒童的職業選擇通常都是配合政府規劃，因此他和妹妹不太有可能討論生涯規劃，答案 (D) 也不可能。

Part 1

Part 2

Part 3

Part 4

Part 5

Part 6

Part 7

Question 2: Which of the following would not be seen in Haka Dance before a rugby game? (Multiple options)

(A) Dancers slapping their thighs.

(B) Dancers kicking in the air.

(C) Dancers inviting audience to join the dance.

(D) Dancers stamping heavily on the ground.

(E) Dancers waving traditional Māori weapons.

解析　哈卡舞有很多肢體上的拍打，以及用力的跺腳，因此選項 (A) 和 (D) 都符合。但哈卡舞並沒有空踢的動作，傳統毛利武器不太可能帶上球場，他們更不會邀請觀眾一起跳舞，因此選項 (B)、(C)、(E) 不符合。

Unit 05

5.1

 Track 09

History of Slave Trade

Slavery systems can be traced back long ago in human history. Ancient Greece, Rome, China, and Egypt all had records showing their usage of slavery. The largest scale of slavery happened during the 16th and 19th century in the Atlantic Slave Trade.

To fill in the laborer shortage, European colonizers **imported** African slaves for their cotton and sugarcane plantation in America. Slave traders captured Africans from the West Coast of Africa and shipped them across the Atlantic to the so called "New World." Slaves were chained like **cattle**, shaved, oiled, examined and branded on their skin like **livestock**. New diseases brought by the Europeans plus **malnutrition** on the journey caused a high death rate among the African slaves.

Those who survived the journey were presented in Slave Auctions for potential buyers from the USA, Spanish, Portuguese America or West Indian Islands. Once they were purchased, they would have no choice but to work for their masters for the rest of their lives. Their descendants also had to carry the same **destinies**:

slaves. **Fugitive** slaves could be beaten, **whipped** or **starved** in darkness, even killed.

Had been practiced for nearly 300 years, the Atlantic Slave Trade was eventually **abolished**, along with the end of the Civil War in the United States. The last Atlantic Slave Voyage took place in 1867.

中文翻譯

奴隸交易史

奴隸制度可以追溯遠至久遠的人類史，古希臘、羅馬、中國、埃及等都有使用奴隸的紀錄。最大規模的奴役發生於十六到十九世紀間，被稱為大西洋奴隸貿易。

為了填滿人力空缺，歐洲殖民者**進口**非洲奴隸去到他們在美洲的棉花田和蔗糖園。奴隸販子從非洲西岸抓捕非洲人，把他們船運橫跨大西洋到所謂的「新世界」。奴隸被像**牲口**一樣用鐵鍊綁住，像**家畜**一樣除毛、抹油、檢驗並在皮膚上烙印。歐洲人帶來的新疾病以及旅程中的**營養不良**，導致非洲奴隸中高死亡率。

那些從運送途中生存下來的人，會在奴隸拍賣會上呈現給從美國、西語或葡萄牙語美洲或西印度群島各地來的潛在買家。一但被買下，他們就沒有任何選擇，得一輩子替主人工作，而他們的後代也必須承襲同樣的命運，當奴隸。**逃跑的**奴隸會被毆打、**鞭撻**、關閉在黑暗中**挨餓**，甚至被殺。

大西洋奴隸貿易在活躍三百年後，終於在美國南北內戰之後被**廢除**，最後一趟大西洋奴隸之旅在 1867 年劃下句點。

 重點字彙

1. **import**（*n.*/*v.*）進口；**export**（*n.*/*v.*）出口

   The expensive import tax makes cars only affordable for very rich people in Singapore.
   昂貴的進口稅使得只有非常有錢的人能在新加坡負擔得起車子。

2. **cattle**（*n.*）牛、牲口

   The young man presented half of his cattle to the family for the permission to marry their daughter.
   這個年輕人將他一半的牲畜獻給女方家人，請他們允許女兒下嫁於他。

3. **livestock**（*n.*）家畜

   Apart from planting crops, the farm also has a section of livestock.
   除了種植穀類作物之外，農場也有家畜區。

4. **nutrition**（*n.*）營養；
   nutritious（*adj.*）營養的；
   malnutrition（*n.*）營養不良

   同義字 ▶ nourish（*v.*）養育；滋養；支持

   ① My mother is an expert in cooking delicious and nutritious meals!

   我母親是烹飪美味又營養的美食專家！

   ② Children in the village generally grow underweight due to malnutrition.

   村子裡的小孩由於營養不良，普遍體重過輕。

   ③ It was the books and music that nourished her through the dark years of loneliness.

   支撐她走過孤獨的黑暗歲月的，是書和音樂。

5. **destiny**（*n.*）命運；**destination**（*n.*）目的地、終點

   ① Despite her broken childhood, she wrote her own destiny by never giving up chasing her ballet dream.

   即使有個破碎的童年，她始終沒有放棄芭蕾舞夢想，終於寫出自己的命運。

   ② The passenger was silent throughout the journey, wondering what would be waiting in his destination.

   這位乘客一路上都很沉默，想著不知道目的地會有什麼在等著他。

6. **fugitive**（*n. / adj.*）逃亡者、亡命之徒；逃跑的

Fled from the abusive employer, the maid hid her identity as a fugitive.

逃離虐待成性的雇主後，女傭成為隱姓埋名的亡命之徒。

7. **whip**（*v.*）鞭撻、抽打；（蛋、奶）攪打

① The worker was shipped by the manager as a punishment for smoking in the cotton mill.

由於在棉花工廠抽菸，工人被經理嚴厲抽打，以示懲戒。

② The cake is layered with whipped cream.

蛋糕中間夾了打發的鮮奶油。

8. **starve**（*v.*）挨餓、餓死；亟需

同義字 crave 渴望、迫切需要

① Thousands of people starved to death in the year of drought.

數以千計的人們在乾旱之年挨餓之死。

② After finishing the whole day work, the team was starving for a good treat.

結束一整天的工作後，整個團隊亟需吃一頓大餐。

③ Orphaned since the age of five, he craves for family life.

他從五歲就成孤兒，渴望家庭生活。

9. **abolish**（*v.*）廢除；**abolishment**（*n.*）廢除

The abolishment of foot binding freed women from centuries of constraints.

廢除纏足終於將女人從好幾世紀以來的束縛中解放。

延伸字彙 annihilate, demolish, eradicate, exterminate

① The enemy has been annihilated.

敵軍已遭殲滅。

② The plant was demolished by explosives.

工廠已被炸毀。

③ The problem needs to be completely eradicated.

此問題需要徹底解決。

④ Cockroaches are difficult to be exterminated.

蟑螂很難被消滅。

Track 10

5.2

The N-Word

Derived from the Spanish and Portuguese word, "negro" which means "black", "nigger" was used to describe African Slaves. Its **literal** meaning is "black-skinned" without a racist **connotation**. Some of the literature records also show that the word was used by other ethnic groups such as Indians, Mexicans and even European people.

The word gradually had become **pejorative** far before the 1900s. As it was associated with an **offensive** context, another word "colored" was used as an **alternative**. During the late 1960s, social groups in the United States identified the word "black" to **denote** black-skinned Americans due to their African **ancestry**. The **compound** term "African American" replaced "black" in the 1990s.

The word "nigger" is now a taboo in the United States. People, especially the Whites, use the "n-word" to replace it. The usages of the n-word are often muted on the television or radio programs. Today, it is used among black people as a sign of solidarity or to **neutralize** the racist impact of the word. The n-word represents the history that cannot be hidden nor be denied. It should be discussed openly as a mirror of self-reflection.

Part
1

Part
2

Part
3

Part
4

Part
5

Part
6

Part
7

中文翻譯

N 開頭的字

衍生自西班牙文和葡萄牙文的「黑色」，Nigger 在過去曾意指非洲黑奴。這個字在**字面上**的意思「黑皮膚的」並沒有種族歧視的**意涵**，有些文學記載也顯示這個字也有用在其他民族上，例如印地安人、墨西哥人，甚至歐洲人。

早在 18 世紀之前，這個字逐就具有**貶抑**，語意**冒犯**，因此「有色人種」成為其替代字眼。1960 年代後期，美國一些社會團體定調用「黑人」**代表**黑皮膚美國人的非洲**血統**。**合成**字眼「非裔美國人」更於 1990 年代取代「黑人」一詞。

Nigger 這個字現在成為美國的禁忌，人們以「N 開頭那個字」簡化取代，特別是白人。這個字通常會在電視或電台節目中被消音。如今的黑人仍然使用這個字以表團結，或**中和**這個字的種族歧視衝擊。這個字代表著那段藏不了也否認不了的歷史，它應該被大大方方的討論，當成一面自我反省的明鏡。

重點字彙

1. **literal**（*v.*）字面上的

When reading poems, you have to think beyond the literal meanings. 讀詩的時候，你得跳脫字面上的意義去思考。

2. **connotation**（*n.*）意涵、言外之意

The professor is notorious for making jokes with sexual connotations.

這個教授是惡名昭彰的愛開黃腔。

3. **pejorative**（*adj.*）輕蔑的、有貶抑的

同義字 insulting, contemptuous, humiliating

① The first groups of women miners had to endure pejorative words from their male colleagues.

最早期的女性礦工必須忍受男性同事的輕蔑言語。

② The same gesture can be found friendly in one culture but insulting in another.

同樣的手勢可能在一個文化中是友善的，但在別的文化卻是冒犯的。

③ She lives like a lone wolf seeing all rules of the society in a contemptuous way.

她像隻孤狼一樣，藐視社會中的一切規矩。

④ Losing the capital was the most humiliating defeat ever happened in the country's history.

首都失陷是這個國家有史以來最大的失敗恥辱。

4. **alternative**（*adj.*）替代的、替代方案；非主流的

同義字 ▶ replacement, substitute

① This project may cost double, but it surely is a safer alternative solution.

這項計畫可能得花費雙倍成本，但確實是比較安全的替代方案。

② The Vice Premier replaced the Premier after the latter resigned from his position.

總理辭去職務後，由副總理取而代之。

③ Soya is a good substitute for milk.

豆漿是取代牛奶很好的替代品。

5. **offense**（*n.*）冒犯；**offensive**（*adj.*）冒犯的、唐突的

① No offense, but I cannot eat your strawberry cheese cake due to my allergy.

沒有冒犯之意，但我有過敏，不能吃你的草莓起司蛋糕。

② Don't use that gesture. It's offensive in this country.

不要做那個手勢，這在這個國家是很沒禮貌的。

6. **denote**（*v.*）代表、指稱

The symbol of lily on the wall denotes the royal identity of the family.

牆上的百合花符號代表著家族的皇室身分。

7. **compound**（*n.*）合成；加重；調停

The drug is strong enough by itself and can even be fatal if mixed with alcohol. 這種藥本身就已經夠強了，若和酒精混合更是致命。

8. **ancestry**（*n.*）列祖列宗、血統

He has a complicated ancestry of Spanish, Scottish, and Ghanaian blood.

他有西班牙、蘇格蘭以及迦納混血血統。

9. **taboo**（*n.*）禁忌

Talking about the loss of the first baby is a taboo in their family.

談論第一個寶寶的夭折是這個家裡的禁忌。

10. **mute**（*v.*）消音

30% of the rapper's performance was muted due to the usage of swear words.

由於大量使用髒話，這個饒舌歌手的表演裡有三成都被消音。

11. **neutralize**（*v.*）中和；使中立化；抵銷

The leather belt neutralized the girlie-ness of that floral chiffon dress.

皮腰帶中和了一點那件碎花雪紡洋裝的女孩子氣。

延伸字彙 ▶ annul, cancel (out),

The effect of the drug has been annulled.

藥力失效。

iBT 新托福字彙閱讀應試技巧

Question 1: Which of the following does not describe African slaves' Atlantic journeys?

(A) The slave traders examined their teeth.

(B) The slave traders measured their heights and weighs.

(C) The slave traders forced them to change new names.

(D) The slave traders burned something on their arms.

> 解析 由於文中描述 "Slaves were chained like cattle, shaved, oiled, examined and branded on their skin",因此選項 (A) 和 (B) 都符合身體檢查的項目,選項 (D) 則代表他們的手臂上被留下烙印,但選項 (C) 並不在其中。事實上,通常都是交易後由新主人給奴隸命名。

Question 2: How did the English language evolve in describing black-skinned people in America?

(A) Nigger → Black → Colored → African American

(B) Nigger → Colored → Black → African American

(C) Black → Nigger → Colored → African American

(D) Colored → Nigger → African American → Black

> 解析 "Nigger" 一詞是最早衍生自西語葡萄牙語的詞彙,1990 年代開

始興起使用 "Colored" 代替，1960 年代改為 "Black"，到 1990 年代才出現 "African American" 這個稱呼，因此正確解答為 (B)。

Question 3: Mary has been a slave for her whole life. She doesn't want her new born baby to get stuck in the same cotton picking life so she runs away in the middle of the night. What could happen to her if she got caught by the master? (Multiple options)

(A) The master might hang her on the tree and punish her with thick lashes.

(B) The master might force her to work overtime.

(C) The master might force her to sign a contract swearing never run again.

(D) The master might lock her in a dark room without her baby.

(E) The master might send the baby away to an adoptive family.

解析 文中提到 "Fugitive slaves could be beaten, whipped or starved in darkness, even killed"，因此選項 (A)，吊在樹上鞭打，以及選項 (D)，把他單獨關在黑暗的房間裡，都有可能是主人會用以懲罰逃跑的手段。

Unit 06

──────── 6.1 ────────   Track 11

The Peranakan Chinese– Baba-Nyonya

The Peranakan Chinese or the Strait Chinese was the Chinese people **migrated** to the Malay Archipelago and British Malaya (now Peninsular Malaysia and Singapore) between the 15th and 17th centuries. The Peranakans are also called, "Baba-Nyonya" which refers to the men and the women **respectively**. The early Peranakans were mainly Han populations of the British Straits Settlements of Malaya and the Dutch-controlled island of Java and other locations, who partially have adopted Malay customs to be **assimilated** into the local communities. As many of them were merchants, traders or **intermediaries** between the British, Chinese and Malays, most of them and the **descendants** are fluent in English, Malay and various Chinese dialects. They also mixed Malay and Chinese dialects into their own language called, "Baba Malay."

Unfortunately, this culture has started to disappear in Malaysia and Singapore. The Singaporean authority classifies the Peranakans to be ethnically Chinese who should receive Mandarin Chinese education instead of Malay as the second language under the "**Mother Tongue** Policy." In Malaysia, the main language,

Bahasa Melayu had been standardized and **assigned** as the official language for all **ethnic** groups which led to the disappearance of Baba Malay. Some of the early Chinese migrants married Malay women and have mix-raced descendants as the Malay then were not necessarily **Muslims**. However, it became a hard decision for non-Malays to marry Malay people in the present Malaysia unless they **convert** to **Islam**. Considering the **linguistic**, religious reasons and other **politic-and-economical** factors, this culture is now struggling to pass down to young Babas and young Nyonyas.

中文翻譯

土生華人峇峇娘惹

The Peranakan Chinese（土生華人）或 Strait Chinese（海峽華人）為十五至十七世紀間，**移民至**馬來群島以及英屬馬來亞（現今馬來西亞半島以及新加坡）的華人。他們又被稱為「峇峇娘惹」，**分別指**男人和女人。早期的土生華人主要是居住在馬來亞英屬海峽殖民地和在爪哇和其他地區的荷屬島嶼的漢人，為了**融入**當地，他們從馬來社會採納了部分文化習俗。由於他們大多為活躍於英國人、華人和馬來人之間的商人、交易人或**中間人**，他們以及**後代**通常都能說流利的英文、馬來文和多種華語方言。他們也融合馬來文和華語方言，成為一種混合語言稱為「峇峇馬來語」。

　　可惜的是，這種文化已逐漸在馬來西亞和新加坡消失。新加坡當局把土生華人歸類為華人，並在「**母語**政策」下，要求他們接受華語普通話而不是馬來語為第二語言學習。在馬來西亞，馬來文被標準化並**指定**成為所有種族族群通用的官方語言，這導致了峇峇馬來語的式微。宗教方面，早期的馬來人並不都是**穆斯林**，當時許多華人移民與馬來女性通婚，生下混血後代；如今，非穆斯林在馬來西亞要與馬來人結婚是一件很困難的事情，除非他們**皈依回教**。在語言、宗教和其他**政經因素**的影響下，這個文化難以傳承給年輕的峇峇、年輕的娘惹。

 重點字彙

1. **migrate / migrant**（*v.* / *n.*）**遷移、移居／移民**

Migrant workers have made a huge contribution to Taiwan's society yet their working environment is not very well-protected.

移民勞工對台灣社會貢獻良多，但工作環境卻不是十分有保障。

延伸字彙

- **immigrate / immigrant**（*v.* / *n.*）遷移入／移民
- **emigrate / emigrant**（*v.* / *n.*）遷移出／移民
- **asylum / asylum seeker**（*n.* / *n.*）政治庇護／尋求政治庇護者
- **expatriate / expat**（*n.* / *n.*）移居國外者／僑民

2. **respectively**（*adv.*）分別地

My mother and father are 45 and 46 years old respectively.

我的母親和父親分別是四十五和四十六歲。

3. **assimilate**（*v.*）吸收；同化

Second generation immigrants become more assimilated into the local community than their parents do.

移民第二代與當地社區的融合通常較父母輩好。

4. **intermediary**（*n.*）中間人；仲介

He has a very good reputation for handling tricky negotiations as an intermediary.

他擔任中間人調解棘手談判的名聲非常好。

延伸字彙

intermediate（*adj. / n.*）中間的、中級的；中間人、調解人

5. **descendant**（*n.*）子孫、後裔

Descendants of Asian immigrants growing in the Western society often struggle to find selfidentity.

在西方社會長大的亞洲移民後代常因自我認同問題而迷惘。

6. **mother tongue**（*n.*）母語

She grew up in Latvia but her mother tongue is Russian.

她出生於拉脫維亞，但母語為俄羅斯語。

同義字 ▶ first language

7. **assign**（*v.*）分配、指定

同義字 ▶ appoint 任命、指派

反義字 ▶ dismiss 解散、遣散

① The team was assigned to organize the annual conference this year.

這個團隊被指定籌劃今年的年度會議。

② The Committee appointed her to lead the new teaching program.

委員會任命她來領導新的教學計畫。

③ The class was dismissed soon after the teacher revealed the results of the exam.

老師公布考試成績後不久就下課了。

8. **ethnic**（*adj.*）種族的、民族的

The pupils in this class are from a wide variety of ethnic origins.

這個班上的學生來自各式各樣的種族背景。

9. Islam/Islamic/Muslim (n./adj./n.)
伊斯蘭教（回教）/回教的/穆斯林（回教徒）

Ramadan is the ninth month of the Islamic calendar when Muslims across the world fast during daytime to develop self-discipline, self-restraint and generosity. It also reminds them of the suffering of the poor, who may rarely get to eat well.

齋戒月是回教曆法的第九個月，全世界的穆斯林都會在白晝禁食一個月，藉以培養自我修養、自制力和仁愛之心。這也提醒他們無法果腹的窮人之苦。

10. convert (v.) 轉換、皈依；改建

① The museum converted an old theatre to a beautiful art gallery.

博物館將一間舊戲院改建成美麗的畫廊。

② The couple converted to Christianity in order to be married in a church.

這對情侶為了要在教堂結婚而皈依基督教。

11. linguistic (adj.) 語言的；語言學的

There is a huge linguistic debate on whether the bilingual environment will benefit children's language ability.

雙語環境對兒童的語言學習究竟有沒有幫助，是語言學界爭論不已的課題。

6.2 Track 12

Peranakan Cuisine

Peranakan Cuisine is a **sparkle** created by Baba Nyonya culture. As cooking was traditionally women's job, the food is also called "Nyonya Food." Since the Strait Chinese migrated to Malaya and some of them married Malay people, they combined Chinese cooking methods with local **ingredients** such as coconut milk, lemon grass, **turmeric**, **tamarind**, **pandan** leaves, chilies and sambal. Most of the dishes look like Chinese food but have much more exciting tastes. For example, Malaysians are very fond of "sambal", chili sauce. They use it in various types of dishes such as sambal shrimps and sambal chicken. Amongst all Nyonya dishes, Asamlaksa represents the cuisine the best.

Asamlaksa is a type of sour and spicy noodle soup cooked with fish and tamarind base. **Shredded** fish, tamarind and **finely sliced** cucumber, onions, red chilies, pineapple, lettuce, common mint and ginger blended with thick rice noodles make up this delicious dish. The mixture of sweetness, sourness, saltiness and a hit of spiciness creates beautifully balanced flavor in one bowl without any **conflict**. Since so, nothing represents the meaning of Nyonya Food better than AsamLaksa. The rich flavor reflects the **harmony** created by people living together **regardless of** races or religions.

Part
1

Part
2

Part
3

Part
4

Part
5

Part
6

Part
7

中文翻譯

土生華人菜

　　土生華人菜是峇峇娘惹文化的**獨特篇章**，由於下廚傳統上是女人的工作，這種料理也被稱為「娘惹菜」。海峽華人移民到馬來亞之後，跟馬來人通婚，結合了華菜與的作法與當地東南亞的食材，例如：椰奶、**檸檬葉**、**薑黃**、羅望子、**七葉蘭**、辣椒和辣椒醬（sambal）。很多菜色乍看都跟中式料理很像，但口味卻有更多變化。馬來西亞人很愛吃辣椒醬（Sambal），所以娘惹菜很多辣椒醬炒菜，例如 Sambal 蝦仁等、Sambal 雞。最具代表性的娘惹菜，莫過於亞參叻沙Asam laksa。

　　亞參叻沙是酸辣麵，湯頭基底由魚和羅望子組成。**碎魚片**、羅望子和切絲的小黃瓜、洋蔥、辣椒、鳳梨、萵苣菜、薄荷和薑，配上粗米粉，就是這道佳餚。酸酸甜甜鹹鹹辣辣的滋味，在碗裡完美的平衡在一起，沒有任何**衝突**。因此，沒有什麼比亞參叻沙更能代表娘惹菜的精神了。這豐富的滋味反映出不同種族、宗教背景的人**和諧地**同居共處。

重點字彙

1. **turmeric**（*n.*）薑黃

2. **tamarind**（*n.*）羅望子

3. **pandan**（*n.*）七葉蘭

4. **sparkle**（*n.*）火花；活力；生氣

   The sparkle on her face disappeared as soon as the judge announced the result of the competition.
   她臉上的光輝在評審宣布比賽結果時瞬間消失殆盡。

5. **ingredient**（*n.*）原料、食材

   It takes only four ingredients to make perfect egg pudding: eggs, milk, cream and sugar.
   做出完美雞蛋布丁只需要四種食材：雞蛋、牛奶、鮮奶油和糖。

6. **shredded**（*adj.*）撕碎的

   The whole office is emptied with only some shredded paper left.
   整間辦公室都清空了，只剩一些碎紙片。

7. **finely sliced**（*adj.*）切絲的

   The finely sliced green papaya is the soul of Thai salad.
   青木瓜絲是泰式沙拉的精華靈魂。

8. **conflict**（*n.*）衝突

Tourists are suggested to avoid going near the conflict zone.

旅客被告知避開衝突危險區。

9. **harmony**（*n.*）和諧

The choir brings the sound of harmony deep into every audience's soul.

合唱團將和諧之音唱到每位聽眾的靈魂深處。

10. **regardless of**（*adv.*）不管、不顧

This is the first school in the country to provide education regardless of the pupils' social classes.

這是全國第一間不論學童的社會階級而提供教育的學校。

Part 1
Part 2
Part 3
Part 4
Part 5
Part 6
Part 7

iBT 新托福字彙閱讀應試技巧

Question 1: What does "Baba" mean?

(A) Father　　　　　　　　(B) Children

(C) Men　　　　　　　　　(D) Women

解析　由 "The Peranakans are also called, "Baba Nyonya" which refers to the men and the women respectively." 可知，Baba 意指男性，Nyonya意指女性。故答案為 (C)。

Question 2: "In Malaysia, the main language, Bahasa Melayu had been standardized and assigned as the official language for all ethnic groups which led to the disappearance of _____." Which of the following answer can fill in the blank?

(A) Baba Nyonya　　　　　(B) Baba Malay

(C) Malay　　　　　　　　(D) English

解析　Bahasa Melayu 本身就是馬來文，所以選項 (C) 不可能；選項 (A) 為族群名稱，並非語言；選項 (D) 並不是該族群特有的語言，與該段落所討論的文化削減現象沒有直接關係，故答案為選項 (B)，峇峇馬來語。

Part
1

Part
2

Part
3

Part
4

Part
5

Part
6

Part
7

Question 3: Which of the following is the most unlikely occupation of the early Peranakan Chinese?

(A) Merchant　　　　　　(B) Trader

(C) Intermediary　　　　　(D) Missionary

解析 由 "As many of them were merchants, traders or intermediaries between the British, Chinese and Malays..." 這句可知，傳教士並不是早期海峽華人所從事的行業，故答案為選項 (D)。

Unit 07

7.1

 Track 13

Collectivism vs. Individualism

While the world is so diverse in different types of cultures, most of them can be divided into two categories: Individualism and Collectivism. This **fundamental** difference of two categories reflects on the education, family structure, and broadly social values. However, here comes the question: should a person's life belong to the individual or should it belong to his/her family, community, society, or even the state?

Individualism focuses on personal achievement **regardless of** the group goals. In Individualism societies, individuals are encouraged to develop their own **uniqueness** and personal identity. Independence is valued. As people are expected to do things on their own, being **dependent** on others may seem to be shameful. Examples of such societies are the USA and Western European countries.

Collectivism **emphasizes** group objectives above each individual's needs and desires. Families, communities and the collective societies have influenced more on individuals and thus have developed rules encouraging **brotherhood**, **sisterhood** and **selflessness**. People in Collectivism societies are more willing to provide help and collaborate with each other. Examples of Collectivism societies are China, Russia and some of the former **Soviet** States.

Either Individualism or Collectivism, each has its **pros and cons**. Individualism societies possess a penchant for offering people chances to express themselves but it's also harder for them to gather a unified will. Collectivism societies work more **efficiently** in achieving the greater goods for the group but this sometime sacrifices some members' personal goals.

中文翻譯

集體主義 vs. 個人主義

世界上的文化這麼多元，大部分都能被歸為兩種分類：個人主義和集體主義。這兩兩存在**根本性的**差異，齊差異反映在教育、家庭結構，以及廣泛的社會價值上。這時問題來了，一個人的生命是屬於他／她自己呢，還是屬於其家庭、社區、社會甚至國家？

個人主義著重在個人成就**勝過**團體目標。在個人主義社會中，每個個人都被鼓勵發展自己的**獨特性**和人格特質。獨立生活是被肯定的。由於人們通常期待凡事自己來，**依賴**他人可能被視為丟臉的事情。這類社會的例子為美國和西歐國家。

集體主義將團體目標**放在**個人需求慾望之上。家庭、社區和整體社會有較多規則,對每個個體有較多影響力,鼓勵**兄弟、姊妹情誼**,以及**無私小我**。集團主義社會的人較願意提供幫助以及互相合作。集體主義社會的例子為中國、俄國以及某些前**蘇聯**國家。

個人主義或集團主義各有有**長處**,也有**短處**。個人主義社會對於人們表達自我比較開放,但他們也比較難彙整出統一的想法意願。集體主義社會追求整體社會福祉上比較有**效率**,但這有時也犧牲內部某些成員的個人目標。

 重點字彙

1. **fundamental**(*adj.*)根本性的

The fundamental issue of the Refugee Crisis is not about housing them but stopping the war in their homelands.
難民危機的根本議題不在於如何安置他們,而是停止他們家鄉的戰亂。

2. **regards**（*n.*）尊重、關心、問候；關係到；
regardless of 無論如何

① Please send my best regards to your family.

請代我像您的家人致意。

② Employees are all invited to the conference regardless of their positions.

不論職位,所有員工都受邀參加會議。

3. **unique**（*adj.*）獨一無二的

She loves the uniqueness of hand-crafted items.

她喜愛手工製作的獨特性。

4. **depend**（*v.*）依賴;取決於;**dependent**（*adj.*）依靠於;
independent（*adj.*）獨立

① The budget of the new project is totally depending on the sponsors.

新企畫的預算完全取決於贊助人。

② Women are encouraged to have financial independence in today's society.

如今社會鼓勵女人經濟獨立。

5. **emphasize**（*v.*）強調

The president skipped some major social issues and only emphasized his achievements in the speech.

總統在演講中略過一些重大社會問題，只強調他的成就。

6. **brotherhood**（*n.*）兄弟情誼；**sisterhood**（*v.*）姊妹情誼；**sibling**（*n.*）手足

① Soldiers form a very strong brotherhood and help look after each other's family.

軍人之間有非常強烈的兄弟情誼，互相照顧彼此的家庭。

② My siblings and I take turn taking of our old father.

我和兄弟姐妹輪流照看年邁的父親。

7. **selfless**（*adj.*）無私；**selfish**（*adj.*）自私

① The Sister spent her whole life to the orphanage selflessly.

那位修女終身都無私的奉獻給孤兒院。

② No one wants to work with that selfish man who never thinks for the group.

沒有人想跟那個自私的人合作，他從不為團體著想。

8. **Soviet**（*n.*）蘇聯

She left Russia after the fall of Soviet Union and never returned again.

她在蘇聯瓦解後離開俄國，從此再沒回去過。

9. **pros and cons**（*n.*）好處與壞處

Living in the city center has its pros and cons. You may be closer to your workplace, but it's also very noisy in the evening.

住在市中心有好處也有壞處，你可能可以離工作地方很近，但晚上也很吵。

10. **efficient**（*adj.*）有效率的；**effective**（*adj.*）有效的；生效

① The new machinery system helps the factory work more efficiently.

新的機械化系統讓工廠工作更有效率。

② A new law has been passed this morning and will be effective from January.

今早通過了一條新法，將於一月起生效。

—————— 7.2 ——————

Child Rearing in Individualism Societies and Collectivism Societies

One of the most fundamental stages that influence a person's whole life is childhood. Different child **rearing patterns** are practiced to develop personalities to fit in Individualism societies and Collectivism societies.

Parents from Individualism societies tend to place **infants** in separate rooms as soon as possible. Babies are trained to self-regulate and self-soothe when they sleep **solitarily**. However, this is not generally allowed in Collectivism societies for health and security concerns. Some also believe that co-sleeping is the most natural practice as it creates more mother-and-child **intimacy**.

Children in Collectivism societies are taught to use titles such as uncle, auntie or teacher instead of names when calling others they are not familiar with. This gives them concept of different interpersonal relationships. Children in Individualism societies are allowed to call people by their names, even their parents' names. This gives them much freedom to treat people without the idea of **hierarchy**.

Unit 07

Part
1

Part
2

Part
3

Part
4

Part
5

Part
6

Part
7

Child rearing conflicts often occur in intercultural families. Even within the same culture, grandparents may still hold different opinions about the upbringing of their grandchildren. To raise the child together properly, the communication with patience is essential. Whether it is in Individualism or Collectivism societies, love is important in everywhere.

中文翻譯

集體主義及個人主義社會的孩童撫養方式

人生中最根本的發展階段之一，就是童年時期。不同的**撫養方式**會訓練出不同的人格特質，以適應個人主義社會或集體主義社會。個人主義社會的父母傾向於盡早讓**嬰兒**獨立一間房間。寶寶從**單獨**睡覺中訓練出自我管理和安撫自己的能力。然而，由於安全和健康考量，這在集體主義社會普遍上是不被允許的。有些人也相信親子同寢是最自然的作法，能增進母子**親密度**。

集體主義社會的孩子被教導要以稱謂叫人，例如叔叔、阿姨、老師等。這讓他們認知到不同人際關係的概念。個人主義社會的孩子則較被容許直呼名號，甚至是父母的名字。這讓他們能較自由的撇開**階級制度**對待別人。

跨文化家庭裡常出現孩子教養觀念的衝突。就算是同一種文化出身，祖父母還是有可能對孫子輩的撫養方式有不同的意見。為了要好好的共同把孩子養大，耐心是溝通中不可或缺的。不論是個人主義或集體主義社會，愛在哪裡都是一樣的。

 重點字彙

1. **rear**（*v.* / *adj.*）撫養、栽培；豎立；後面的

   ① Please familiarize yourself with the safety exits. There are two at the front and two at the rear of the aircraft.

   請熟悉一下逃生出口的位置，飛機的前方和後方各有兩個出口。

   ② He was reared by his grandmother due to his parents' absence for work.

   由於父母長年工作，他是由祖母撫養長大的。

2. **pattern**（*n.*）模式；樣式

   ① This company set a good patter of a successful social enterprise.

   這間公司立下了成功的社會企業模範。

   ② I prefer check to floral pattern for bags.

   比起碎花圖案，我比較喜歡格紋包。

3. **infant**（*n.*）嬰幼兒；**toddler**（*n.*）學步的小孩

Mothers often get exhausted by waking up every night to breastfeed the infants.

每晚起來替嬰兒哺乳通常都會讓母親疲憊不堪。

4. **solitary**（*adj.*）單獨的、孤獨的

He lives a solitary life with little contact with the society.

他獨居生活，跟社會少有接觸。

5. **intimacy**（*n.*）親密感

Intimacy comes without words.

親密感是無需文字述說的。

6. **hierarchy**（*n.*）階級、等級制度

Soldiers need to follow strict hierarchy in the army.

軍人在軍中必須遵守嚴格的階級制度。

iBT 新托福字彙閱讀應試技巧

Question 1: Paula grew up in a big family with lots of blessing from uncles and aunties. Her parents convinced her to study accounting. She graduated and got employed by a large firm. She works in a big team. Her colleagues all find her very easy to collaborate with. Where is Paula from?

(A) New York　　　　　(B) London
(C) Kiev　　　　　　　(D) Berlin

解析　寶拉成長於有眾多叔伯阿姨疼愛的大家庭，她的父母替她安排生涯規劃，她進入大公司工作，團隊中的同事都認為她很容易合作，由此可見寶拉很有可能是集體主義社會出身，而紐約在美國、倫敦在英國、柏林在德國，都是屬於較個人主義的社會，因此答案為 (C)，基輔為前蘇聯國家烏克蘭的首都。

Part
1

Part
2

Part
3

Part
4

Part
5

Part
6

Part
7

Question 2: Aiko is Japanese. She married to an American man and recently gave birth to a baby. She worries that her mother-in-law might disagree with how she would raise the child. Which of the following shouldn't be her concern?

(A) She wants to sleep with the baby but the grandma says the baby would grow too attached to her.

(B) The old lady wants to be called by her name when the baby learns to speak but Aiko thinks it's too rude.

(C) She was taught to follow the rules at school but her husband encourages the child not to be afraid of challenging teachers in the classroom.

(D) She wants to breastfeed the baby but the mother-in-law believes that baby formula is more nutritious.

解析　Aiko 是日本人，由於日本是集體主義社會但美國是個人主義社會，她擔心會和她的美國家庭會在孩子教養上有些歧見。選項 (A)、(B)、(C) 都是有可能會發生的問題，但母乳和配方奶的選擇，和集體主義社會或個人主義社會並沒有太大關聯，因此答案為選項 (D)。

Unit 08

8.1

Track 15

Intercultural Communication – High Context vs. Low Context

Miscommunication happens a lot between people from different cultural backgrounds. Communication styles can be categorized into high context and low context.

High context cultures tend to use fewer words to **convey** complex messages, which work effectively between people sharing the same cultural knowledge, since the similarity in their knowledge could be **omitted** in the conversation. **Understatement** is very commonly used in high context communication. However, this type of expression may sound confusing for people from lower-context culture. People outside of the group either struggle to figure out the unspoken things or underestimate the significance of the messages and make wrong **judgments**.

People in low context cultures are more **explicit** in their expressions. People tend to be **wordier** in giving details with lots of **exaggerations** such as "Oh my GOD!" "Best friends FOREVER". From the marketing perspective, this type of communication methods may make the audience tired easily when getting too much excitement.

The difference between high context and low context culture only shows by comparison. For instance, British people may find it challenging to **negotiate** with Japanese people as both tend to hold their expressions. But for the American people, British humor is **puzzling**! Thus, it is harder to translate the higher context into lower context languages than the other way around.

中文翻譯

高情境文化與低情境文化

溝通不良的情況常發生在不同文化背景出身的人之間，不同的溝通習慣可分為高情境和低情境。

高情境文化傾向於用較少的篇幅**傳達**複雜的訊息，這在具備同樣文化知識的人之間很有效，由於知識相似，因此對談中可以**省略**許多彼此都知道的事情。保守的**輕描淡寫**也很常在高情境溝通中出現。然而，這種表達方式對於較低情境文化出身的人來說就比較難懂了，外人要不是搞不懂那些沒說出來的事情，就是低估訊息的重要性，進而做出錯誤的**判斷**。

低情境文化表達的時候比較**詳盡**，比較會給**冗長的**細節描述，還有很多**誇張**的言詞例如「我的天啊！」「永遠都是最好的朋友」。以行銷的角度來說，這種溝通方式給太多刺激，讓觀眾容易一下就疲勞。

　　高情境和低情境文化的差異只有比較才會出現。舉例來說，英國人可能覺得和日本人**談判**很有挑戰性，因為他們傾向於保守的表達方式。但對美國人來說，英式幽默又太難懂了！因此，從高情境語言翻譯到低情境語言比較難，反之則易。

 重點字彙

1. **miscommunication**（*n.*）溝通不良

They have miscommunication issues due to each other's accent.
他們因為雙方的口音而產生溝通不良的問題。

2. **convey**（*v.*）傳達、表達

She conveyed her disagreement firmly with grace.
她優雅但堅定地表達無法認同。

3. **omit**（*v.*）省略

The author raged at the publisher who omitted a paragraph without asking her.
作者對於出版社沒問過她就刪去一個段落感到怒火中燒。

同義字 neglect 忽略

His poor health condition is not to be neglected.

他的健康問題不容忽視。

4. understatement（*n.*）保守說法、輕描淡寫

反義字 overstate, exaggerate 誇大

① "Pretty" would be an understatement. You look stunning today.

說「漂亮」太含蓄了，你今天看起來明豔動人。

② Don't exaggerate the obstacles. You are still responsible for your mistake.

不要把那些障礙講的那麼誇張，你還是得為你的錯誤負責。

5. explicit（*adj.*）詳盡的、明確的

He presented an explicit report on the practices of the new project.

他針對新企畫的執行方法，提供了一份非常詳盡的報告。

6. **judgment**（*n.*）判斷

No matter what people tell you, you must trust your own judgment.

不論別人怎麼跟你說，你都要相信自己的判斷。

7. **wordy**（*adj.*）嘮叨、冗長

同義字 ➤ lengthy 長的；冗長的

① He always found his mother's preaching too wordy until he started his own life.

他老是嫌媽媽的教誨太嘮叨，直到他開始自己的新生活為止。

② Everyone is tired of the chairman's lengthy speech.

每個人都受不了主席冗長的演講。

8. **exaggerate**（*v.*）誇大；
   exaggeration（*n.*）誇張的言詞、手法

① Don't exaggerate your loss. It's just a broken plate!

不要把你的損失講得這麼誇張，只是破了一個盤子！

② The young blogger's articles are full of exaggerations with little content.

那個年輕部落客的文章充滿一堆誇張的言詞，沒什麼內容。

9. **negotiation**（*n.*）談判

It's been a year since the war started yet there's still no sign of negotiation!

戰爭都打一年了，談判還是連個影都沒有！

10. **puzzle**（*n.*）謎題、難解之事；使人困惑；
puzzling（*adj.*）令人困惑不解的

① Each challenge comes with a puzzle.

每個關卡都有一道謎題。

② This professor is known for giving puzzling, yet inspiring advices.

這個教授以給人難懂但充滿啟發性的建議聞名。

Part 1

Part 2

Part 3

Part 4

Part 5

Part 6

Part 7

8.2

British Humor

Apart from fish n'chips and castles, the UK has another thing which is well-known to the world – British Humor. British Humor can be found everywhere from advertisements, films, dramas, stand-up comedies to politician's speeches.

Britain is notorious for dividing the social classes and people within the classes. To make their statuses and **differentiate** themselves from others, each class develops their own ways of expression. For example, upper class people speak in a different accent to show their superiority. Traditionally, working class people in London developed their **dialect** "Cockney" so that outsiders couldn't understand their conversation. Cockney now became the Londoner accent. British people like to mock each other's regional accent, too. For instance, Birmingham accent is called, "Brummie"; Liverpool accent, "Scouse"; Newcastle accent, "Geordie", and so on.

British people are the master of **sarcasm** which reflects on their rich works of **satire**. Harsh words are used between close friends and family members to show intimacy, which could seem rather shocking to outsiders. However, there is only a fine line between humor and **bullying**. Young **pupils tease** each other's race, region, hair color or any kind of **stereotype** at school to have fun. Victims often suffer years of inferiority until finding confidence in life.

中文翻譯

英式幽默

除了炸魚薯條和城堡之外，英國還有一件世界聞名的特產——英式幽默。英式幽默無所不在，從廣告、電影、戲劇、脫口秀到政治人物演講都能找的到。

英國是出了名的會內部劃分社會階級，以及身在其中的群眾。為了要把自己的身分跟別人有所**區分**，每個階級都會發展出自己的表達方式。傳統來說，倫敦的工人階級發展出一種**方言**「考克尼」，好讓外人聽不懂他們的對話內容，如今考克尼儼然成為倫敦口音。英國人也喜歡嘲笑彼此的地區口音，例如伯明罕腔被稱為 "Brummie"，利物浦腔是 "Souse"，紐卡索腔則是 "Geordie"。

英國人是**諷刺**大師，這反映在豐富的**諷刺**作品上。好友、家人之間常會用特別刺耳難聽的言詞來表達親密感，對外人來說大概會滿驚訝的。不過，幽默和**霸凌**之間只有一線之隔，小學生在學校裡會為了好玩而拿彼此的種族、出身地區、髮色或任何**刻板印象**來大肆奚落。受害者通常都得要過了好幾年的自卑歲月，才能再次找到自信。

重點字彙

1. **differentiate**（*v.*）區別

   They use colorful vests to differentiate teams of different roles.
   他們用彩色背心區分不同團隊的功能。

2. **dialect**（*n.*）方言

   Born and raised in Malaysia, he can speak Malay, English, and several Chinese dialects.
   自幼在馬來西亞長大的他能說馬來語、英文以及數種中文方言。

3. **tease**（*v.*）戲弄、欺負

   同義字 ▸ annoy 惹惱、使煩擾；bother 打擾、煩擾

   ① The boys tease the girl by pulling her ponytail.
      那些男生拉女生的馬尾藉以欺負她。
   ② I find his rude swearwords very annoying.
      我覺得他粗魯的髒話非常討厭。
   ③ Mosquitoes really bother me at night.
      我晚上都被蚊子煩得受不了。

4. **sarcasm**（*n.*）挖苦、諷刺

   The comedian is known for criticizing politics with sarcasm.
   那位喜劇演員以諷刺批評政治知名。

5. **satire**（*n.*）諷刺文學、諷刺劇

Living in the age with no freedom of speech, the writer put all his anger in this masterpiece of satire.

這位作家生在沒有言論自由的年代，只能把所有不滿投注在這部諷刺文學大作上。

6. **bully**（*v.*）霸凌

She suffered from kids bullying her red hair throughout her teenage years.

整個青春期她都因為紅頭髮而在其他孩子霸凌下度過。

7. **pupil**（*n.*）小學生、未成年人；弟子

This is a very small village. The local school only has five pupils this year.

這是個很小的村子，當地學校今年只有五位學生。

8. **stereotype**（*n.*）刻板印象

She doesn't apply to the most usual French stereotype - she doesn't eat cheese!

她並不符合最普遍的法國刻板印象 — 她不吃起司！

iBT 新托福字彙閱讀應試技巧

Question 1: Which of the following is a lower context communication method?

(A) Alice likes to bring up historical references of her country.

(B) Ben borrows some lines from classic literature to write in his love letters.

(C) Eric prefers giving people tips than providing complete solutions.

(D) The old cookbook explains every step of the recipe in detail.

解析　(A) 愛莉絲喜歡提起歷史典故，但外國人未必聽得懂；(B) 班從古典文學中借了幾句寫進去情書裡，他的情人必須讀過這些名著才能看得懂；(C) 艾瑞克偏向給人提點，卻不說完整的解決方案，這會給人很大的揣測空間。因此答案為 (D)，烹飪書把食譜每個步驟都解釋得非常仔細，這是最容易讓人理解的表達方式。

Question 2: Which are the reasons for British people to develop accents and dialects? (Multiple options)

(A) To show their statuses.
(B) To keep secrets from others.
(C) To improve the cultural diversity.
(D) To create group identity.

解析 英國人之所以發展出口音和方言，有些是因為強調自己的身分、有些是不讓外人得知秘密、有些是為了凝聚群體意識，這些造就了今日的文化多元社會，而不是當初為了發展多元化而培養口音的，因此答案為選項 (A)、(B)、(D)。

Part 1

Part 2

Part 3

Part 4

Part 5

Part 6

Part 7

Unit **09**

9.1 **Track 17**

Culture Shock

Culture shock is a type of personal **disorientation** happened when a person travel or migrate to a different social environment. This can be divided into four stages: Honeymoon, **Frustration**, Adjustment, and Mastery.

Honeymoon refers to the joy upon arrival when the person is amused by all the novelties. The person is **thrilled** to **embrace** everything new from tasting local food, meeting new friends, learning local languages to visiting local attractions, etc.

Followed by the romantic Honeymoon, the second stage is Frustration or called, Negotiation. The person might be frustrated by social **obstacles** like language barrier. Local traffic system could be dangerous to new comers. All kind of pressure, together with **homesickness**, can be so **overwhelming** that some people even suffer from anxiety.

After fighting the second stage for a while, the person either goes back or adjusts himself/herself to stay. This is called,

Adjustment stage. The person needs to learn humbly from the locals about how to dress to deal with the local weather, how to cook with local ingredient and how to behave in local manners, etc.

Finally, the newcomer develops a way to live in the new environment with ease and comfort. This doesn't require the person to abandon his or her roots. Many people in this situation maintain good connections with their origins. In some cases, people may have the fifth stage – **Reverse** Culture Shock – by returning to their origins.

中文翻譯

文化衝擊

文化衝擊是一種人格**失調**，發生在一個人旅行或遷移到不同的社交環境時。這可以被分為四階段：蜜月期、**沮喪期**、適應期和融入期。

蜜月期指的是抵達時，面對所有新奇事物而產生的歡樂感。此人**迫不及待的接受**一切新事物，品嚐當地食物、認識新朋友、學當地語言、參訪當地景點等等。

緊接浪漫的蜜月期後，第二階段是沮喪期，或稱抗拒期。此人可能因各種諸如語言隔閡的社交**障礙**感到喪氣，當地交通系統對初來乍到的新人更是充滿危險。種種壓力加上**思鄉病**，可能會太過強烈壓的有些人甚至被焦慮所苦。

抗拒一段時間後，此人要不是回去，就是要自我調整好繼續待下來，這也就是適應期。此人必須謙虛地向當地人學習如何因應當地氣候搭配衣著、如何烹飪當地食材、如何讓行為符合當地規範等等。

最後，新人終於在新環境發展出輕鬆又舒服的生活方式，也就是融入期。這不代表一定要拋去元生本性，許多人在這種情況仍然和原生環境保持良好的連結。有些情況下，人們可能發展出第五階段——文化再衝擊——也就是**回到**原生地後的重新適應。

 重點字彙

1. **orientation**（*n.*）定位；確定；（開學）介紹；
   disorientation（*n.*）失序、迷惘

   ① She moved to the University two days before the semester to attend orientation events.
   她在學習前兩天就搬進大學，參加始業典禮。
   ② The horrible experience in the war left him with lifelong anxiety and disorientation.
   戰時的恐怖經歷給他一輩子揮之不去的焦慮和失調。

與 disorient 相關的 延伸字彙

baffle, bamboozle, bemuse, bewilder, buffalo, confound

He's completely bamboozled by the latest changes in policies.

政策上的改變讓他非常困惑。

2. **frustrate**（*v.*）重挫；**frustrated**（*adj.*）灰心喪氣；**frustration**（*n.*）挫折

① He was frustrated as the boss just sacked him.

被老闆開除讓他灰心喪氣。

② He cried in frustration, worrying the bills and rents to pay.

他受挫而泣，擔心那些還沒繳交的租金和帳單。

延伸字彙

同義字　aggravation, exasperation, annoyance, nuisance

① The noise is the source of aggravation.

噪音是焦躁的原因。

② The exasperation and frustration of holiday shopping has been an experience commonly shared.

假日購物帶來的憤怒和沮喪是大眾共同的經驗。

3. **thrill**（*v.*）使興奮、使激動；使緊張、毛骨悚然；
   thriller（*n.*）恐怖小說、令人毛骨悚然的事物

   ① The actress was thrilled by the news that she was nominated as the best actress of the year.
   那位女演員接到年度最佳女演員的提名，興奮的不得了。

   ② The latest thriller used a haunted house..
   最新驚悚片將一座鬼屋搬上了大銀幕。

4. **embrace**（*v.*）擁抱；（機會、協議、宗教）接受、抓住

   ① They embraced each other and forgave what had happened before.
   他們擁抱彼此，原諒過去發生的事情。

   ② The young man embraced this opportunity with no hesitation.
   這個年輕人毫不猶豫地接受這個好機會。

   同義字 grasp 抓牢、緊緊抓住
   He grasped an umbrella in a rush, not knowing it was broken.
   他匆忙抓起一把雨傘，不知道傘是壞的。

5. **obstacle**（*n.*）障礙

   Despite a series of obstacles, she managed to graduate with the highest grade from the University.
   儘管有重重障礙，她還是以最高分從大學畢業了。

6. **homesickness**（*n.*）思鄉病

She never liked bubble tea before but now that's the only thing to ease the homesickness.

她從來不喜歡珍珠奶茶的，但現在這卻是唯一能一解思鄉情懷的東西。

7. **overwhelm**（*v.*）淹沒、壓倒、戰勝；
   overwhelming（*adj.*）壓倒性的

① She was overwhelmed by the news and couldn't find a word to say.

她被新聞震懾到說不出一句話。

② Team Taiwan won the game with an overwhelming score.

台灣隊以超高分在比賽中獲得壓倒性的勝利。

8. **reverse**（*v.*）反轉、反面、顛倒

Cooking used to be the wife's job but the position reversed after she started a new job and needed to work later than the husband.

煮飯原本是太太的工作，但在她換了一份比先生還晚下班的工作後，角色就顛倒了。

9.2

 Track 18

How to Overcome Culture Shock

Going to study abroad? **Relocating** to an overseas office? Here are a few tips to help **overcome** culture shock in a foreign country:

1. *Learn the Language.* Being capable to speak local languages can help you get used to local life a lot easier. Attend a language course. Listen to radio and read local newspaper. It may sound challenging but definitely easier than you thought.

2. *Don't Apply Your Values to Other People.* Every culture is different in how people approach and interact with others. In some cultures, sharing family backgrounds and financial situation are acceptable. But in others, these topics may **intrude** into personal privacy. Always respect values that are different from yours.

3. *Make new Friends!* Join clubs to meet people with the same hobbies. Be active in local events. Make friends with local people and blend in their society!

4. *Develop a Sense of Stability*. Establish a healthy daily **routine**.

Unit 09

Part 1

Part 2

Part 3

Part 4

Part 5

Part 6

Part 7

Become a regular to a local club. A stable life can help you develop the sense of belonging.

5. *Be Open to New Things.* There will be a lot of unexpected surprises. Just ask people if you ever find confused instead of making **assumptions**. If you are moving from a warm place to a cold one, ask people how to use the heater **economically**. If you are moving from a dry country to a damp one, ask people how to avoid **moldy** wall and **rotten** furniture.

如何克服文化衝擊

要出國留學嗎？**調職**到海外分公司？這裡有幾個小建議，幫助你在異鄉**克服**文化衝擊，展開新生活：

1. *學習語言*。能使用當地語言會讓你更容易適應當地生活。上語言課程，聽收音機、讀當地報紙，也許聽起來很難，但絕對比你想的容易。

2. *不要把你的價值加諸他人身上*。每個文化中，人們相處的方式都不大相同。有些文化裡，分享家族背景和財務情況是可接受的，但在其他文化中，這些話題可能有侵犯他人隱私的疑慮。尊重與你不同的價值觀。

3. 交**新朋友**！加入社團，認識些有相同嗜好的人。多多參加當地活動。交些朋友並打進他們的社會吧！

4. *發展**穩定性***。立下一個健康的**日常作息**，成為當地酒吧的常客。安定的生活可以幫助你發展出歸屬感。

5. 對新事物保持開放。一定會有很多料想不到的驚喜，不要擅作**預設立場**，如果感到困惑，就多問問其他人。如果你從溫暖的地方搬到很冷的地方，問別人如何節約使用暖氣。如果是從乾燥的國家搬到潮濕的國家，問別人該如何避免**壁癌**和家具**壞掉**。

 重點字彙

1. **relocate**（*n.*）搬遷、調動

   The whole village relocated to the other side of the river.
   整村都遷移到河的另一岸。

2. **overcome**（*n.*）克服

   It took her a great deal of courage to overcome the fear of giving a public speech.
   她鼓起好大的勇氣才克服公開演講的恐懼。

3. **intrude**（*v.*）侵入、侵犯、闖入

The house was intruded by a thief while the family was all sleeping.

小偷趁這家人全部睡著時闖入屋內。

4. **stable**（*adj.*）穩定；**stability**（*n.*）穩定性

① Gold is the most stable metal.

金是最穩定的金屬。

② She longs for a family that gives her the sense of stability.

她渴望有一個能讓她有安定感的家庭。

5. **routine**（*n.*）固定作息、例行公事；固定舞步

His daily routine starts by a coffee at 8am.

他每日作息以早上八點一杯咖啡開始。

6. **assume**（*v.*）設想、假想；**assumption**（*n.*）預設想法

From the way you stare at me now, I assume you won't accept any explanation.

從你現在瞪著我的樣子來看，我想你大概聽不進任何解釋吧。

Part 1

Part 2

Part 3

Part 4

Part 5

Part 6

Part 7

7. **economy**（*v.*）經濟；**economical**（*adj.*）節省的

① The new government started its rule by improving the tough economy.

新政府上任便先從改善艱困的經濟開始。

② Though expensive, this is the most economical air-conditioner in the market.

雖然貴了些，這卻是市面上最節能的冷氣機。

8. **mold**（*n.*）霉；**moldy**（*adj.*）發霉的

The stingy landlord refused to pay the cost of cleaning the mold on the wall.

小氣的房東拒絕負擔除壁癌的費用。

9. **rotten**（*adj.*）腐爛的、腐朽的

They stored too much food in the fridge. Some of the apples were already rotten.

他們在冰箱裡堆太多食物了，有些蘋果都已經壞了。

iBT 新托福字彙閱讀應試技巧

Part 1

Part 2

Part 3

Part 4

Part 5

Part 6

Part 7

Question 1: Gary really hates the taste of animal organs but he recently learned the origin of Scottish haggis and started to appreciate its down-to-earth culture. Which stage is he experiencing in adapting the Scottish culture?

(A) Honeymoon　　　　　(B) Frustration

(C) Adjustment　　　　　(D) Mastery

> 解析 能夠克服原本對動物內臟的障礙，學習從文化的角度品嘗當地特產，這代表蓋瑞已經過了衝擊／抗拒期，進入適應期，因此答案為 (C)。

Question 2: "Make friends with local people and _____ their society" Which of the following can be put in the sentence? (Multiple options)

(A) Integrate into　　　　(B) Sneak in

(C) Be part of　　　　　(D) Stick with

> 解析 文章中 "Make friends with local people and blend in their society" 中的 "blend in" 可以替換為 (A) 結合、與社會結為一體，或 (C) 成為一份子，但選項 (B) 意思為偷偷溜進，(D) 為緊緊跟著不離開，意思不符合，因此答案為選項 (A) 和 (C)。

Unit 10

10.1 Track 19

Stereotypes

Stereotypes are generalized ideas that associate certain **characteristics** with the whole group of people which aren't always **applicable**. These characteristics can be anything from skin color, religion to nationality, accent, sexual orientation, etc. Not all stereotypes are negative but they often cause **prejudgment** and discrimination which enlarge the gap between different cultures.

Stereotypes are **prevalent** in mainstream media and affect how people are treated in the society. For instance, teachers show bias toward students from the largest ethnic backgrounds; children with homosexual tendency may be bullied at school; employers can exclude applicants with foreign-sounding names from the interview; police officers tend to target people with color to check on the street.

To break the stereotypes, it is important to focus on individuals instead of the culture behind. This method is also called "non-**essentialism**" point of view which applies to any specific **entity**, that is, there is no necessity to meet the whole set of **attributes** that represent the identity and function of the group of origin. Critical thinking is required to avoid being **manipulated** by the media. Always be alert to the non-relevant elements used in commercial advertisements and question their purposes. Keep sharp when receiving **propaganda** as the authorities may use stereotypes as the tool to **polarize** people.

Although being 100% free from stereotypes is almost impossible, people can still learn to take stereotypes lightly and treat each other as equally as possible. After all, there is one thing that we always share equally, humanity.

中文翻譯

刻板印象

刻板印象是概括的想法，將特定**特徵**聯想到整個族群中的所有人，但那些人不一定都符合這些特徵。這些特徵可能是膚色、宗教或國籍、口音、性向等等。刻板印象並不全是負面的，但時常導致**偏見**和歧視，讓不同文化之間產生隔閡。

刻板印象**充斥於**主流媒體，影響人們在社會中的待遇。舉例來說，老師有可能對出身多數族群背景的學生偏心；有同志傾向的小孩可能在學校遭受霸凌；雇主可以排除名字聽起來像外國人的應徵者，不讓其面試；警察在街上傾向於針對有色人種臨檢。

　　要破除刻板印象的話，專注於個人而非背後的文化，是非常重要的。這個方法也被稱為「非**精粹主義**」觀點，意指不論任何特定**個體**，都沒有必要完全符合代表出身族群的身分和功能的每一項**特質**。要避免被媒體**操控**，批判性思考在是不可或缺的，對於在商業廣告中看似無關的元素保持警覺，並質疑其扮演的目的。對於政府的**文令宣傳**也要謹慎以待，因為當權者也有可能利用刻板印象**分化**民眾。

　　雖然要 100% 沒有刻板印象是幾乎不可能的，人們還是可以學著不要太看重刻板印象，對待別人時越平等越好。畢竟，有一樣事是我們不論如何都平等共有的，那就是人性。

 重點字彙

1. **character**（*n.*）人物、角色；性格、個性；
   characteristic（*n.*）特色、特徵

   ① Jean Valjean is the soul character in Les Misérables.
   尚萬強是悲慘世界中的靈魂人物。
   ② Though small, Taiwan has sharp characteristics.
   台灣雖小，卻有非常鮮明的特色。

2. **applicable**（*adj.*）適用的、可應用的、合適的

   The sim card comes with a 3-in-1 package. Surely you can find an applicable size for your phone.

SIM卡送來就是三合一的包裝，你一定可以找到手機適用的尺寸。

3. **prejudgment**（*n.*）**偏見；預先判斷、未審先判**

同義字 prejudice 偏見

① Stereotypes and prejudgments are the things that hold people back from understanding each other.

刻板印象和偏見是阻止人們了解彼此的癥結。

② Pride and Prejudice is one of Jane Austen's masterpieces.

《傲慢與偏見》是珍‧奧斯汀的經典作之一。

4. **prevalent**（*adj.*）**普遍的、盛行的**

Drugs are so prevalent in this country that the government decided to legalize it in order to better control its usage.

藥物在這個國家盛行到政府決定合法或，以更有效管制其使用。

5. **homosexual**（*adj.*）**同性戀的；homophobia**（*n.*）**恐同症**

① Thousands of homosexual people joined the Pride Parade to celebrate love and life.

數以千計的同志參加同志大遊行，慶祝愛與生命。

② The homophobic civil servant was sentenced to jail for refusing to issue marriage licenses to the same-sex couple.

那個歧視同志的公務員因為拒絕發給同性情侶結婚證書，被判刑入獄。

6. **essential** 必要的、不可或缺的；
   essentialism（*n.*）精粹主義

   ① Reading good books is essential to the making of a good writer.

   廣閱好書是造就好作家的必要工作。

   ② Essentialism may explain social behaviors to a certain degree but doesn't apply to every single individual in a group.

   精粹主義也許能在某種程度上解釋社交行為，但並不能套用到團體中的每一個個體。

7. **entity**（*n.*）實體、存在

   It's sad to see a once successful business being segmented into small entities for sell to buyers.

   看到一個曾經成功一時的企業，被切割成小個體出售給買家，真是令人不勝唏噓。

8. **attribute**（*n.*）屬性、特質；標誌、象徵

   White gold and silver look similar but are very different in attributes.

   白金和銀看起來很像，但卻有非常不同的特質。

9. **manipulate**（*v.*）操縱

The obsession of diamond rings is totally manipulated by the diamond industry.

鑽戒的迷思完全是鑽石企業操作出來的。

10. **propaganda**（*n.*）宣傳

The TV show is always praising the government like propaganda.

這個電視節目總是在吹捧政府，簡直就是政令宣導。

11. **polarize**（*v.*）分化、使極化

My family always gets polarized when it comes to politics.

每談到政治，我們家總是非常兩極。

Part 1

Part 2

Part 3

Part 4

Part 5

Part 6

Part 7

10.2 Track 20

Whitewashing in Hollywood

How did Cleopatra look like? Was she black, brown or light-skinned? In Hollywood films, she is white, played by Elizabeth Taylor.

Hollywood has a bad name of Whitewashing people of colors. Some of the **casts** used White people and use special makeup to fake **minority** groups' **features**. Others simply change the characters' identities. *Breakfast at Tiffany*'s in 1961 was criticized for having Mickey Rooney wearing fake buck teeth to play a Japanese businessman. *A Mighty Heart* in 2007 darkened Angelina Jolie's skin to fit a mixed race journalist. *Prince of Persia: The Sands of Time* in 2010 had the Persian prince played by Jake Gyllenhaal. The 2014 *Exodus: Gods and Kings* received numerous complaints about the absence of North African actors among the Egyptian roles. Even the **biblical** Hebrew leader, Moses, was played by Christian Bale.

The truth is, Hollywood is a business industry that money is the first priority when it comes to casting consideration. Whitewashing might work in the past when people with colors had little voices. Nowadays the markets have grown largely outside of the US and the audience can speak freely on the Internet for changes. It is time for Hollywood to stop hiring **Caucasian** actors to play characters with colors. It is time for actors/actresses of all shapes and colors to shine on the big screen.

中文翻譯

漂白的好萊塢

埃及豔后克利歐佩特拉長什麼應子？她的膚色是黝黑的、深褐色的還是小麥色？在好萊塢電影中她是白人，由伊莉莎白泰勒飾演。

好萊塢以「漂白」有色人種為人詬病。有些劇組用特殊化妝術，把白人假扮成**角色裡少數民族**的長相，有些則乾脆把故事裡的角色直接改掉。1961 年的《第凡內早餐》因為幫米基魯尼戴上暴牙，假裝日本商人而受批評。2007 年的《無畏之心》將安潔莉娜裘莉的膚色加深，讓她扮演混血記者。2010 年的《波斯王子：時之刃》讓傑克葛倫霍扮演波斯王子。2014 年的《出埃及記：天地王者》因為埃及角色中完全沒有北非演員而備受不滿，甚至連**聖經**故事裡的希伯來領袖摩西，都由克里斯汀貝爾飾演。

事實是，好萊塢是一個商業產業，金錢是選角的第一考量。「漂白」在過去可能行得通，當時有色人種還沒有什麼發聲管道。但現在美國以外的市場蓬勃發展，觀眾也能在網路上自由的呼籲改變。該是時候讓好萊塢停止用**高加索血統的**演員假扮有色人種了該是時候讓所有不同體型、膚色的男女演員登上大螢幕大放異彩了。

重點字彙

1. **cast**（*n.*/*v.*）卡司、演員選派；投擲、投射

The director will announce the cast of his new film in the press conference later.

導演等一下會在記者會上公布新電影的演員名單。

延伸字彙

- **director** 導演
- **screenplay** 電影劇本
- **playwright** 劇作家
- **producer** 製片、製作人
- **leading actor** / **actress** 男主角/女主角
- **supporting actor** / **actress** 男配角/女配角
- **voice over** 旁白
- **dub** 配音

The playwright has a very sharp eye in picking novels and making classic screenplay adaptions.

這位劇作家挑小說的眼光非常精準，寫出不少經典改編電影劇本。

2. **minority**（*n.*）少數；**majority**（*n.*）多數

More than 95% of the total income in the country is hold by the minority group of people.

超過95%的國內總收入為少數人所持有。

3. **feature**（*v.*）特徵、長相；以……為特色

① The new theme park featured in the crazy rollercoaster attracts thousands of visitors per day.

以瘋狂雲霄飛車為名的新主題公園，每天都吸引上千人來訪。

② The dark mascara strengthened her striking feature.

漆黑的睫毛膏讓她吸引人的五官更加突出。

4. **Bible**（*n.*）聖經；**biblical**（*adj.*）聖經中的

① As the daughter of a priest, she started reading the Bible since the age of 5.

身為牧師的女兒，她從五歲就開始讀聖經。

② Many artists find inspirations from biblical stories.

許多藝術家從聖經故事中找靈感。

5. **Caucasian**（*n.*）高加索人、白種人

Her blue eyes expose the Caucasian blood passed down by her grandmother.

她的藍眼睛透露出祖母傳下來的高加索血統。

Part 1
Part 2
Part 3
Part 4
Part 5
Part 6
Part 7

iBT 新托福字彙閱讀應試技巧

Question 1: What does "stereotypes" mean?

(A) Bad images people hold towards different groups of people.

(B) First impression appears when people meet each other.

(C) Ideas that are generalized to the whole group of people.

(D) Business strategies used in the media.

解析　刻板印象意思是被概括投射到整個群體的一些想法，因此答案為 (C)。刻板印象不一定是負面的訊息，因此選項 (A) 不對；刻板印象有可能影響人與人的第一印象，但不完全等於第一印象，因此選項 (B) 並不正確；媒體有時會利用刻板印象操控大眾的想法，但刻板印象本身並不等於商業策略，因此選項 (D) 也不對。

Part
1

Part
2

Part
3

Part
4

Part
5

Part
6

Part
7

Question 2: What does the statement "being 100% free from stereotypes is almost impossible" mean in the article?

(A) It is impossible to be free from stereotypes.

(B) It is possible to live without stereotypes as long as people don't watch commercial advertisements.

(C) To abandon stereotypes is a basic task that everyone should learn to do.

(D) A world without stereotypes is the ideal that people should try to achieve.

解析 「100% 沒有刻板印象是幾乎不可能的」指的是完全消除刻板印象是個理想的狀態，雖然要達到理想非常困難，但值得朝目標前進，因此答案為 (D)。這句話並沒有完全否定可能性，選項 (A) 不對；商業廣告是鼓吹刻板印象的元兇之一，但不是唯一，因此選項 (B) 不對；拋棄刻板印象並不是一件容易的事情，文中也沒有要求每個人都應該這麼做，因此選項 (C) 也不對。

Unit **11**

11.1

 Track 21

3D Printing - a New Page of Manufacturing Industry

Can you imagine how to "print" out a toy? Not from busy **assembly lines** in massive factories but in an office, by a desk-top printer? With the most **cutting-edge** 3D printing technologies, printers now can do more than putting **two dimensional** images on a piece of paper. 3D printers opened a new page in manufacturing history since the **Industrial Revolution**.

3D printers use **melting** or **softening** material to produce the layers of the objects. 3D printing technology can be classified into 7 **categories**: **Vat Photo Polymerization**, **Material Jetting**, **Binder Jetting**, **Material Extrusion**, **Powder Bed Fusion**, **Sheet Lamination** and **Directed Energy Deposition**. 3D printers can produce objects with different colors, different degrees of **transparency**, hardness or flexibility. To print out the objects, 3D printers require **virtual** design for the production. The virtual designs are made in CAD (**Computer Aided Design**) files using 3D modeling programs.

3D printing technologies have been applied to various fields including medical industry, **aerospace** and **aviation** industries, **automotive** industry and other industrial printings. For the users who are not **capable** to design their own 3D models, they can use 3D scanners to make digital 3D copies of existing objects. They can also join 3D **marketplaces** to download 3D model files.

中文翻譯

3D 列印技術開創製造產業新的一頁

你能想像「列印」出一個玩具嗎？不是從忙碌的工廠**生產線**中製造出來，而是桌上型的印表機？在**最新的**3D列印科技發展下，印表機的功能超越了**二維的**平面紙上影像列印。3D印表機開創了自**工業革命**以來，製造業歷史上新的一頁。

3D 印表機利用**熔化**或**軟化**材料，層疊製造出物件。3D 列印可以分為七大技術：**光聚合、噴嘴成形、黏著劑噴膠成型、材料擠製成型、粉體熔化成型、層疊製造成型、定向能量沉積**。3D 印表機可以製造出結合不同顏色、**透明度**、硬度或彈性的物件。3D 印表機需要有物件的**虛擬**設計以進行列印，虛擬設計是由 3D 製模程式寫出的 CAD（**電腦輔助設計**）檔案。

3D 列印技術應用在不同領域，包含醫療業、**航太業**、**汽車業**，以及其他工業列印。對於**無法**自己設計 3D 模型的使用者，他們可以使用 3D 掃描機，將現有的物件做出副本，他們也可以加入 3D 市集下載 3D 模型檔案。

重點字彙

1. **vat photo polymerization** 光聚合

2. **material jetting** 噴嘴成形

3. **binder jetting** 黏著劑噴膠成型

4. **material extrusion** 材料擠製成型

5. **powder bed fusion** 粉體熔化成型

6. **sheet lamination** 層疊製造成型

7. **directed energy deposition** 定向能量沉積

8. **assembly line**（*n.*）裝配線、生產線

   Her first job was working in an assembly line in a toy factory. The job was simple yet very boring. 她的第一份工作是在玩具工廠裡的生產線做事。工作很簡單，但是很無趣。

9. **cutting-edge**（*adj.*）最前線、尖端的

   He is always changing mobile phones to catch up with the most cutting edge technologies. 為了跟上尖端科技，他總是在換手機。

10. **dimension**（*n.*）尺寸；規模；維度；**scale**（*n.*）等級、規模；比例、尺度

The artist makes amazing paintings with two dimensional illusions of three dimensional spaces. 這位藝術家創作出神奇的畫作，讓二維平面看起來就像具有立體空間的幻覺。

11. Industrial Revolution（*n.*）工業革命

Manchester is the birthplace of the Industrial Revolution. The red-brick cotton mills record the history of the city.
曼徹斯特是工業革命的起源地。紅磚棉花工廠紀錄著城市的歷史。

12. melt（*v.*）熔化

The tip of this easy chocolate brownie recipe is to melt the dark chocolate with some milk.
這個簡易巧克力布朗尼食譜的秘訣，就是用一些牛奶熔化黑巧克力。

13. soft（*adj.*）軟、柔軟；soften（*v.*）軟化；softener（*n.*）（衣物）柔軟劑

She sings with such a very soft voice that it can soften even the hearts of stone. 她的歌喉如此柔美，連鐵石心腸都會被軟化。

14. category（*n.*）種類、範疇

延伸字彙

● type（*n.*／*v.*）種類、類型；打字
● class（*n.*）班級；階級；classify（*v.*）分類、分級；classification（*n.*）分類、分級、類別

Part 1

Part 2

Part 3

Part 4

Part 5

Part 6

Part 7

The local library received a large amount of book donation. They aim to classify the books into categories.
當地圖書館收到了大量捐贈書，他們希望能將這些書分門別類。

15. **transparency**（*n.*）透明度

The NGO requests the government for improving the budget transparency. 非政府組織要求政府改善預算透明度。

16. **virtual**（*adj.*）虛擬的

She spends a lot of money in upgrading her computer to play virtual reality games. 為了玩虛擬實境遊戲，她花很多錢升級電腦。

17. **Computer Aided Design** 電腦輔助設計；**Computer Aided Engineering** 電腦輔助工程；**Computer Aided Translation** 電腦輔助翻譯

Computer aided design is widely used in various fields including the interior designs.
電腦輔助設計在許多領域內被廣泛使用，包括室內設計。

18. **aerospace**（*n.*）航空、太空

NASA is the biggest aerospace research center with the most advanced technologies in the world.
美國航太總署（National Aeronautics and Space Administration,

USA）是最大的航太研究中心，有著全球最先進的科技。

19. **aviation**（*n.*）航空、飛機製造業

The attempt to fly in the sky started thousands of years ago in human history. But it was since some basic technical problems being solved in the early 20th century, the technologies have been developed quickly in military as well as civil aviation industries. 在空中飛翔的渴望早在數千年前就已經存在於人類史上。但是在二十世紀初克服某些基本技術性問題之後，航空業才快速的發展於軍事以及民間用途上。

20. **automotive**（*adj.*）汽車的

The automotive industrial development played a crucial role in Japan's postwar economy renaissance.
汽車業發展在日本戰後的經濟復甦扮演重要的角色。

21. **capable**（*adj.*）有能力、可勝任；**capability**（*n.*）能力

① This team of ten people is capable of doing large campaigns.
這個十人團隊可勝任處理大型企劃案。
② Considering her high education and solid experiences of working in the industry, it's no doubt that she has the capability of leading the department. 考量她的高學歷以及業界豐富的工作經驗，毫無疑問，她絕對有能力領導這個部門。

—————— 11.2 ——————

3D Printed Gun

3D printing opened a new possibility in the manufacturing world. Like the invention of personal computers allowed the public to use the technology that was once used only by the **authorities** for **military** purposes, 3D printers may also allow end users to produce their own objects instead of **relying on** manufacturers.

Apart from the convenience, there might also be risks. Once the public have access to such technology, they might use it to execute dangerous means such as weapons. The first 3D printed prototype gun was made in 2013 and was named "the Liberator". The Liberator is an actual gun that can fire standard handgun bullets. The developer released not only the video of the gun, but also its CAD files online.

The Liberator attracts 3D printing users to download the CAD files and further started their own experiments. Now anyone with a 3D printer and having access to the required materials can produce their own **firearms** at home. The Liberator is mainly made out of plastic but requires one metal **component**. The **objectors** of 3D printing are concerned about the future development of fully plastic 3D printed guns that can trick **metal detectors**. The trend of 3D printed weapons **triggered** the debates on whether 3D printers should be allowed to the public, and if so, how the authorities should set regulations of its usage. But for now, the price of 3D printers is still beyond normal public's budget.

中文翻譯

3D 列印手槍

3D 列印開啟了製造業世界的新契機。就像個人型電腦讓曾經只限於**當局軍事**用途的科技，普及給大眾使用，3D 列印機也可以讓終端使用者自己製造物品，不再**依靠**製造商。

除了方便性之外，這也有些風險。一旦民眾有能力使用這種科技，他們有可能將之用在危險的用途上，例如武器。在2013年，第一把3D列印手槍原型問世，被稱為 The Liberator。The Liberator 是一把真槍，可以發射標準手槍子彈。開發者不只公布手槍的影片，也把其CAD檔案發布在網路上。

The Liberator吸引3D列印使用者下載CAD檔案，進一步各自實驗。現在任何人只要有一台3D列印機，而且有所需的材料，就能夠在家製造自己的**槍枝**。The Liberator主要是塑膠製，但需要一個金屬**零件**。3D列印的**反對者**非常擔心未來可能會發展出能躲過**金屬探測器**的全塑膠3D列印手槍。3D列印武器的潮流**引發**3D列印機是否應該普及化的爭論，以及如果普及化,當局該如何規範其使用。不過目前來說,3D列印機的價格仍然超出一般大眾的負擔範圍。

 重點字彙

1. **authority**（*n.*）職權;當局;官方

   ① Only the CEO has the authority to approve such a huge project.

   只有執行長有批准這麼大案子的權限。

   ② The authorities are criticized for cutting the funding on social benefits.

   當局政府因為刪減社會福利預算而備受批評。

2. **military**（*adj./n.*）軍事的;軍隊、軍方;**army**（*n.*）軍隊

   ① Every man in this country needs to take one year military service.

   在這個國家,每個男人都必須服一年的兵役。

   ② Thousands of protesters went on street against the military rule.

   上千名抗議人士上街反對軍政府。

3. **rely on**（*v.*）依靠、信賴

延伸字彙

- **depend on**（*v.*）依賴；取決於；**dependent**（*adj.*）受撫養的眷
- **independent**（*adj.*）獨立的；**independence**（*n.*）獨立

  The whole family's well-being is relying on the single mother's income.

  整個家庭的幸福都依靠在單親媽媽的收入上。

- **reliable**（*adj.*）可靠的

  Though not very talkative, he is a very reliable partner to work with.

  雖然不是很健談，但他是個非常可靠的工作夥伴。

4. **firearm**（*n.*）火器、槍枝

The police discovered dozens of firearms in the suspect's house.

警方在嫌犯家中查獲數十隻槍枝。

5. **component**（*n.*）零件、組成要素

The factory produces components for bicycles.

工廠出品腳踏車專用的零件。

6. **object**（*n.*／*v.*）物品；反對；**objector**（*n.*）反對者

延伸字彙

- **dissident**（*n.*）異議人士；**protester**（*n.*）抗議人士；**activist**（*n.*）社運人士

① The security officer received a report of an unknown object in the airport.

安檢人員接獲一起機場不明物體的通報。

② The parents object their relationship despite the love between the couple.

儘管這對情侶深深相愛，父母仍然反對他們的戀情。

③ Many objectors from local residents stood up to boycott the latest council housing plan.

當地居民中有許多反對者站出來反對最新的社會住宅案。

 iBT 新托福字彙閱讀應試技巧

Question 1: Which of the following is not used in 3D printing?

(A) Binder Jetting　　　　(B) Line Cutting

(C) Material Extrusion　　(D) Sheet Lamination

解析　由於 3D 列印採層疊堆積的方式，材料都是熱熔凝固，因此不需要切割，答案為 (B)。

Question 2: Which of the following are the ways to use 3D printers?

(A) Manually control

(B) Photograph the object

(C) Computer aided detection (CAD)

(D) 3D scan the object

解析 目前 3D 列印還不能 (A) 手動操作,也不能 (B) 用物體的照片當作設計檔案輸入,3D 列印的 CAD 指的是 Computer Aided Design 設計而不是 Computer Aided Detection(電腦輔助檢測),故答案為 (D) 3D 掃描物件。

Question 3: According to the article, 3D printing has not been used in which industry below?

(A) Aircrafts

(B) Cars

(C) Dentist

(D) Jewelry

解析 文中提到 3D 列印目前應用在醫學界、航太業以及汽車業,因此,選項 (A)、(B)、(C) 的飛機、汽車、牙醫都包含在內,答案為選項 (D) 的珠寶。

Part 1

Part 2

Part 3

Part 4

Part 5

Part 6

Part 7

Unit **12**

12.1 Track 23

Astronomy and Aerospace Engineering

Have you ever wondered the mystery of the Universe? Have you ever dreamed of traveling through the galaxies? Astronomy is the study of phenomena outside of Earth's atmosphere and **celestial** objects including, but not limited to stars, **galaxies**, planets, moons, **asteroids**, **comets** and **nebulae**. Aerospace engineering is the study and industry that aims to create artificial objects for human beings to explore the **atmosphere** and space. The tools that aerospace engineering utilize cover airplanes, helicopters, rockets and **satellites**.

Airplanes and helicopters are used as the transportation means on Earth. Some rockets and missiles are usually sent to atmosphere but more are sent to space. Rockets work by expelling the **exhaust** of the engine and push the aircraft to the opposite direction at high speed. Chemical rockets are the most common high speed rockets using fuel and an **oxidizer.** When fuel and the oxidizer contact, the reaction will start spontaneously and spout exhaust to generate power. Satellites are artificial objects placed into **orbits** to rotate around the Earth. Satellites can be used for military usages, weather forecast, communication, **navigation** and so on. Some satellites are **habitable** and serve as space stations for **astronauts**. The orbits vary by the function of the satellites. Some rotate below-Earth orbit; others medium-Earth orbit (at 20,000 km) or **geostationary** orbit.

中文翻譯

天文學與航太工程

你是否曾幻想過宇宙的奧秘？是否曾夢想過銀河旅行？天文學是專注於地球大氣層以外的現象以及**天際間的**物體，包括星辰、**銀河**、星球、月亮、**小行星**、**彗星**、**星雲**等以外的物體。航太工程是創造人工物體讓人類可以探索**大氣**以及太空的學科以及行業。這包括飛機、直升機、火箭和**衛星**。

飛機和直升機被用在地球上的運輸。有些火箭也在大氣層使用，例如飛彈，但大多被送到外太空。火箭以排放引擎的排氣將火箭體往反方向推進，化學火箭是最常見的高速火箭，利用燃料和氧化劑接觸反應時，自然產生的氣體製造動能。衛星是被放在**軌道**上的人工物體，提供不同功能，可以用在軍事用途、氣象預測、通訊、**導航**等領域。有些衛星**可以住人**，成為太空人的太空站。運行軌道依衛星的功能而異，有些是低軌道、有些是中軌道（兩萬公里高）或與**地球同步的**高軌道。

重點字彙

1. **celestial**（*adj.*）天空的

   The 10-year-old little girl is fascinated by celestial bodies and is able to name all the stars in the sky.

   這個十歲小女孩對天空中的事物著迷，可以講出天空中所有星星的名字。

2. **galaxy**（*n.*）銀河、星系

   So far, aerospace engineers are still searching for ways to reach other galaxies.

   目前為止，航太工程師仍在尋找接觸其他星系的方式。

3. **asteroid**（*n.*）小行星

   The new asteroid was named after the astronomer who discovered it.

   新的小行星被命名為發現它的天文學家之名。

4. **comet**（*n.*）彗星

   Comets are very rare phenomena that can only be seen from Earth once in decades.

   彗星是非常罕見的現象，數十年才能從地球看見一次。

5. **nebula**（*n.*）星雲（複數：**nebulae / nebulas**）

Some nebulae shine by the radiation within. Some reflects the light of nearby objects. Others are dark nebulae.

有些星雲由內部的輻射發光，有些反射周圍物體的光芒，有些則是暗星雲。

6. **satellite**（*n.*）衛星

The cabin is equipped with a satellite phone for the passengers' usages.

客艙中備有衛星電話可供乘客使用。

7. **atmosphere**（*n.*）大氣層；空氣；氣氛

70% of the atmosphere in Earth is nitrogen.

地球大氣中有七成都是氮氣。

8. **missile**（*n.*）飛彈

The report revealed that the passenger plane was shot down by a missile.

報告揭露出客機是被飛彈擊落的。

9. **exhaust**（*n.*）排氣、排氣管；抽空、耗盡；
exhausted（*adj.*）筋疲力盡

She was burnt by the exhaust when walking by a motorbike.
她走過一輛機車時，被排氣管燙到了。

10. **oxygen**（*n.*）氧氣；**oxidizer**（*n.*）氧化劑

Everyone was given two oxygen cylinders to reduce altitude sickness.
每人配給兩個氧氣筒以緩和高山症。

11. **spontaneous**（*adj.*）自發的、自然的；主動的

Hearing the music, he started dancing spontaneously in the coffee shop.
聽到音樂，他就在咖啡店裡自然的跳起舞來。

12. **orbit**（*n.*）運行軌道；知識範疇；眼窩

The satellite fell from its low-Earth orbit and crashed in a field.
那個衛星從原本的低空軌道落下，摔在一片田裡。

13. **navigation** （*n.*）航行；導航

Despite being a good driver, he can't go anywhere without the GPS's navigation.
儘管開車技術很好，他沒有 GPS 導航依然哪都去不了。

14. **inhabitant**（*n.*）居民；
habitable（*adj.*）可居住的、宜居的

① The local inhabitants are highly concerned with the environmental damages made by the tourists.

當地居民高度擔憂觀光客對環境造成的傷害。

② Our ancestors found this place near the river very habitable and built our village here.

我們的祖先覺得這個傍河而居的地方非常適合居住，於是便把村莊蓋在這裡。

15. **astronaut**（*n.*）太空人

The rocket that departed today sent five astronauts to their mission on Mars.

今天出發的火箭將五位太空人送往火星執行任務。

16. **geostationary**（*adj.*）與地球旋轉同步的

The telecommunication services have improved greatly since the new geostationary started to work.

自從新的同步衛星開始運作後，通訊服務有了大幅的改善。

Track 24

12.2

Scientific Facts in Movie: *Interstellar*

In the movie *Interstellar*, the astronaut Cooper travels through a **wormhole** and managed to send a message to his daughter in the past from the future which eventually saved human beings from **extinction**. In reality, is this mission **feasible** from the scientific view?

Gravity plays a key role in the story. Theoretically, if time was added to the three-dimensional space, it would create a four-dimensional time space. The time space can be described as a flat sheet. Hit by a heavy object, the surface of the sheet may hollow and the time space would be twisted by gravity.

If the time space was bended so much that it's almost folded over, it could create a wormhole. The distance to go through from point A to point B can be skipped by simply crossing through the wormhole. In theory, the wormhole can help travel between galaxies within seconds, which as we can see, is the way used by Cooper and his fellow astronauts. However, some **physicists** claim that nothing with **mass** can go through wormholes. Others believe that it is possible to travel from one galaxy to another through the

Part 1

Part 2

Part 3

Part 4

Part 5

Part 6

Part 7

wormhole but the return trip may not lead to the original galaxy.

So far, no human beings have ever entered a wormhole. The truth remains a mystery.

中文翻譯

電影《星際效應》的科學事實

電影《星際效應》中，太空人庫柏穿越**蟲洞**，將訊息從未來傳送給身在過去時空的女兒，最後拯救人類免於**滅絕**。現實中，從科學角度來看，這個任務是**可行的**嗎？

重力在這個故事中扮演關鍵的角色。理論上來說，如果三維空間加上時間，就成為四維的時空。時空可以形容為一張平的薄紙，若被重物重擊，表面會下凹，時空則會被重力扭曲。

如果時空被彎曲到幾乎快要摺過來，就可能形成蟲洞。穿越蟲洞後，可省下 A 點到 B 點的距離之間的距離。理論上，蟲洞讓星際旅行僅需數秒便能達成，我們也能看到這這也就是庫柏和他的太空人同伴所採用的方式。不過，有些**物理學家**宣稱沒有任何有**質量**的物體能夠穿過蟲洞，其他物理學家相信利用蟲洞做星際旅行是有可能的，但回程不一定能回到原本的星系。

目前為止，還沒有任何人類曾進入過蟲洞，真相仍是一個謎。

重點字彙

1. **interstellar**（*adj.*）星際的 **stellar**（*adj.*）星型的；顯著的；恆星的

The time length required for interstellar journey is often longer than a human lifetime.

星際航程所需的時間通常都比人的一生還要長。

2. **mission**（*n.*）任務；使命

延伸字彙

● **missionary** 傳教士

① She looks like a tourist but her real identity is a spy on mission.

她看起來像個觀光客，但真實身分是任務在身的間諜。

② The old man takes the children in the orphanage as his life mission.

老人將孤兒院的孩子視為他一生的使命。

③ European missionaries created the earliest written language for tribes in Taiwan with Roman alphabets.

歐洲傳教士以羅馬字母替台灣的部落發明出最早的書寫語言。

3. **feasible**（*adj.*）可行的、合理的

He was disappointed because the manager didn't deem his proposal very feasible in the meeting.

他非常失望，因為在會議中經理不認為他的提案很具可行性。

4. **extinction**（*n.*）滅絕

The unique leopards are facing extinction due to the disappearance of their habitat.

這種獨特的豹因為棲息地的消失而面臨絕種。

5. **black hole**（*n.*）黑洞

His endless greed is like a black hole where all the money disappears.

他無止盡的貪婪就像黑洞一樣，所有錢都消失殆盡。

6. **wormhole**（*n.*）蟲洞

Many researchers aim to study wormhole but none of them ever ge in one.

很多研究員都致力於研究蟲洞，但沒有人真的進入過蟲洞。

7. **gravity**（*n.*）重力

① Newton's law of universal gravity was inspired by an apple.
牛頓因一顆蘋果而啟發了他的萬有引力論。

② Astronauts need to be trained to work under zero gravity environment.
太空人必須接受訓練以在無重力環境下工作。

8. **physics**（*n.*）物理學；**physicist**（*n.*）物理學家

The physicist combines the knowledge of physics and some humor to create lots of amusing magic tricks.
那位物理學家結合物理知識和一些幽默，做出許多好玩的魔術。

9. **mass**（*n.*）質量；眾多、大量、大部分

The only way to reduce average cost is to make mass production.
減低平均成本的唯一方法就是大量製造。

iBT 新托福字彙閱讀應試技巧

Question 1: What is an orbit?

(A) The station for a satellite to be settled in.

(B) The aircraft that carries a satellite to rotate around the Earth.

(C) The rocket that sends a satellite to the atmosphere.

(D) The elliptical course that the satellite rotates around the earth on.

解析 如文中所述 "Satellites are artificial objects placed into orbits to rotate around the Earth"，軌道是人工衛星繞行地球所依據的圓形路線，因此答案為 (D)。

Question 2: What is the key that leads Cooper to his success?

(A) Gratitude

(B) Gravy

(C) Gratuity

(D) Gravity

解析 「重力」是庫柏成功的關鍵，因此答案為 (D)。選項 (A) 為感激之情，(B) 是肉汁、(C) 是賞錢。

Part 1

Part 2

Part 3

Part 4

Part 5

Part 6

Part 7

Unit 13

13.1

 Track 25

Generic Codes - DNA

Some of our characters are **congenital**, some are **acquired**. Those inborn characters are written as generic codes in our body, which is called, **DNA**.

A **chromosome** is the packed structure made by DNA **molecule** in the cell's **nucleus**. The unit of a short DNA section is called a gene which codes for a specific **protein** and defines the creature's feature. Human body cells have 23 pairs of chromosome in the nucleus. Some chromosomes are shorter with fewer sets of genes. The longer ones can carry up to 2000 genes.

Every person is born with a unique set of DNA sequences, except for **identical twins**. Inheritance patterns of certain traits do not always pass from parents since it still needs to see if the patterns are dominant or recessive genes. Some of the gene traits have been identified such as eye colors, skin colors and some specific diseases. But the **biotechnologists** around the world are still working on decoding human being's gene codes.

The present technology can examine some major diseases from DNA tests. For instance, **Down syndrome** is now as a routine part of **prenatal** test. However, some genes can only suggest the tendency of certain diseases but the traits does not definitely express.

中文翻譯

基因密碼 - DNA

有些特質是**先天的**，有些是**後天習得的**。那些天生的特質以基因密碼寫在我們的體內，也就是 DNA。

染色體是**細胞核**中，由 DNA **分子**組成的結構組。DNA 組成的單位稱為基因，編碼負責特定**蛋白質**，決定生物的特質。人體的細胞核有二十三對染色體，有些較短，只有比較少的基因組，較長的可以有高達兩千組基因。

每個人生來都有獨一無二的 DNA 組合，除了**同卵雙胞胎**之外。基因依顯性或隱性而異，遺傳序列傳下的特定性徵並不一定會從雙親傳下，有些基因特徵能夠識別出來，例如眼睛顏色、膚色或罹患某些疾病的風險。但世界各地的**生物工程學家**仍在努力解開人類基因密碼的秘密，

當前的科技已經能用 DNA 檢測驗出某些重大疾病，例如**唐氏症**現在就是產前檢查的一項例行檢驗。不過，有些基因只能代表此人較有可能罹患某些疾病，但這種病徵不一定會顯現出來。

重點字彙

1. **congenital**（*adj.*）先天性的

   Born in a family with the history of diabetes, he also suffers from this congenital disease.

   出身在有糖尿病史的家族裡，他也深受這種先天疾病所苦。

   延伸字彙　born, native, natural

2. **acquire**（*v.*）取得；習得；**acquired**（*adj.*）養成的、習得的

   ① It took her three weeks to acquire all the books needed for her thesis from different libraries.

   她費了三周才從不同圖書館取得論文所需的書。

   ② He acquired the taste of cheese from the summer holiday in France.

   他從暑假的法國行養成了對乳酪的品味。

3. **DNA**（deoxyribonucleic acid）脫氧核醣核酸

   延伸字彙

   ● **acid** 酸的；**alkaline** 鹼性的

   ① The secret of the family is hidden in their DNA.

   這個家族的秘密藏在他們的 DNA 裡。

   ② The area endured acid rain due to over industrialization.

   這個區域因為過度工業化而深受酸雨所苦。

   ③ Sometime eating alkaline-forming food can calm an upset stomach. 有時吃些鹼性食物能緩和腸胃不適。

4. **chromosome**（*n.*）染色體

Human cells have 22 pairs of autosomes and one pair of sex chromosomes

人類細胞有 22 對正染色體以及一對性別染色體。

5. **molecule**（*n.*）分子

Water molecules are made of hydrogen and oxygen.

水分子由氫和氧組成。

延伸字彙

● **nucleus** 核、核心；原子核；細胞核（複數：**Nuclei / Nucleus**）

① The committee is the nucleus of the domestic film industry.

委員會是國內電影產業的核心。

② The gene codes are hidden in cell nucleus.

基因密碼被藏在細胞核中。

6. **protein**（*n.*）蛋白、蛋白質

Soya milk is a good source of protein.

豆漿是好的蛋白質來源。

7. **identical twins**（*n.*）同卵雙胞胎；
fraternal twins（*n.*）異卵雙胞胎

① The teachers are always confused by the identical twins in the class.

老師們總是被班上那對同卵雙胞胎搞得相當糊塗。

② She looks nothing like her fraternal twin sister.

她跟她的異卵雙胞胎姊姊長得一點都不像。

延伸字彙

● **triplets** 三胞胎

The parents are delighted to have triplets from trying test-tube babies.

這對雙親嘗試試管嬰兒，很高興地得到了三胞胎。

8. biotechnology（*n.*）生物工程；biotechnologist（*n.*）生物工程學家

The biotechnologist is so passionate to his work that even dinner cannot interrupt his thoughts around the experiments.

這個生物工程學家對工作熱忱到就連晚餐也無法打斷他滿腦子實驗的思路。

9. Down syndrome（*n.*）唐氏症

The parents decided to deliver the baby although the prenatal test shows that it carries Down syndrome.

那對父母決定生下孩子，即便產前檢查顯示出孩子得了唐氏症。

10. prenatal（*adj.*）產前的

I need to ask for a half-day leave for my prenatal test.

我必須請半天假去做產前檢查。

---------- 13.2 ---------- Track 26

Part 1
Part 2
Part 3
Part 4
Part 5
Part 6
Part 7

Genetically Modified Food

Would you want apples to be bigger, sweeter, and better not to turn brown brown after sliced? With the help of genetic engineering, an **antioxidant** gene may help to make the last request come true.

Genetic engineering technologies allow scientists to improve **organisms** by changing their DNA sequences and inserting genes from either animal to plants, plants to animal, animal to animal or plants to plants. By being developed the ability to delay the ripening after picking up, the first genetically modified (GM) tomato was introduced in 1994. Nowadays, 80% of the soybeans, 35% of the corn and 80% of the cotton in the world are genetically modified.

GM food can be designed to be bigger, longer-lasting, more nutritious or even better **immune** to diseases and **pests**. Although this technique has enhanced the plants' market values **tremendously**, its risk to harm human body is still unknown. GM food can also break the balance of food market and change natural environment. Therefore, more and more countries are now asked to set strict regulations on GM food's production.

中文翻譯

基因改造食物

你希望蘋果變得更大、更甜，切開後最好不要變色嗎？有了基因工程，一個**抗氧化的**基因就有可能讓第三樣願望成真。

生物工程科技讓科學家可以藉由改變 DNA 序列來改善**物種**，不論是從動物身上取出基因插入植物基因中，或植物到動物、動物到動物或植物到植物之間。最早上市的基因改造（簡稱基改）食物是 1994 年的番茄，那種番茄從摘下後可以延遲成熟時間。現今世界上有 80% 的黃豆、35% 的玉米和 80% 的棉花都是基改作物。

基改食物可以被設計的更大、保存期更久、更有營養，甚至能對疾病和**害蟲免疫**。然而，即便這種技術讓產物的市值**大幅**提升，這樣對人體可能造成的傷害風險仍是未知數。基改食品可以打亂食品市場的平衡，也會改變自然生態。因此，越來越多國家被要求針對基改食品的生產設下嚴格規範。

重點字彙

1. **antioxidant**（*n.*）抗氧化劑

   Lemons and onions are both antioxidants that are tasty and easy to collect.
   檸檬和洋蔥都是好吃又容易取得的抗氧化食物。

2. **organism**（*n.*）生物、有機體

   The water pollution killed many organisms in the sea.
   水汙染殺死了許多海洋裡的生物。

3. **ripe**（*adj.*）成熟的、適宜實用的；圓滑的；
   ripen（*v.*）使成熟、催熟

   The tip of ripening bananas is to place them with rice.
   催熟香蕉的小訣竅是把香蕉跟米放在一起。

4. **immune**（*adj.*）免疫的

   After working for two months, the secretary grows immune to the boss's bad temper.
   工作兩個月後，秘書就對老闆的壞脾氣免疫了。

5. **pest**（*n.*）害蟲；**pesticide**（*n.*）殺蟲劑、農藥

   You have to soak the greens in water longer to get rid of the pesticide on the leaves.

   你得把綠色蔬菜泡在水裡久一點，才能去除掉葉子上的農藥。

6. **tremendous**（*n.*）極度的、巨大的

   Your donation has helped our charity campaign tremendously.

   您的捐款對我們的慈善運動幫助極大。

   延伸字彙 astronomical , colossal, cosmic

   ① It's an astronomical number beyond imagination.

   這是一個超乎想像的天文數字。

   ② The new statue has a colossal size.

   新雕像相當巨大。

iBT 新托福字彙閱讀應試技巧

Question 1: Which of the following order describes the relationship between Chromosome, Cell, DNA and Nucleus?

(A) Nucleus> Cell >Chromosome>DNA

(B) Cell >Nucleus>Chromosome> DNA

(C) Cell >Chromosome>Nucleus> DNA

(D) Cell >Chromosome> DNA>Nucleus

解析 染色體由 DNA 組成，位於細胞核中，也就是細胞的核心，因此答案為細胞 > 細胞核 > 染色體 > DNA，答案為 (B)。

Question 2: Which of the following is not the reason for the authorities to set regulations in GM food?

(A) To maintain the balance on food market.

(B) To protect natural environment.

(C) To protect people's health.

(D) To help promote GM food.

解析 設定基改食物規範的用意在於 (A) 維持食品市場的平衡、(B) 保護自然環境以及 (C) 保障民眾的健康，而不是配合推銷基改食品，因此答案為 (D)。

Part 1

Part 2

Part 3

Part 4

Part 5

Part 6

Part 7

Unit 14

14.1

 Track 27

Artificial Intelligence

Can machines think like human brains? Engineers aim to create computers and computer software that can **simulate** human intelligence and even be capable of intelligent behavior. This type of technologies is called, "Artificial Intelligence (AI)".

AI requires complex researches encompassing numerous fields of science and professions including Computer Science, **Mathematics**, Psychology, **Linguistics**, **Philosophy**, **Neuroscience** and Artificial Psychology. Some AI technologies can read oral/written languages and respond in human languages. And such functions can be applied to answering machines, call centers, and online assistants. Some software developers also produce computer-aided translation/interpreting programs. Combined with other technologies, intelligent agents can observe through **sensors** and interact with the environment to achieve certain goals.

Artificial **neural** networks are computer programs simulating human brains to analyze **comprehensive** database, proceed in structural decision making processes and are capable of learning new things.

While AI technologies grow rapidly, some people are concerned about the potential risk of computer overtaking human being's power. Can computers really "think" like human brains? If so, can they be "smarter" than human beings? Will they be able to control or even rule us in the future? If we aim to prevent it, can we start again without the convenience of AI technologies? This is the **dilemma** we have to face in this digital era.

中文翻譯

人工智慧

機器可以像人腦一樣思考嗎？工程師致力於創造出能夠模仿人類智慧，甚至有能力做出智能行為的電腦和電腦軟體，這類科技稱為「人工智慧 (AI)」。

人工智慧需要橫跨多種科學以及專業領域的複雜研究，包括電腦科學、**數學**、心理學、**語言學**、哲學、**神經科學**和人工心理學。有些人工智慧科技可以讀取口語／書寫語言，並以人類語言做出回應，這樣的功能可以應用在答錄機、客服中心和線上服務。有些軟體工程師也發展電腦輔助翻譯／口譯程式。和其他科技結合在一起，智能代理可以藉由感應器觀察環境並達到作用。

　　人工類神經網路是一種模仿人腦的電腦程式，可以分析**廣泛綜合的**資料庫，進行結構性的的決策，還有學習新事物的能力。

　　在人工智慧科技快速成長的同時，有些人也擔心電腦超越人類的潛在風險。電腦真的可以像人腦一樣「思考」嗎？如果可以的話，它們會不會比人類「聰明」？它們未來會不會足以控制甚至統治我們？如果我們想要阻止這發生的話，我們有辦法回到沒有便利的人工智慧科技的生活嗎？這是我們在此數位化年代所面臨的**困境**。

重點字彙

1. **simulate**（*v.*）模仿；冒充

   He simulates the crack voice to ask for a day off.

   他裝出發啞的聲音去請一天假。

   同義字 imitate 模仿

   He makes amazing beatbox imitating sounds of instruments.

   他可以模仿各種樂器的聲音做出超讚的節奏口技。

2. **mathematics**（*n.*）數學（簡稱 Math）

   The manager tends to hire people with mathematic backgrounds to be the business analysts.

   經理偏向請有數學背景的人來當商業分析員。

   延伸字彙

   ● **plus / minus / times / divide** 加減乘除

   Three times five minus one and divided by two equals seven.

   三乘五減一再除以二等於七。

   ● **equation** 方程式

   The math student stays up all night to figure out the tricky equation.

   這個數學系學生熬了一夜解這題棘手的方程式。

3. **linguistics**（*n.*）語言學；**linguist**（*n.*）語言學家

The archeologists invited linguists to decode the ancient language.

考古學家邀請語言學家來解析古語言的密碼。

4. **philosophy**（*n.*）哲學

① Socrates was one of the founders of Western philosophy.

蘇格拉底是西方哲學的創始人之一。

② Cook with hunger, eat with passion, bake with love - that is my philosophy.

餓肚子就煮飯，用熱情享用食物，用愛烘培─這就是我的人生哲學。

5. **nerve**（*n.*）神經；沉著、膽量；
neural（*adj.*）神經的、神經中樞的

① Giving the speech in our company meeting today was testing my nerve.

今天公司會議上發表演講簡直就是挑戰我的膽量。

② The severe injury on his head left permanent damage on his neural network.

頭部的嚴重創傷讓他留下永久的神經網路傷害。

6. **neuroscience**（*n.*）神經科學

Finding a cure for her father's Alzheimer's disease was the reason to study neuroscience.

替她父親的阿茲海默症找出療法，是她研究神經科學的原因。

7. **sensor**（*n.*）感應器

The sensors detect temperature changes in the house.

多處感應器可偵測到屋內的溫度變化。

8. **comprehensive**（*adj.*）廣泛的、綜合的

It took her one week to read through this comprehensive report.

她花了一整周才讀完這一份完整的報告。

延伸字彙

同義字　coherent, explicit, understandable

反義字　ambiguous, equivocal

---　14.2　--- **Track 28**

Military Robots

While Artificial Intelligence (AI) has been applied to so many fields including education, medical, and games, military also intend to use it on their forces. In fact, some governments have already been building and using military robots. But is it really appropriate to have **autonomous** weapons?

Not all military robots are offensive. Some military robots are defensive such as **landmine detection** robots and bomb **disposal** robots that assist soldiers in handling dangerous tasks. **Surgical** robots which are used in civilian hospitals also work in operation rooms in **combat** zones. However, even more robots are indeed heavily armed without any trace of humanity. Some military robots are semi-autonomous. Some requires **remote** control. Some can work autonomously once switched-on.

Biomimetic robots are designed with natural biological attributes to do movements like crawling or climbing naturally. AI neuro network also allows robots to recognize human interaction and even learn and memorize new things.

Unit 14

Part
1

Part
2

Part
3

Part
4

Part
5

Part
6

Part
7

Concerned that these "killing machines" might bring damage to human societies in the near future, over 1000 world leading AI experts signed an open letter calling for a ban on offensive autonomous weapons in July, 2015. After all, robots, however intelligent, are no human beings.

中文翻譯

軍事機器人

AI 人工智慧不只應用在教育、醫療、遊戲等領域，軍隊也有意用在軍備上。事實上，有些政府早就開始建造使用軍用機器人了。但具有**自主能力的**武器，真的妥當嗎？

並不是所有的軍用機器人都具攻擊性，有些不具攻擊性，例如協助軍人處理危險任務的**地雷偵查**機器人、**拆彈**機器人，民間醫院使用的**手術**機器人也在**戰區**的手術室中派上用場。不過，的確有更多機器人是重度武裝，不具一絲人性。有些軍用機器人是半自主的，有些需要遠端遙控，有些一旦打開開關就能自主工作。**仿生**機器人是以自然生物特性設計的，能夠自然的移動，如爬行或攀爬。人工智慧類神經網路也賦予機器人認知人類互動的能力，甚至能夠學習並記住新事物。

超過一千名引領世界的人工智慧專家在 2015 年七月簽屬一封公開信，因為深深擔憂對這些「殺人機器」可能在未來對人類社會帶來的傷害，呼籲禁止自主攻擊性武器。到頭來，機器人，不論再怎麼高智能，仍舊不是人類。

重點字彙

1. **autonomous**（*adj.*）自主的、自治的

The central government agrees to set an autonomous area for the aboriginal people.

中央政府同意設立原住民自治區。

2. **landmine**（*n.*）地雷

Princess Diana was devoted to banning landmines.

黛安娜王妃生前致力於推動禁止地雷。

延伸字彙

● torpedo 魚雷、水雷

The new submarine is equipped with a number of lethal torpedoes.

新的潛艇配有數支致命的水雷。

3. **detect**（*v.*）發現、察覺；**detective**（*n.*）偵探；**detection**（*n.*）偵查

① The radar detected an unknown object approaching the island.

雷達偵測到一個不明物體正靠近島嶼中。

② The entrepreneur hired a detective to find out who stole his secret formula.

企業家雇了一個偵探去查出是誰偷了他的秘密配方。

4. **dispose**（*v.*）；**disposal**（*n.*）處理；配置；
   disposable（*adj.*）可任意處理的；可拋棄的

   ① The couple argued about the disposal of the furniture for their new house.

   這對情侶為了新家的家具配置爭執。

   ② The takeaway food comes with disposable chopsticks.

   外帶食物有附贈拋棄式的筷子。

5. **surgery**（*n.*）外科醫學、（外科）手術；
   surgeon（*n.*）外科醫生；
   surgical（*adj.*）外科的、外科醫生的；手術用的

   ① Her mother died because the family couldn't afford the surgery.

   她的母親因為家裡負擔不起手術費用而過世。

   ② As a surgeon, she is always on call.

   身為外科醫生，她隨時都要隨傳隨到。

   ③ He started his internship from working in the surgical unit.

   他從在外科工作開始他的實習生涯。

6. **biomimetic**（*adj.*）仿生的

   The new museum is a biomimetic building that can self-adjust the inner temperature.

   新的博物館是座仿生建築，可以自己調節內部溫度。

iBT 新托福字彙閱讀應試技巧

Question 1: According to the article, which of the following services may not be available in AI technology?

(A) Virtual Receptionist

(B) Restaurant Reservation

(C) Language teacher

(D) Interactive Dictionary

> 解析　文中提到有些人工智慧軟體能夠辨識人類語言，並做出自然的回應，可用在答錄機、客服中心，甚至提供翻譯服務，因此 (A) 虛擬接待員，(B) 餐廳訂位和 (D) 互動式字典都是有可能的，但目前還沒有發展到可以擔任教學工作的軟體，因此答案為 (C)，語言老師。

Question 2: What is the function of bomb disposal robots?

(A) Testing experimental bombs in the laboratory.

(B) Dissembling bombs in combat zones.

(C) Setting bombs in combat zones.

(D) Detecting landmines in the field.

解析 文中提到有些機器人不具攻擊性，可以協助軍人處理危險的工作，選項 (C) 放置炸彈是具有威脅性的工作，因此不對，選項 (A) 的實驗室工作不一定在軍人的工作範圍內，選項 (D) 則是地雷偵查機器人，因此答案為 (B)，在戰區拆卸炸彈。

Question 3: What is the dilemma people have towards AI technology?

(A) It can save a lot of effort in life but most of the people cannot afford the price.

(B) It is so convenient that people might lose some basic skills.

(C) It's reached the peak that engineers struggle to make further development.

(D) It grows so fast that one day people may lose control over it.

解析 人工智慧科技發展迅速，提供人類生活許多便利，而且還有很好的發展前景，但目前最大的困境在於擔憂發展過度有可能超越人類智慧，讓人類陷入無法控制的局面，因此答案為選項 (D)。

Unit **15**

15.1 **Track 29**

Material Science and Engineering

Material Science and Engineering is the profession that focuses on the attributes and applications of different materials. This is an **interdisciplinary** field highly related to chemistry, physics, **metallurgy**, and **mineralogy**. It also requires good knowledge in engineering, electronic engineering and biology to develop applications for various purposes.

Materials can be classified into organic and inorganic materials. The former includes metal and non-metal materials such as **ceramics**. The latter covers everything that comes from plants, animals and their waste products in the environment. Materials can also be divided by their **mechanical** properties, chemical properties, electrical properties, **thermal** properties, **optical** properties, **magnetic** properties and so on.

Forensic sciences are another field that requires Material Science a lot. The material evidence from the crime or incident scenes can be as massive as the dust left from a factory explosion or as small as the **saliva** left by a suspect on a glass. Scientists can analyze the evidence and trace it back to the source.

Supporting the rapidly growing engineering technology, Material Science also evolves to meet new developments' needs. Therefore, apart from analyzing the existing materials, scientists also work on exploring and developing new materials including **nanomaterials** and **biomaterials**.

中文翻譯

材料科學以及材料工程

材料科學以及材料工程是一門針對不同材料的屬性以及應用方式的專業，這是個**跨領域的**學科，與化學、物理、**冶金學**、**礦物學**等息息相關，且須熟悉工程、電子工程和生物學等領域的知識，才能替不同需求做出應用方案。

材料可以分為有機和無機，前者包括金屬和非金屬物質，如**陶瓷**。後者含括所有來自動、植物以及它們留在環境中的排泄物等物質。材料也可以依不同性質做區分，可能是其**物理機械**屬性、化學屬性、電子屬性、**保暖性**、**光學**屬性、**磁性**等特性分類。

鑑識科學也是亟需材料科學的一門範疇，犯罪現場或事故現場的物質證據可以大到工廠爆炸遺留的塵土，小至嫌疑犯在杯子上留下的**唾液**。科學家可以研究這些證據，並追溯到來源。

為了支援工程科技的快速發展，材料科學也不斷進步以達到新發展的需求。因此，除了研究既有的材料以外，科學家也努力找尋和發展新材料，包括**奈米材料**和**生物材料**。

 ## 重點字彙

1. **interdisciplinary**（*adj.*）跨領域的、跨學科的

   Information Management is an interdisciplinary subject that requires programming skills and business knowledge.

   資訊管理是一門跨領域的學科，需要具備寫程式的能力和商業知識。

2. **metal**（*n.*）金屬；**metallurgy**（*n.*）冶金學；冶金術

   ① In this rural village, everyone knows how to purify gold with ancient metallurgy.

   在這個偏遠的村莊裡，每個人都知道提煉黃金的古老煉金術。

   ② The Taiwanese heavy metal band is very popular around the world.

   這個台灣重金屬樂團紅遍全球。

3. **mineral**（*n.*）礦物；**mineralogy**（*n.*）礦物學

① This university is famous of its long history of Mineralogy.
這所大學以礦物學歷史悠久聞名。

② The mountain stream is the source of mineral water.
這條山裡的溪流是礦泉水的源頭。

4. **ceramics**（*n.*）陶瓷

The little girl accidentally broke a vintage ceramic bowl while playing in the kitchen.
小女孩在廚房裡玩時，不小心打破了一只骨董瓷碗。

5. **mechanical**（*adj.*）機械的；物理的

The clock seems complex with the decoration but the mechanical concept is very simple.
時鐘的裝飾看起來很複雜，但機械原理很簡單。

6. **property**（*n.*）特性、屬性；財產；房地產

① Scientists discovered that some elements' properties change under high pressure.
科學家發現有些元素的屬性在高壓下會改變。

② Apart from the house she lives in, she owns another two properties in town.
除了她自住的房子之外，她在城裡還有另外兩棟房地產。

7. **thermal**（*adj.*）熱的、溫泉的；保暖的

She can't go out without thermal underwear in winter.
她在冬天沒有發熱內衣就不能出門。

8. **optical**（*adj.*）眼睛的、勢力的；光學的

He was born with poor eye sight and has to rely on optical aids on a daily basis.
他天生視力就很差，每天都得依賴視力輔助器。

9. **magnet**（*n.*）磁鐵；
   magnetic（*adj.*）磁性的、地磁的；富有吸引力的

① He always collects magnets as souvenirs from his trips.
他總是在旅途中蒐集磁鐵當紀念品。
② She has a powerful and magnetic voice.
她的聲音有力又具磁性。

10. **forensic**（*adj.*）法庭的、法醫鑑識的；辯論的；
   forensics（*n.*）辯論、辯論學

The victim was told not to touch anything to keep all the forensic evidence on site.
受害者被告知不要碰任何東西，保持現場所有的辨識證據。

11. **saliva**（*n.*）唾液

The suspect was required to take a saliva test.

嫌犯被要求做唾液檢查。

12. **nanomaterial**（*n.*）奈米材料

Nanomaterial clothes improve traditional sportswear's shortage.

奈米材料衣物改善許多傳統運動服裝的缺陷。

13. **biomaterial**（*n.*）生物材料

The hospital is very short of biomaterial for the surgeries.

醫院極缺手術需要的生物材料。

Part 1
Part 2
Part 3
Part 4
Part 5
Part 6
Part 7

15.2

Nanotechnology

Nanotechnology is the subfield under Material Science that manipulates materials in the molecular scale. It can also be referred more **precisely** as **Molecular** Nanotechnology.

Atom is the smallest bits of any matter, made from **protons, neutrons** and **electrons**. The substance made from only one atom is an element such as hydrogen. A molecule is made of one or more than one atoms and makes the most basic unit of every material in the world. Most of the molecules are formed with multiple atoms and are called **compounds**. Only since decades ago that scientists discovered the possibility of building things by gathering single molecules and how the materials' properties changed in such microscale.

Nanotechnology helps material engineers overcome numerous obstacles by purifying materials to the most basic units. For instance, the smaller electronic **circuits** are, the faster they can process data. Therefore, nanowires are developed millions of times smaller in **diameter** than a human hair and with extremely low resistance. More opportunities are being investigated to apply concepts of nanotechnology. Even chefs are crazy about molecular **gastronomy**. Next time when you have a chance to try a molecular tiramisu, taste the difference!

中文翻譯

奈米科技

奈米科技是材料科學下的一個子領域，以分子單位來操作材料，更**精確**來說，也被稱為**分子**奈米科技。

原子是所有物質中最小的東西，以**質子**、**中子**、**電子**組成。由單一原子組成的物質即為元素，例如氫。分子由一個或多個原子組成，是世上所有材料最小的單位，大部分的分子由多原子組成，稱為**化合物**。直到數十年前，科學家才發現把單一分子聚集在一起製造東西的可能性，以及在極微小的分度裡，物質屬性如何改變。

奈米科技讓材料工程師藉由純化物質到最小單位，克服許多障礙。舉例來說，**電路**越小，處理資料的速度就越快。因此，奈米電線做的只有人類毛髮的數百萬之一**直徑**粗，做到幾乎零電阻。還有很多應用奈米科技概念的機會正在研究中，連廚師都在瘋分子美食**料理**。下次有機會吃到分子提拉米蘇時，好好嚐嚐有什麼特別之處！

重點字彙

1. **molecule**（*n.*）分子；**molecular**（*adj.*）分子的

   ① Diatomichydrogen (H2) is the smallest molecule.

   雙原子氫 (H2) 是最小的分子。

   ② Microscopes are essential in studying molecular biology.

   顯微鏡在研究分子生物學是不可或缺的。

2. **precise**（*adj.*）精確的、準確的

   She modified her draft several times to ensure every word is precise in for the speech.

   她把稿子修改多次，確保演講的每個字都夠精確。

3. **proton**（*n.*）質子；
   neutron（*n.*）中子；
   electron（*n.*）電子

   The number of protons and electrons are always equal to balance the positive and negative charge of the atom. Neutrons have no charge.

   質子和電子的數量一定相等，平衡原子的正電價和負電價。中子不帶電價。

4. **compound**（*n.*）化合物、複合物；混合、合成；加重

The green material company developed a new compound that is solid enough for constructions and still eco-friendly.

這間綠色材料公司發展出一種新的複合物，既夠堅硬可做建築，又環保。

5. **circuit**（*n.*）環道、巡迴路線；電路；環行

The circuit used in this lab is as complicated as a maze.

這間實驗室的電路圖跟迷宮一樣複雜。

6. **diameter**（*n.*）直徑

The globe theater is 100 feet in diameter.

圓形劇場的直徑有一百英尺。

延伸字彙

● **radius** 半徑

● **circumference** 圓周

The circumference of Earth at the equator is about 40,075 km.

地球赤道的圓周大約為 40,075公里。

7. **gastronomy**（*n.*）美食、烹飪法

Her trip in France was literally a gastronomy journey.

她的法國行根本就是美食之旅。

iBT 新托福字彙閱讀應試技巧

Question 1: Which of the following is least related to Material Science?

(A) Chemistry
(B) Physics
(C) Methodology
(D) Mineralogy

> 解析 文中提到 "This is an interdisciplinary field highly related to chemistry, physics, metallurgy, mineralogy",因此選項 (A)、(B)、(D) 皆符合,選項 (C) 為方法論、教學方法,與材料科學並無太大關聯,因此答案為 (C)。

Question 2: Apple, glass, wood, gelatin, silk, nylon, paper, jade. How many of these are organic materials?

(A) 3
(B) 4
(C) 5
(D) 6

> 解析 水果、木頭和紙都是植物的產物,吉利丁是動物膠,絲是由蠶繭抽絲而成,因此答案為 (C)。

Question 3: Which of the following describes the relationship among molecules, atoms, neutrons and compounds?

(A) Molecules < Atoms < Neutrons < Compounds

(B) Atoms < Molecules < Neutrons < Compounds

(C) Neutrons < Atoms < Molecules < Compounds

(D) None of these above

解析　原子為質子、電子、中子組成，分子由一個或多個原子組成。化合物是由兩種或兩種以上的元素所組成的，像碳元素 (C) 和氧 (O) 合成後會成為二氧化碳 ($CO2$)，這裡的二氧化碳就是合成物，而碳跟氧分別為元素。答案為 (C)。

Unit 16

16.1

 Track 31

Marketing

Marketing is the strategy that companies used to communicate with consumers to **promote** their products, services and the brands. Every business needs to evaluate its own business scale, products or services and **target buyers** to define the marketing strategies. The traditional marketing includes printing, **broadcast**, direct mail and telephone. Some of the traditional methods are still widely used today but there are also other options to promote businesses now.

Thanks to the digital technologies and global economy, more methods are developed to promote businesses. Some businesses use Direct Marketing including e-mail, texts or fliers to reach the vast market directly. **Partnership** Marketing, also known as **Alliance** Marketing, links the business to **complementary** brands to create strategic partnerships that benefit both parties. Community Marketing requires businesses that already have existing consumers to gather more consumers. This is also called, "**Word of Mouth Marketing**". **Guerrilla** Marketing is to use creative surprises to get attention such as **flash mobs**. Some brands boost their businesses by giving **freebies** or free samples.

To manage consumer information more systematically, Database Marketing can be used to create customized communication approaches. Big Data plays a crucial part in today's business environment. It can help analyze existing consumers and even predict future trends.

Part 1

Part 2

Part 3

Part 4

Part 5

Part 6

Part 7

中文翻譯

關於行銷

行銷是公司與客戶溝通，**推銷**產品、服務以及品牌本身的策略。每一個企業都需要衡量自身的規模、產品或服務，以及**目標市場**以訂定策略。傳統的行銷方案包括印刷刊物、**廣播**、郵寄信函和電話行銷。有些傳統方法仍廣泛使用，但現在也有更多其他的推廣方法可以選擇了。

拜數位科技及全球經濟所賜，越來越多不同推廣生意的方法因而發展出來。有些企業用直效行銷，以電子郵件、簡訊或傳單直接接觸廣大市場。**夥伴關係**行銷，或稱**聯盟行銷**、共同行銷，是將公司和互補或相配的品牌連結在一起，以達到雙方**互利**共生的方式。社群行銷則需要企業已有客戶，用現有的客源聚集更多的客戶，這也被稱為「**口耳相傳**」。**游擊**行銷是用創意驚喜來吸引注意，例如**快閃活動**。有些品牌會用發**免費周邊產品**或免費試用品來促銷。

為了更有系統的管理客戶資料，資料庫行銷可以用來建立更客製化的客戶溝通方法。大數據在現今的商業環境扮演舉足輕重的角色，它可以有助於分析現有客戶，甚至預測未來潮流。

 重點字彙

1. **target buyer / audience / consumer**（*n.*）目標客群、目標族群

The luxury brand introduced a new series that may appeal to new target audience amongst middle-class young professionals.

精品品牌推出了一個新的系列，有望在中產階級的年輕上班族群中，吸引新的目標客群。

延伸字彙

● **end user** 終端使用者、直接用戶

This is the price for end users. We can provide another quote for your business.

這是賣給終端使用者的價錢，我們可以給您的公司提供另一個報價。

2. **promote**（*v.*）宣傳、促銷；升遷、提拔

① The supermarket is on a buy-one-get-one-free promotion.
超市現在促銷買一送一。

② Her hard work totally deserves the promotion.
她這麼努力工作，升遷真的是實至名歸。

3. **broadcast**（*n.*／*v.*）廣播；播送、散播

① Radio broadcast is one of the most influential communication methods during war times. Two of the most famous examples are an American DJ's story in Vietnam War "Good Morning, Vietnam" and Winston Churchill's wartime speeches.
電台廣播是戰時最具影響力的溝通管道之一。兩個最有名的例子是美國 DJ 在越戰的故事「早安越南」，以及邱吉爾的戰時演講。

② The wedding of the royal family was broadcasted live on television channels globally and made the palace one of the most popular touristic attractions in the world.
皇室婚禮在全球各大電視台現場直播，讓皇宮成為全世界最受歡迎的觀光景點之一。

4. **partnership**（*n.*）合夥關係、合作關係

The partnership between the chain convenience shop and the coffee brand created a new trend of coffee experience.
連鎖便利商店與咖啡品牌的合作，開創了咖啡體驗的新潮流。

Part 1

Part 2

Part 3

Part 4

Part 5

Part 6

Part 7

5. **ally**（*n.*）同盟、同盟國、夥伴；**alliance**（*n.*）結盟；聯姻

① The two states used to be allies but the friendship broke after the war started.

這兩國原本是同盟國，但友誼隨著戰爭開打破裂了。

② The truth behind the wedding is the alliance of two politician families.

婚禮背後的真相是兩個政治家庭的聯姻。

反義字 competition 競爭 ；competitive 競爭的；愛好競爭的

It's very competitive in this industry that we need to always keep an eye on our competitors' prices.

這行競爭非常激烈，我們必須隨時注意對手的價格。

6. **complementary**（*adj.*）互補的；相配的

Gene modification biotechnology can match complementary DNA molecules to create better species. However, the impact of that on the species development is still unknown.

基因改造生物科技可以組合互補的 DNA 分子以創造更好的物種。然而，這對於物種發展的衝擊仍然是未知數。

7. **Word of Mouth Marketing**（*n.*）口耳相傳

Her business started from selling dumplings in a small stall but the news about the delicious taste spread out quickly. The world of mouth marketing eventually made the small business develop into a big restaurant.

她從擺攤子賣水餃做起生意，但好吃的名聲一下就傳開了，口耳相傳讓她的小生意最後成長成大餐廳。

8. **guerrilla**（*n.*）游擊的；游擊隊員

① The famous band started chasing their dreams by guerrilla gigging on the streets.

這支熱門樂團當初是從街上打游擊表演起家築夢的。

② Facing the foreign invasion, local people ran into the jungle and became guerrillas to defend the homeland.

面對異族的入侵，當地人逃進了叢林裡，成為游擊隊員以捍衛家園。

9. **flash mob**（*n.*）快閃活動

The dancers arranged a flash mob at the train station to raise funds for a charity.

這群舞者策劃了一場快閃活動，在火車站替慈善團體募款。

10. **freebie**（*n.*）免費物

The new bookshop's strategy is giving away freebies, such as sticky notes.

新書局的策略是送便利貼之類的免費東西。

16.2

Search Engine Marketing

Amongst all the different types of digital marketing strategies, Search Engine Marketing starts a new wave in the online competition. Google is the largest search engine in the world. To earn more **traffic**, websites need to **optimize** themselves to rank higher in search results. If a company aims to do so, it needs to improve on-page development as well as off-page link-building. This marketing method is called Search Engine Optimization (SEO).

On-page development can be divided into two parts: structure analysis and content building. The website requires a well-organized index with clear logic so that Google spider can "**crawl**" through every page. Quality content needs to be written with enough but not excessive keywords relative to the topics so they don't look **suspicious**. If a website uses **shady** means, such as stuffing keywords marked in the same color that blends with the background, the website may show up more frequently in the result temporarily but soon would be blocked to the **blacklist** after the web analysts from the search engine **manually** check the website.

Off-page SEO is all about link building. Some search engines focus more on the **quantity** of the traffic whilst others are more concerned about the **quality**. Useful tips to increasing the traffic are asking business partners for link exchange, posting articles on forums and blogging. However, in this ever-changing Internet world, SEO analysts need to keep up with the latest news and be prepared for new challenges.

中文翻譯

搜尋引擎行銷

在所有不同的數位行銷策略中，搜尋引擎行銷在線上競爭中掀起一股新的潮流。谷歌是全球最大的搜尋引擎。為了贏得更多造訪**流量**，網站必須**優化**自身以在搜尋結果中擠進排行前名。要達到這個目標，企業得從站內優化做起，也要發展站外的點進連結。這種行銷策略被稱為搜尋引擎優化（SEO）。

站內優化可以分成兩個部分：架構分析以及內容建立。網站需要具有系統化的索引結構，谷歌蜘蛛才能「**爬**」過每一頁。優質的網站內容必須有貼切主題的關鍵字，而關鍵字的數量要夠多，但不能太多，以免看起來很**可疑**。如果網站使用**不光彩的**手段，例如大量堆積與背景同色的隱藏式關鍵字，網站也許短時間內會竄升到很高的排名，不過一旦搜尋引擎的網路分析師**人工**檢查過，就會被列入封鎖**黑名單**。

　　站外 SEO 幾乎都是在於建立連結。有些搜尋引擎重視流量的**數量**，有些則**重品質**。建立連結可從一些地方下手，例如邀請商業夥伴交換連結，在論壇發表文章或經營部落格。不過，在瞬息萬變的網路世界中，SEO分析師必須跟上最新潮流，隨時準備因應改變而作調整。

 重點字彙

1. **traffic**（*n.*）交通；流量

   ① The speaker was stuck in the traffic and caused the speech one hour late.

   　講師塞車被困在路上，演講因此延誤了一個小時。

   ② The fashion blog receives tens of thousands of traffic a day because of its frequently updated news.

   　這個時尚部落格因為頻繁更新新聞，每天都有數以萬計的流量。

2. **optimize**（*n.*）優化；使⋯⋯最優化

   We hired a new project manager to optimize the productivity.

   我們聘了一個新的專案經理以優化生產力。

3. **crawl**（*n.*）爬行；移動

   She fell down the stairs and crawled forward to open the door.

   她從樓梯摔下，往前爬去開門。

4. **suspicious**（*adj.*）可疑的

Statistics shows that police officers tend to find black people more suspicious out of racist reasons.

數據顯示出因為種族歧視原因，造成警察傾向於認為黑人較為可疑。

延伸字彙

● **skeptical** 懷疑的、多疑的

Voters are skeptical about the candidate's proposals.

選民對候選人的政見相當懷疑。

5. **shady**（*adj.*）陰暗的；可疑的、名聲不佳的、見不得人的

The committee passed some shady trading agreements under the table.

委員會在檯面下通過了一些見不得人的交易協定。

6. **manually**（*adj.*）手工的；人工的

Due to some technical problems, the railway technicians need to check each and every line manually to ensure the system is safe to start again. 由於一些技術性問題，技術人員必須以人力檢查每一條鐵路支線，以確保系統可以安全重新啟動。

反義字 automatic 自動的

Instead of creating the report manually every time, you can schedule a weekly report which let the system send it to you automatically. 與其每次都要手動製作報表，你可以排程讓系統自動寄給你每周報告。

iBT 新托福字彙閱讀應試技巧

Question 1: Which of the following couldn't be good practices for Partnership Marketing?

(A) Car rental companies and travel agencies

(B) Language schools and reference book publishers

(C) Gyms and nutritionists

(D) Airlines and football teams

解析　夥伴關係行銷，是將公司和互補或相配的品牌連結在一起，以達到雙方互利共生的方式，因此 (A) 租車公司可以和旅行社達到提供旅客互補的服務關係；(B) 語言學校可以提供出版社購買參考書的讀者；(C) 營養師可以給健身用戶飲食諮詢。但航空公司和足球隊並沒有互補或相配的服務，而是屬於贊助關係，故答案選 (D)。

Question 2: Which of the following is not the crucial element that made the marketing strategies today?

(A) Internet

(B) Broadcast

(C) International development

(D) Bid data

解析 由於文中提到"Thanks for the digital technologies and global economy, more methods are developed to promote businesses."，網路、大數據皆包含在數位科技中，而國際發展則和全球經濟息息相關，因此答案為存在已久的 (B) 電台廣播。

Question 3: To optimize a website for Search Engine Marketing, which of the following methods is not suggested to do?

(A) Build the website with clear structure.

(B) Write content with lots of different topics.

(C) Use the keyword in the website title.

(D) Repeat the keywords frequently in the content.

解析 為了讓網站更適於搜尋引擎行銷，網站一定要有 (A) 清楚的架構，也要在內容中 (D) 使用重複的關鍵字，如果網站名稱中 (C) 包含關鍵字的話，也會有幫助。然而內容如果 (B) 涉及太多不同主題，可能會讓搜尋引擎不知如何歸類，因此答案選 (B)。

Part
1

Part
2

Part
3

Part
4

Part
5

Part
6

Part
7

Unit **17**

17.1

Capitalism and Socialism

Although the world became more globalized now, each country still varies so much in its economic systems. The two major divisions between economies are **Capitalism** and **Socialism**.

In Capitalism economies, every individual or business can have private ownerships and the control over their **capitals**. They work to maximize their own profit. Capitalism is also called Market System since the prices are determined by the interaction between buyers and sellers in the market rather than by the state's control. This system allows individuals to **pursue** self-development. But the downside of it is wealth inequality and social instability caused by people's selfish desire. The typical economy of Capitalism is the United States.

Socialism is also known as **Command** System. In a Socialism economy, the government decides the price and the allocation of resources. Ideally speaking, the system aims to **eliminate** social class **divisions** and have everyone share work and be paid by the government to **allocate** the resources equally. None of the individuals or businesses can **monopolize** the market. Although paid more equally, people do not necessarily have higher living standards in Socialism economies than that of average people in Capitalism economies. An example of Socialism economy is the former Soviet Union.

Part 1

Part 2

Part 3

Part 4

Part 5

Part 6

Part 7

中文翻譯

資本主義與社會主義

儘管世界越發全球化，每個國家之間仍然在經濟體系上差異頗大，不同經濟體間可以分為兩大派別，**資本主義**和**社會主義**。

資本主義經濟體中，每個個體或企業都可以持有並掌控私人**資本**，並工作以達到各自利潤最大化。資本主義又稱市場經濟，因為所有價格都由市場上賣方與買方的互動決定，而不是由國家控制。這種體系讓個體能夠**追求**各自的發展，但缺點就是人的自私慾望導致貧富不均和社會不穩定。資本主義的典型範例是美國。

社會主義又稱**計畫**經濟。在社會主義經濟體中，政府決定價格和資源分配方式。理想來說，這種體系的目標為**消滅**社會**階級**，讓政府分配工作和配發薪水，並平等的**配給**資源給每個人。沒有任何人或企業可以**壟斷**市場。雖然待遇較平等，社會主義居民享有的生活水準並不會高於於資本主義社會的平均值。社會主義經濟體的例子之一就是前蘇聯。

重點字彙

1. **Socialism**（*n.*）社會主義

延伸字彙

capital（*n.*）資本；首都、首府；**capitalism**（*n.*）資本主義

① Their business lost half their capital in this financial crisis.

他們的公司在金融危機損失了一半的資本。

② You can find more opportunities in the capital but the living expenses are also higher there.

你可以在首都找到較多發展機會，但那邊的生活費也比較高。

2. **pursue**（*v.*）追趕；追求；繼續

He spent thirty years pursuing fame and wealth but lost the most important thing, love.

他花了三十年追逐名利，卻失去了最重要的東西，愛。

3. **allocate**（*v.*）分配、配給

延伸字彙

同義字　allot, assign, distribute

① The fund is so short that we are unable to allocate any resource to the advertisement department.

資金短缺到我們沒有辦法分配任何資源給廣告部門。

② Every candidate is allocated 10 minutes to express his/ her idea.

每位候選人都有10分鐘發表自己的意見。

③ Every team member has been assigned to a different task.

每位成員都分配不同的任務。

4. **command**（*v.* / *n.*）命令；指揮、統帥；
commander（*n.*）指揮官、領導人

① Do not underestimate her. She is the one in command.

不要小看她，這裡她作主。

② Unlike the last one, the new commander accepts no excuses for failure.

不像他的前任，新的指揮官不接受任何失敗的藉口。

5. **eliminate**（*v.*）排除、消滅、淘汰

延伸字彙　abolish, conquer, crush, overthrow

① The strategy currently available can only reduce but not entirely eliminate the problem of food shortage.

目前可用的策略只能緩和但不能完全排除食物短缺的問題。

② Any ideas about discrimination needs to be abolished.

任何關於歧視的想法都需廢除。

③ All the difficulties can be conquered.

所有的困難都能被克服。

Part
1

Part
2

Part
3

Part
4

Part
5

Part
6

Part
7

6. **divide**（*v.*）劃分；隔開；使對立；
   division（*n.*）分割、分派；分歧

   ① There's barely anything dividing people working here that everyone can hear each other in the office.
   這裡人跟人之間幾乎沒有任何隔間，每個人在辦公室工作時都可以聽到彼此的聲音。

   ② They used to be best friends in the school, but a small misunderstanding started to make division in the group.
   他們曾是學校裡最好的朋友，但一個小小的誤會讓團體裡開始有了岐異。

   延伸字彙　disconnect, disjoin, disjoint

   ① The Internet is disconnected.
   網路斷線了。

   ② The disjointed information makes the comprehension of it difficult.
   資訊太過片斷讓解讀變得困難。

7. **utility**（*n.*）用品；公用事業

The last straw crashed the family was the utility bills.

壓垮這個家庭的最後一根稻草，是水電費帳單。

延伸字彙

utilitarian（*adj.*）有用的

utilitarianism（*n.*）功利主義

① Plans have to be utilitarian instead of being shallow.

計劃必須有用，而非看來膚淺。

② A country that practices utilitarianism tends to have policies benefit the public.

功利主義的國家的政策較偏圖利大眾。

8. **monopolize**（*v.*）壟斷

同義字　monotonous, dreary, boring, repetitious, dull

反義字　bright, lively

① The global food industry is almost monopolized by international fast food franchises.

全球食物產業幾乎被國際素食連鎖店給壟斷了。

② Her tone during the speech sounds monotonous.

她在演講的語調聽起來非常單調。

—————————— 17.2 —————————— Track 34

Neoliberalism

Neoliberalism is an economic philosophy widespread since the 1970s. Neoliberalism objects the government to **intervene** in the domestic market but encourages the usage of political, economic, military and **diplomatic** means to put pressure on foreign markets.

The theory of economic **liberalism** was introduced by the Scottish economist, Adam Smith in 1776. He **advocated** the **abolition** of governmental control over economic matters. The theory was challenged during the Great Depression in the 1930s. The experience of unemployment and **poverty** then forced people to rethink the government's role in the market **mechanism**. After that, the new wave of economic philosophy was therefore called, Neoliberalism.

Neoliberalism supports free trade and private ownership and opposes state's policies intervening the market such as minimum wage, welfare program, union **negotiation** rights, trading protection or environment protection. In fact, Neoliberalism is strongly associated with **austerity** that reduces governmental **expenditure** on maintaining the market mechanism. Therefore, the economic growth under such societies is partially based on sacrificing social benefits provided by the government. Neoliberalism no doubt allows the rich to grow richer but also makes the poor suffer from **poverty**.

Part
1

Part
2

Part
3

Part
4

Part
5

Part
6

Part
7

中文翻譯

新自由主義

新自由主義是個從 1970 年代開始擴張的經濟意識形態。新自由主義反對政府**干預**國內市場，但鼓勵使用政治、經濟、軍事和**外交**手段給外國市場施加壓力。

自由主義經濟理論是從 1776 年由蘇格蘭經濟學家亞當史密斯發起的，他**主張**應該**廢除**政府對經濟事務的控制。這個理論在 1930 年代的經濟大蕭條受到強烈的挑戰，高失業和**貧窮**讓人們不禁反思政府在市場**機制**中的角色。之後，新的一波自由主義經濟型態就被稱為：新自由主義。

新自由主義支持自由貿易和財產私有化，反對干預市場的政府政策，例如最低薪資、福利制度、工會**談判權**、交易保護或環境保護等。事實上，新自由主義和**樽節主義**息息相關，減少政府保持市場機制的支出**預算**，因此，這種社會的經濟成長一部分是建築在犧牲政府提供的社會福利。新自由主義毫無疑問的讓有錢人持續得更有錢，但也讓窮人更受貧困所苦。

重點字彙

1. **liberalism**（*n.*）自由主義；**neoliberalism**（*n.*）新自由主義

   One of the main concepts in liberalism is free market.
   自由主義的中心思想之一，就是自由市場。

2. **intervene**（*v.*）干涉、介入

   Kids learn not to intervene in parents' fights since very young age.
   小孩很早就學會不要介入父母吵架。

3. **mechanism**（*n.*）機械作用；結構、機制

   The sacked factory workers decided to fight against the unfair employment mechanism.
   被遣散的工廠工人決定對抗這不公的就業機制。

4. **diplomacy**（*n.*）外交；**diplomat**（*n.*）外交官；**diplomatic**（*adj.*）外交的；圓滑的

   ① Despite the lack of an official ambassador, we still have a diplomat in that country.
   即便沒有一位正式使節，我們仍在此國駐有一位外交官。

   ② After spending a few years in the industry, she learnt to speak in a more diplomatic tone.
   在業界打滾幾年後，她學會更圓滑的說話方式。

5. **advocate**（*v.*）提倡、主張；
   advocator（*n.*）提倡者、擁護者

The poet society is advocators for freedom and passion.
這個詩社提倡自由和熱情。

延伸字彙

● **abolish**（*v.*）廢除；**abolition**（*n.*）廢除
Some believe that the married partner column should be abolished from the national ID card.
有些人認為配偶欄應從身分證上廢除。

6. **austerity**（*n.*）樽節

Hundreds of thousands of people's lives were hit by the benefit cuts introduced by the austerity policy.
成千上萬的人，因為樽節政策帶來的福利減免而生計受阻。

延伸字彙

● **austere**（*adj.*）簡樸的
He lives an austere life. 他過著簡樸的生活。

與 austere 相關的 延伸字彙 severe, stern, tough
His stern look always gave others' an impression that he's strict, but he's actually a nice person.
他嚴肅的表情總讓人覺得他很嚴格，但他人其實很不錯。

7. **negotiate**（v.）談判；**negotiation**（v.）談判

The police officers are on a negotiation hoping to help some hostage out.

警察正在談判，希望能救出一些人質。

8. **expenditure**（n.）經費、支出

The living expenditure is at least 200 per week in London.

倫敦的生活費至少是每周200鎊。

9. **poverty**（n.）貧窮、貧困

Over 50% of the popularity in this area lives under poverty line.

這區的人口裡有超過 50% 在貧窮線下生存。

iBT 新托福字彙閱讀應試技巧

Question 1: Which of the following description is not true?

(A) People in Capitalism societies can set up their own companies more easily.

(B) Companies in Socialism societies may have more restrictions over their business.

(C) Because resources are shared more equally, people's living standard is usually better in Socialism economies than that is Capitalism economies.

(D) The authority decides the price in Socialism economies.

解析　資本主義鼓勵私有制，因此人們要成立公司比較容易；社會主義的環境下，私人公司營運上通常有較多限制；社會主義的經濟體下，當局可以決定價格。但儘管資源分配較為平均，社會主義下的平均生活水準通常較資本主義社會低，因此答案為 (C)。

Question 2: "The system aims to _____ social class divisions and have everyone share work and be paid by the government to allocate the resources equally" Which of the following does not fit in the sentence?

(A) Remove

(B) Get rid of

(C) Abolish

(D) Emphasize

解析 本文中 "The system aims to eliminate social class divisions and have everyone share work and be paid by the government to allocate the resourcesequally"，"Eliminate" 可以以選項 (A) 的「消除」代替，或選項 (B) 的「擺脫」，或選項 (C) 的「廢除」，但選項 (D) 的「強調」卻意思完全相反，因此答案為 (D)。

Unit 17

Part
1

Part
2

Part
3

Part
4

Part
5

Part
6

Part
7

Question 3: What does the word "austerity" mean in the article?

(A) Cutting governmental budgets on military projects.

(B) Cutting public spending on maintaining the domestic market.

(C) Harsh economic conditions that discourage people from spending money.

(D) State policies that encourage private ownerships.

解析　新自由主義支持以軍事等手段影響外國市場，因此選項 (A) 減少政府軍事預算並不符合；雖然 "Austerity" 的確有簡樸、禁慾生活的意思，但與本文探討經濟政策不符，因此選項 (C) 也不對；新自由主義和自由主義一樣鼓勵私有化，但和樽節政策無直接關係，因此答案為選項 (B)，樽節政策主張減少用來維持國內市場的公共支出。

Unit 18

18.1

Track 35

Economic Indicators

In this globalized world, every country's development is so closely associated with each other. The global economy may be too complicated to follow but learning some **indicators** can help get a whole picture of it.

GWP stands for **gross** world product which equals the total global GDP (gross domestic product). Comparing the GWP statistics of different periods can help understand the growth and decline in global development.

Inflation is the increase in the general price level of goods or services. As the higher the price rises, the fewer goods and services can be purchased; the inflation reflects the reduction in the purchasing power. Most economies favor lower and steadier inflation rate.

Generally speaking, the more industrialized a country is, the higher employment rate this country will have. On the opposite, the unemployment rate reflects the lack of industrialization. Therefore, industrial production growth rate and unemployment rate show not just the industrial development but also the social

Unit 18

Part
1

Part
2

Part
3

Part
4

Part
5

Part
6

Part
7

development in an economy.

Balance of trade (BOT) is the difference between the country's imports and its exports. If the imported goods of a country are more than exported goods and services, the country has a trade **deficit**. The opposite **scenario** is a trade **surplus**.

中文翻譯

經濟指標

在這全球化的世界裡，每個國家的發展都和彼此密不可分。要跟上全球經濟也許太過複雜，但學會一些**指標**能夠幫助搞懂整體情況。

GWP 代表世界生產**總值**，等於全球 GDP（國民生產總額）的總和。比較不同時期的 GWP 數據可以幫助了解全球發展的成長和衰退。

通貨膨脹指的是貨品或服務的平均價格水準上漲。由於價格越高，能購買的貨品和服務就越少，因此通貨膨脹也反映出購買力的下降。大部分的經濟體都傾向較小幅或穩定的通貨膨脹率。

一般來說，一個國家的產業發展越高，該國的就業率就越高。反之，失業率也反映出工業發展的匱乏。因此，工業生產成長率和失業率表現出的不只是產業發展，也反映出經濟體中的社會發展。

國際收支平衡（BOT）是國家進口和出口的差額，如果進口的貨品和服務大於出口，該國的貿易就出現**赤字**，相反的**情況**則是**貿易順差**。

重點字彙

1. **indicate**（*v.*）指示、指出；**indicator**（*n.*）指標

① The latest report indicates that the major factor of air pollution is the chemistry factories around the city.

最新報告指出空氣汙染的最大因素是城市周圍的化學工廠。

② Unemployment rate is one of the most important economic indicators.

失業率是最重要的經濟指標之一。

2. **gross**（*n.* / *adj.*）總和、毛利的（數據）；粗略的；低俗的、惡劣

① The gross profit grows as soon as they cut down the transportation cost.

他們一把運輸費用減低，毛利潤就成長起來了。

② The whole bureaucracy system is full of gross corruption.

整個官僚體系充斥著惡劣的貪腐。

3. **per capita** 每人均值

The country spends the most education investment per capita in the world.

這個國家花費的平均每人教育投資是全球之冠。

4. **inflation**（*n.*）**通貨膨脹**

延伸字彙

同義字　boost, escalate, exaggerate, inflate,

反義字　abridge, diminish

The country experiences severe inflation after the war.

此國在戰後經濟了嚴重的通貨膨脹。

5. **currency**（*n.*）**幣值、貨幣**

As a frequent traveler, he is always following the exchange rate fluctuation between currencies.

由於時常旅行，他總是注意著幣值間的匯率變動。

6. **deficit**（*n.*）**赤字、不足**

The large amount of people retiring in the last decade has created a deficit in the pension scheme.

過去十年來大量退休的人潮造成退休金制度的赤字。

7. **surplus**（*n.*）**盈餘、順差；過剩**

The restaurant always brings the food to the nearby orphanage when there's surplus by the end of the day.

餐廳在每天結束時，如果還有過剩的食物，就會帶去附近的孤兒院。

Part 1

Part 2

Part 3

Part 4

Part 5

Part 6

Part 7

18.2

The Great Depression

In the 1930s, the world suffered a severe economic depression. The period is called the Great Depression.

After WWI, the USA replaced Britain and became the most powerful economy in the world. The economy boosted the **prosperity** of all industries. People became confident in taking chances. Sales were **promoted** through buying **credit**. However, the good time didn't last long. While consumer spending dropped and unsold goods started to pile up, the stock price continued to grow. On October 24, 1929, the stock market bubble finally **burst**. The day was called, "Black Thursday".

The stock market crashed consumer confidence. The lack of spending and **investment** led factories to slow down their productions and **constructions**. Businesses began firing their workers and reducing wages of those who remained employed. Many people who made purchases credits fell into **debts**. Farmers couldn't afford to harvest their crops and had to leave them to rot in the field while **starvation** started to spread in the society. Thousands of banks were forced to close.

The USA government eventually had to intervene the economy to create jobs by building a series of **infrastructures**. The Great Depression also forced the government to provide unemployment insurance and **pensions** to the citizens.

Part 1

Part 2

Part 3

Part 4

Part 5

Part 6

Part 7

中文翻譯

經濟大蕭條

全球在 1930 年代經歷一場嚴重的經濟蕭條，被稱為「經濟大蕭條」。

一次世界大戰後，美國取代英國成為世界上最富強的經濟體，連帶所有產業都**發展興旺**。人們變得勇於擁抱機會，商業行銷鼓勵**借貸購買**。然而，好日子沒有延續太久，當消費者的購買力開始下降，賣不出去的產品開始滯銷時，股票價格持續上漲。直到 1929 年十月二十四日，股市終於**崩盤**，這一天被稱為「黑色星期四」。

股市崩盤摧毀了消費者信心，消費和**投資**資金的減少讓工廠必須減緩生產和**建設**速度。公司開始開除員工，並且減少剩餘員工的薪水。許多曾經借款以做消費的人開始背上**債務**。農夫無法負擔收割，只能任由穀物在田裡腐壞，而**飢餓**開始在社會上蔓延。數以千計的銀行被迫倒閉。

美國政府最終必須干預經濟，政府以建造一系列的**基礎建設**為由創造工作機會，經濟大蕭條也逼迫政府提供國民失業保險和**退休金**。

重點字彙

1. **prosperous**（*adj.*）繁榮的、興旺的；
   prosperity（*n.*）繁榮、興旺、成功

   ① Wish you a very prosperous new year!
   祝您新年旺旺來！

   ② They believe in planting flowers to bring prosperity.
   他們相信種花可以帶來興旺。

2. **promote**（*v.*）晉升、升級；促銷、宣傳

   ① She was promoted to be senior manager on her two year working anniversary.
   她在工作滿兩年時被升為資深經理。

   ② The shop introduced "Buy one, get one free" promotion to boost the winter sale.
   這間店在冬季特賣時推出「買一送一」促銷活動。

3. **burst**（*v.*）爆炸、破裂；爆發；脹破

   ① The dam burst after a whole week of nonstop rain.
   下了連續一周的雨後，水壩終於潰堤。

   ③ The audience burst out laughing as the comedian fell on the floor.
   喜劇員跌倒在地引起觀眾哄堂大笑。

4. **vanish**（*v.*）消失；絕跡

Dinosaurs once dominated the Earth but vanished approximately 65 million years ago.

恐龍曾一度稱霸地球，但在大約六千五百萬年前絕跡了。

5. **invest**（*v.*）投資

"Don't put all your eggs in one basket" is the rule number one for making investment.

「不要把雞蛋全放在一個籃子裡」是做投資的第一項原則。

6. **construction**（*n.*）建設；建築

He learned all the skills from working in construction sites and eventually set up his own company.

他從在工地工作學會所有技能，最後成立自己的公司。

7. **credit**（*n.*）賒債；信譽；信用；銀行存款；
debit（*n.*）（會計）借方；**debt**（*n.*）債款、負債；情義

① She is very cautious in using credit card, never exceeding her credit limit.

她用信用卡非常小心，絕不超出信用額度。

② The accountant examines the record carefully by all the debit and credit entries.

會計師非常仔細的檢視紀錄上所有借方與貸方的帳目。

③ It took him five years of hard work to pay back the debt from student loan.

他辛苦工作五年才還清就學貸款的債務。

8. **starve**（*n.*）捱餓、餓死；極度需要；
starvation（*n.*）飢餓、餓死

① You should work out more instead of starving yourself to lose weight.

你應該多運動而不是捱餓減肥。

② The unusual drought led to severe starvation throughout the country.

反常的乾旱導致全國上下嚴重的飢餓。

9. **infrastructure**（*n.*）公共設施；基礎建設

The new mayor introduced a series of new infrastructures including WIFI hot spots in every metro station.

新市長引進一系列的新建設，包括每個地鐵站的 WIFI 熱點。

10. **pension**（*n.*）退休金、養老金

He doesn't trust the state pension so he decides to join a private pension scheme.

他不相信國家退休金，所以選擇加入一個私人的退休金方案。

iBT 新托福字彙閱讀應試技巧

Question 1: Which of the following indicators doesn't tell the purchase power per capita in an economy?

(A) Balance of trade (BOT)
(B) GDP (gross domestic product)
(C) Unemployment rate
(D) Inflation rate

解析　一個經濟體中的每人平均購買力可以由不同指標中觀察到，例如選項 (B) 的國民生產總額，國民生產總額越高，通常就越有餘力進行購買；選項 (C) 失業率則通常和購買力成反比，失業率越高，就越多人無法負擔消費；選項 (D) 通貨膨脹則影響到同樣金額的錢能購買到的商品總額，如果通貨膨脹太嚴重，則人民就算有錢也買不了太多。但選項 (A) 的國際收支平衡指的是該國進口和出口貿易的差額，和國民平均購買力沒有直接關係，因此答案為 (A)。

Part 1

Part 2

Part 3

Part 4

Part 5

Part 6

Part 7

Question 2: Which of the following was not the reason that caused the Great Depression?

(A) The banks gave away too many credits.

(B) The stock market puffed up too much like a bubble.

(C) Food shortage on the market.

(D) The market lost balance between supplying and demanding.

解析 經濟大蕭條由許多背景因素造成，銀行給出太多貸款、股票市場嚴重膨脹、市場上供需失衡等都是原因，但食物短缺是因為經濟大蕭條期間，農夫無法負擔收割成本，只能任由農作物在田裡腐爛，農產品無法進入市面上，才導致食物短缺，因此選項 (C) 並不是經濟大蕭條的原因，而是連帶社會的影響。

Part 1

Part 2

Part 3

Part 4

Part 5

Part 6

Part 7

Question 3: John grew up during the Great Depression. Which of the following may describe his childhood? (Multiple options)

(A) John's father lost his job in a metal company.

(B) John's baby sister was starved to death.

(C) John's mother was promoted to be the bank manager.

(D) John works during summer holiday by helping in the farms.

(E) John's uncle ran away because he couldn't pay back the debt.

解析　約翰是在經濟大蕭條期間長大的，他小時候可能經歷父親失業、妹妹於襁褓中餓死、叔叔躲債潛逃，但當時百業蕭條，母親不大可能在銀行裡仍然有升遷，農場也未必還能請約翰暑假去打工，因此答案為 (A)、(B)、(E)。

Unit 19

19.1

Track 37

Earthquake

An earthquake is the shaking of the surface of the Earth by which the energy in the Earth's crust is released and creates **seismic waves**. Sometime it is barely **perceptible** but sometime it can be violent enough to destroy buildings and constructions.

Earthquakes can happen in various conditions. Most of the earthquakes are caused by the structure movements of Earth which are called "**tectonic** earthquakes". Tectonic earthquakes happen in different types of **faults**, which are normal, reserve and strike-slip faults. Once the fault has locked, the continuous motion between plates increase stress and store strain energy near the fault surface. When **accumulated** to a certain limit, the energy makes the fault to press the locked fault and even crack the rocks to release the energy. Caused by the movement of magma in volcanoes, earthquakes also often occur in **volcanic** regions. In fact, earthquakes can provide an early warning of volcanic eruptions.

Earthquakes are measured by **seismometers** in Richter **magnitude** scale. Most of the time people can only sense ground shakes at least magnitude-3. The damage of an earthquake varies by the scale and also by the depth. Earthquakes beyond magnitude-7 can destroy a city. The largest recorded earthquake in history was the magnitude-9.5 quake in Chile in 1960.

中文翻譯

地震

地震是地殼內釋放能量而在地表產生地震波而成的**震動**。有時地震幾乎**感覺**不到，但有時地震可以強烈到足以摧毀建築物或大型建設。

地震可能在不同情況下發生，大部分的地震都是由地球結構移動造成的，稱為「**構造型**地震」。構造型地震發生在不同**斷層**上：**正斷層、逆斷層**和**平移斷層**。一旦斷層被鎖住，板塊間的連續移動會增加壓力，在斷層表面累積緊繃的能量。當能量**累積**到一定的極限時，就會擠壓斷層從鎖住的狀態滑開，甚至**崩破**岩石以釋放能量。地震也常出現在**火山**地區，由火山**岩漿**的流動造成。事實上，地震可以提供為火山爆發的前兆警訊。

地震可由**地震儀**測量，以芮氏**地震規模**表示。通常要至少三級以上，人們才會感覺的到地表晃動。地震的災害因震級而異，也受深度影響。超過七級的地震可以摧毀一座城市。有史以來紀錄中最大的地震，是 1960年智利的 9.5 級大地震。

重點字彙

1. **seismic wave** 地震波；**seismometer** 地震儀

① The seismometer recorded dozens of mild seismic waves on a daily basis.

地震儀每天都記錄下數十筆微小的地震波。

② Animals and insects are more sensitive to mild seismic waves than human beings can.

動物和昆蟲比人類還能察覺到細微的地震波。

2. **perceive**（*n.*）察覺、感知；**perceptible (perceivable)**（*adj.*）可察覺的、可辨的

① The little boy perceived the tension between his parents and ran back to his room.

小男孩察覺到父母間緊張的氣氛，於是跑回自己的房間。

② They try to hide the conspiracy, but there are still some perceivable clues in their interaction.

他們試著隱藏陰謀，但互動間仍察覺的出一些蛛絲馬跡。

3. **tectonic**（*adj.*）構造的；地殼構造的

The complex tectonic settings in this area make its unique scenery.

這個區域的複雜地殼構造，造就其獨一無二的景觀。

4. **fault**（*n.*）錯誤、缺陷；地質斷層

① The computer crashed this morning due to an electric fault.

今早的電腦當機是由電力故障造成的。

② Stop blaming yourself. This is not your fault.

別再自責了，這不是你的錯。

③ The government promised to rebuild the village which used to be on the major earthquake fault line.

政府承諾重建那座原本位於重大地震斷層帶上的村莊。

5. **accumulate**（*v.*）累積

Within two years of graduation from the University, she has already accumulated solid working experience in the industry.

大學畢業後兩年內，她就在業界累積了扎實的工作經驗。

6. **volcanic**（*adj.*）地震的

① The volcanic eruption of Mount Vesuvius destroyed the Roman city Pompeii.

維蘇威山的火山爆發摧毀了羅馬古城龐貝城。

② Seven Star Mountain is a dormant volcano in Yangmingshan National Park.

七星山是陽明山國家公園內的一座休火山。

延伸字彙

● **active volcano** 活火山
● **dormant volcano** 休火山
● **extinct volcano** 死火山

其它延伸字彙

explosive, ferocious, fierce, tempestuous, tumultuous, turbulent, violent

7. **magma**（*n.*）岩漿

The photographer insists on entering the volcano area to capture the image of magma.

攝影師執意要進入火山區去捕捉岩漿的畫面。

8. **magnitude**（*n.*）（地震）震級

The whole city was woken up by the magnitude-5 shake at 3am last night.

整座城市昨晚都被凌晨三點的五級地震震醒了。

其它相關字彙　volcanic, eruption, debris, avalanche

① Volcanic activities are frequent in this area.

這區的火山活動非常頻繁。

② The alert system will go off if the sign of volcanic eruption is detected.

火山一旦有爆發的徵兆，警報系統就會啟動。

③ The debris were scattered after the flood.

淹水後四處可見殘骸。

Part 1

Part 2

Part 3

Part 4

Part 5

Part 6

Part 7

Track 38

19.2

Japan Earthquake and Tsunami of 2011

Japan was hit by a **devastating** earthquake which **unleashed** a **savage tsunami** in 2011. Until now, the residents are still recovering from the disaster.

The magnitude-9 earthquake occurred in north eastern Japan with the **epicenter** approximately 79 km off the coast and the **hypocenter** 30 km depth underwater. The unexpected earthquake was followed by tsunami waves up to 40.5 meters high. The country's early earthquake warning system sent out warning a minute before the shake and stopped high speed trains and factory assembly lines. People also receive text alerts about the earthquake and the coming tsunami from their mobile phones. Despite such efficient system, the disaster along with the tsunami still took away over 15,000 lives. The tsunami also caused **nuclear** accidents in the Fukushima Daiichi Nuclear Power Plant and forced hundreds of thousands of residents to **evacuate** from the area.

The impact of this disaster was deep and long. Nuclear plants were shut down due to the damage. Four years later, Japan decided to reactivate a nuclear plant on 11th August, 2015 which would surely provide the nation with more sufficient electricity but also put people back to the shadow of nuclear accident.

Part 1

Part 2

Part 3

Part 4

Part 5

Part 6

Part 7

中文翻譯

日本地震和 2011 年的海嘯

日本在 2011 年遭到一場**毀滅性的**地震打擊，地震並**引發殘酷的海嘯**。四年過去了，居民仍在從那場災難中慢慢恢復。

這場震級九級的地震發生在日本東北，**震央**在離岸約 79 公里，**震源**在海底 30 公里深。這毫無預料的地震隨之跟來的是高達 40.5 公尺高的海嘯。國內的地震警告系統在地震發生前一分鐘發出警告，停止高速鐵路和工廠生產線運作。民眾也在手機上收到簡訊警告地震和海嘯。儘管有這麼有效率的系統，災難仍然奪走了 15,000 條生命，大部分是因為海嘯。海嘯也在福島第一核電廠引發了**核能**災害，迫使數十萬居民**撤離**當地。

這場災難的影響既深又遠。核電廠因為受損而關閉，四年過去了，日本決定於 2015 年八月十一日重啟座核電廠，這無庸置疑可以提供國家更充足的電力，但也將人民帶回核災的陰影中。

重點字彙

1. **devastating**（*adj.*）毀滅性的

The devastating storm sank the whole city in flood.
毀滅性的暴風雨讓整座城市淹在水裡。

2. **unleash**（*v.*）解開束縛、宣洩情緒

The new benefit cuts unleashed a storm of protests in the UK.
最新的社會福利縮減引發英國境內一連串的抗議。

3. **savage**（*adj.*）殘暴的、猛烈的；未開化的

The formal debate between party leaders turned out to be a politicians' savage attack between each other.
各黨領導人的正式辯論演變成政客間的互相猛烈攻擊。

4. **Tsunami**（*n.*）海嘯

He lost all his family in the tsunami three years ago.
他在三年前的海嘯失去了所有家人。

延伸字彙 ▶ ruin, decimate, demolish

同義字 ▶ catastrophic, calamitous, disastrous, fatal

反義字 ▶ advantageous, fortunate

Part 1

Part 2

Part 3

Part 4

Part 5

Part 6

Part 7

5. **epicenter** （*n.*）震央、中心

Although not very strong by scale, the earthquake still caused some damage due to its epicenter in the city.

儘管震度規模並不強，這次地震仍然造成一些災害，因為震央在城裡。

6. **hypocenter**（*n.*）震源

The hypocenter of the earthquake this time was very near the surface.

這次地震的震源非常靠近地表。

7. **nuclear**（*adj.*）原子核的；核能的

The country claimed to have developed powerful nuclear weapon.

此國宣稱發展出強大的核子武器。

8. **evacuate**（*v.*）撤離、撤退

The authority sent the army to evacuate the flooding area.

當局派出軍隊徹空淹水區域。

延伸字彙　ruin, decimate, demolish

同義字　catastrophic, calamitous, disastrous, fatal

反義字　advantageous, fortunate

iBT 新托福字彙閱讀應試技巧

Question 1: What does "Tectonic Earthquakes" mean?

(A) Earthquakes caused by construction accidents.

(B) Earthquakes caused by nuclear explosions.

(C) Earthquakes caused by volcanic eruptions.

(D) Earthquakes caused by motions of plates.

解析 構造型地震是由地殼板塊的移動造成的，並非工程意外造成，也非核能爆炸，而火山爆發雖然也可能與地殼板塊移動相關，但並不完全等於「構造型地震」，因此答案為 (D)。

Question 2: What does "faults" mean in the article?

(A) The cracks in the rocks between plates.

(B) Natural borders between continents.

(C) The flaws in natural sceneries.

(D) The ruins left by human activities in natural environment.

解析 "Faults"在本文為「斷層」的意思，也就是只板塊間岩石的斷裂處。斷層並不是指不同大陸間的天然邊界，也不是自然景觀的瑕疵，更不是人類活動在自然環境中留下的遺跡，因此答案為 (A)。

Question 3: What is the difference between epicenter and hypocenter?

Part 3

(A) They are synonyms.

(B) Epicenter is used to plotting earthquake's location on the map. Hypocenter is the true point where earthquake occurs and is always located at some depth underground.

(C) Both epicenter and hypocenter stand for earthquake's location but the former is used to emphasize the epic scale of the shake.

(D) Both epicenter and hypocenter stand for earthquake's location but the latter is used when earthquake happens underwater.

解析　震央和震源的差別在於前者是地圖上平面定位的地震所在，後者為地震實際發生的點，且一定在具有一定深度的地底下。因此，震央和震源並不是同義字，前者和晃動的劇烈程度並無強調作用，而後者並不代表地震一定發生在水底，因此答案為 (B)。

Unit 20

20.1 Track 39

Climate Changes

Observing the record from the past, scientists have already figured the changes of weather patterns millions years ago. They apply the statistics from the past to the present conditions in order to predict the possible changes in the future. Moreover, scientists hope to find solutions to prevent **irreversible** weather changes that may endanger human survival, such as dramatic global warming.

Climate changes can be caused by internal mechanisms such as ocean **currents** and life cycle of **carbon** and water circulation. Weather conditions can also be affected by various external mechanisms including **orbital** variation, **solar** output, volcanic activities, plate tectonics and human influences. Of course, it is not very likely to reject solar radiation, change the Earth's orbit or prevent volcanic eruptions with the present human forces. However, we surely have control over artificial factors that make climate changes and prevent the deterioration of global warming. For instance, we can restrict **fossil fuel** consumptions, CO2 emissions; drag on the increasing speed of **ozone** depletion and

Unit 20

Part
1

Part
2

Part
3

Part
4

Part
5

Part
6

Part
7

illegal usage of land; accelerate the efficiency of trees planting rather than that of **deforestation**, etc.

Although industrial development has contributed a huge part in modern civilization, we still need to consider the impact of that on natural environment. Human beings must find a way to respect the environment while developing more innovations.

中文翻譯

氣候變遷

從觀察過去的紀錄中，科學家研究出了過去數百萬年來的氣候變遷規律，他們將這些過往的數據應用到現今的情況，用以預測未來的可能變化。科學家甚至希望能找到預防措施，以防危及人類生存的**不可逆**氣候變化，例如劇烈的全球暖化。

氣候變遷可以被內部機制影響，例如海洋**洋流**和生命中的碳和水循環等。氣候條件也會受不同的外在機制影響，例如地球**軌道變異**、**太陽能**輻射、火山活動、地殼活動和人類影響等。當然，目前人類的力量仍不太足以阻擋太陽能輻射、改變地球運行軌道或阻止火山爆發，但我們絕對有能力控制改變氣候的人為因素，避免全球暖化更加惡化。舉例來說，我們可以控制石化燃料用量、二氧化碳排放量、延緩臭氧層的消耗和不合法的土地使用、加快種植樹木而非砍伐樹木的效率和砍伐等。

　　儘管工業發展對現代文明貢獻良多，我們仍須考量這對自然環境的衝擊。人類一定要找到創新發展下仍然尊重環境的方式。

 重點字彙

1. **reverse**（*adj.*）顛倒的、相反的；倒轉；
   irreversible（*adj.*）不可逆的

   ① The damage cannot be reversed. You can only try to make up for it. 傷害已鑄成無法迴轉，你只能試著彌補。

   ② It took the country ten years to build up the economy from the irreversible damage caused by that notorious policy. 那惡名昭彰的政策造成不可逆的傷害，國家花了十年才重振經濟。

2. **current**（*n.*）洋流；目前的

   ① The island is in a perfect location with the warm current adjusting the sea surface temperature.
   這座島嶼位居完美的位置，溫暖的洋流調節海面溫度。

   ② She is currently unavailable to see you. 她目前不方便見您。

3. **carbon**（*n.*）碳

   She tends to buy fruits and vegetable from local farms to reduce the carbon footprint in her diet.
   她盡量向當地農場購買水果蔬菜以減低飲食中的碳足跡。

4. **orbit**（*n.*）（天體）運行軌道；繞行；範圍；眼窩；
   orbital（*adj.*）軌道的

   The higher the orbit is, the longer it takes to circulate the Earth. 軌道越高，繞行地球所需的時間就越長。

5. **solar**（*adj.*）太陽能的、日光的

   The building is known for using solar energy for electricity usage. 這棟建築以太陽能發電聞名。

6. **fossil**（*n.*）化石；**fossil fuel**（*n.*）化石燃料

   ① The fish fossils show that this area used to be under water. 這些魚化石證明這個地區曾在水中。
   ② Fossil fuel supplies the majority of the energy needed in the area. 化石燃料提供此地主要的能量來源。

7. **ozone**（*n.*）臭氧

   Ozone provides the Earth with natural UV protection.
   臭氧層是地球自然的紫外線保護。

8. **forest**（*n.*）森林；**forestation**（*n.*）造林；
   deforestation（*n.*）砍伐森林

   The extensive deforestation in the country led to the result of mass desertification.
   國內的大規模森林砍伐造成大範圍沙漠化的結果。

Part 1
Part 2
Part 3
Part 4
Part 5
Part 6
Part 7

20.2

 Track 40

Climate Anomalies - El Nino

We all think the nature has its rule in making four seasons just as how they should be. Plants **sprout** to welcome the New Year in spring. Everyone should enjoy **sunbath** on the beach for summer holidays. Trees change colors in autumn. Everything should be concealed under white snow on Christmas day. However, disordered global climate system has triggered climate **anomalies** with various factors.

El Nino Southern Oscillation (ENSO) is irregularly periodic climate change caused by the temperature variations of the tropical eastern Pacific Ocean's sea surface. El Nino refers to the warming phenomenon. The cooling phase is called **La Nina**. El Nino happens often in winters with abnormally higher temperatures. The temperature variations on the Pacific Ocean near the **equator** affect the weather around the globe. As the ocean currents circle around the globe, El Nino and La Nina bring the influence to other parts of the world that causes strange weathers such as warm winter or cold summer.

The frequency of El Nino and La Nina has increased in the last

Part 1

Part 2

Part 3

Part 4

Part 5

Part 6

Part 7

few decades and aggravated other climate variations such as the melting of the **Arctic**. This phenomenon makes it even harder to predict weather changes.

中文翻譯

氣候變異－聖嬰現象

　　我們都認為自然有其規則，讓四季都有該有的樣貌。植物在春天**發芽**迎接新年，暑假就是要大家一起到沙灘上做**日光浴**，樹葉變色預告秋天的來臨，而聖誕節就是萬物都覆蓋在白雪底下。然而，全球系統因為不同因素而失調，造成氣候**異常**。

　　聖嬰現象 (ENSO)是熱帶東太平洋海面溫度變化造成的間歇性的不規律氣候變化。聖嬰現象指的是暖化現象，而冷事件則被稱為**反聖嬰現象**。聖嬰現象常發生在冬季，造成反常的高溫。**赤道**附近太平洋的溫差影響全球天氣。由於海洋洋流繞著全球循環，聖嬰現象和反聖嬰現象就把影響帶到世界不同地方，造成奇怪的天氣，例如暖冬或冷夏。

　　聖嬰現象和反聖嬰現象發生的頻率在過去幾十年增加不少，而氣候變異，如北極的融化也隨之惡化，這種現象也讓氣候變化更加難以預測。

重點字彙

1. **sprout**（v.）發芽；嫩枝

   The students are excited to see their plants to sprout.
   學生們都對他們種的植物發芽非常期待。

2. **sunbathe**（v.）日光浴（名詞：sunbath）

   She forgot to apply some lotion before taking sunbath.
   她忘了曬日光浴前要先擦防曬油。

3. **anomaly**（n.）異常、反常的事物

   The small company's success made a positive anomaly in the market.
   這個小公司的成功在市場上造成反常態的正面效應。

4. **Celsius**（溫度）攝氏；**Fahrenheit**（溫度）華氏

   1 degree Celsius is equal to 33.8 degrees Fahrenheit.
   攝氏一度等於華氏 33.8 度。

5. **El Nino Southern Oscillation** 聖嬰現象；
   La Nina 反聖嬰現象

   A record storm occurred this summer due to the El Nino effect.
   聖嬰現象在今年夏天造成一個破紀錄的暴風雨。

6. **equator**（*n.*）赤道

   Located near the equator, the island is warm throughout the year.
   位居接近赤道，這座島一年到頭都很溫暖。

   延伸字彙

   ● **Tropic of Cancer** 北迴歸線；**Tropic of Capricorn** 南迴歸線
   The Tropic of Cancer crosses through Taiwan and divides the island into tropical and semi-tropical zones.
   北回歸線穿越台灣，將島區分為熱帶與副熱帶。

7. **Arctic**（*adj. / n.*）北極 (North Pole)

   Her dream is to take an Arctic adventure!
   她的夢想是到北極探險！

Part 1

Part 2

Part 3

Part 4

Part 5

Part 6

Part 7

iBT 新托福字彙閱讀應試技巧

Question 1: Which of the following are factors that people can control over the global climate? (Multiple Options)

(A) Volcanic Eruption
(B) Trees plantation
(C) Petrol consumption
(D) Greenhouse gas emission
(E) Solar radiation

解析 人為可以控制的全球氣候因子包括植樹、石油用量、溫室氣體排放量等，但火山爆發和太陽能輻射並不是人類可以控制的因素，因此答案為 (B)、(C)、(D)。

Question 2: What can fill in the blank in "Scientists hope to find solutions to prevent _____ weather changes"?

(A) Unrepairable
(B) Dramatic
(C) Irresistible
(D) Irritating

Part 1

Part 2

Part 3

Part 4

Part 5

Part 6

Part 7

解析　文中這句話原本用的是"Irreversible"，也就是不可逆轉的意思，選項(B) 為「劇烈的」，(C) 為「不可抗拒的」，(D) 為「令人惱怒的」，因此答案為(A)「不可修復的」。

Question 3: What does "Anomaly" mean in the article?

(A) Dramatic global warming phenomenon.
(B) Abnormal temperature changes.
(C) Devastating weather disasters.
(D) Temperature changes on the Pacific Ocean.

解析　文中的「異常」指的是不正常的氣溫變化，而不是單指劇烈的全球暖化、毀滅性的天氣災害或太平洋的溫度變化，因此，答案為選項(B)。

Unit **21**

—————————— **21.1** —————————— **Track 41**

Food Chains

Food chains are not just about who eats whom in the wild nature. Food chains also describe the **calorific** energy flow in the cycle of life.

In the **ecosystem**, the feeding relationships among different species are critical in balancing the system. The base of the food pyramid is green plants called Primary Producers. They use **photosynthesis** to convert solar energy, air and water into nutrition. Species that eat green plants are Primary Consumers. They **absorb** the nutrition through digestion and then use **respiration** to produce the energy needed. Secondary Consumers are those who consume the Primary Consumers. Because of their diet on meat, they are also called **Carnivores**. For those consuming Primary Consumers and Primary Producers, they are **Omnivores**. As Primary Consumers, Secondary Consumers also practice digestion and respiration to absorb the energy for growth and storage. Finally, **Decomposers** break down plants, **herbivores**, omnivores, carnivores and release the energy back to the soil.

In this system, the energy will be gradually depleted in every stage of the food chains. Thus, warm-blooded animals require nutrition to maintain body temperature. The evaporation of body heat contributes to one of energy losses. Since the loss of energy at each chain limits creatures' activities, the links of food chains will be confined into four to six.

中文翻譯

食物鏈

食物鏈不只是野生自然中誰吃誰而已，更描述出生命循環中的**熱量能源**流動關係。

在**生態環境**中，不同物種間的食性關係扮演平衡系統非常重要的角色。食物金字塔的基礎是綠色食物，稱為生產者。他們用**光合作用**，將太陽能、空氣和水，轉變為養分。吃綠色植物的物種為一級消費者，他們消化**吸收**營養，並行**呼吸作用**產生需要的能量。次級消費者就是吃一級消費者的物種，由於肉食習慣，他們也被稱為**肉食性動/植物**。而一級消費者和生產者通吃的物種，則稱為**雜食類動/植物**。次級消費者和一級消費者一樣，都透過消化和呼吸作用，吸收能量以利成長和儲存。最後，**分解者**將植物、**草食類動/植物**、雜食類動/植物和肉食類動/植物分解，並將能量釋放回到土壤中。

系統在食物鏈的每個階段都會流失能量。因此，恆溫動物需要養分來保持體溫，而能量就隨體溫散去。每階失去的能量成為限制，讓大部分的食物鏈都不超過四到六階。

 重點字彙

1. **calorie**（*n.*）卡路里；**calorific**（*adj.*）熱卡的

① She controls her diet by strictly calculating the calorie consumed.

她嚴格計算所有吃下去的卡路里以控制飲食。

② Apart from the high calorific content, this bread doesn't have much nutrition.

除了高卡路里之外，這麵包沒什麼營養。

和 calorie 相關的 延伸字彙

● **cardiograph**（*n.*）心電圖儀

● **cardiovascular**（*adj.*）心血管的

You need to carefully measure how much calories you have taken each meal or you will get cardiovascular diseases easily.

你必須謹慎計算每餐所攝取的卡路里，否得你容易會有心血管疾病。

2. **ecosystem**（*n.*）生態系統

The NGO is dedicated to protecting the ecosystem in the rain forest.

這個無政府組織致力於保護雨林的生態系統。

3. **species**（*n.*）物種、品種

The orchid foundation named the new species after the first lady.

蘭花協會替新品種命名為第一夫人之名。

4. **photosynthesis**（*n.*）光合作用

Students are told to put some plants outside and some in the dark room to compare the outcome of photosynthesis.

學生被教導把一些植物放外頭，一些放暗室，藉此比較光合作用的效果。

與 synthesis 相關的　延伸字彙

alloy, amalgam, amalgamation, combination, composite, compound, fusion, mixture, blend

① The company is in the process of amalgamation with other two companies.

該公司正在和其它兩家公司合併中。

② The material is made by alloying tin with copper.

該物質是由錫和銅混合而成。

5. **absorb**（*v.*）**吸收；吸引；併吞**

The chicken has absorbed all the herbs' flavors and became super delicious.

雞肉吸收了所有香料的味道，好吃的不得了。

6. **respire**（*v.*）**呼吸；respiration**（*n.*）**呼吸作用**

① The hikers respire supplemental oxygen to keep their strengths.

登山者呼吸補給氧氣以保持體力。

② Most of the people know that plants practice photosynthesis during daytime but little do they know about respiration that happens all day on the plants.

人們大多知道植物在白天行光合作用，但很少人知道植物整天都在行呼吸作用。

延伸字彙 breathe, exhale, inhale

7. **carnivore**（*n.*）**肉食性動物；肉食性植物**

He is totally a carnivore who eats steak three times a week.

他是個徹徹底底的肉食性動物，一周要吃三次牛排。

與 carni- 字首相關的 延伸字彙 carnival

8. **omnivore**（*n.*）雜食性動物

They feed their chickens with their leftovers as chickens are omnivores.

因為雞是雜食性動物，他們都用廚餘餵雞。

與 omni- 字首相關　延伸字彙

- **omnipotent**（*adj.*）全能的
- **omnicompetent**（*adj.*）能處理各種狀況的
- **omnibus**（*n.*）（英）公車

9. **herbivore**（*n.*）草食性動物

Most herbivores are harmless. They won't attack you as long as you don't attack them.

大部分的草食性動物都沒有傷害性，只要你不攻擊他們，他們就不會攻擊你。

Part 1
Part 2
Part 3
Part 4
Part 5
Part 6
Part 7

—————— 21.2 ——————

Animals on the Verge of Extinction - Tropical Rainforests

Every species has its own role in the ecosystem. Although hunting is a brutal game, either the **predators** or the **preys** plays a necessary role to maintain the system. However, as human territory expands, the rising number of species are on the **verge** of **extinction**. The extinction rates have been particularly **accelerated** in the last two centuries.

All species rely greatly on their habitats to survive. However, human parties occupy natural territories to satisfy their own demands. For example, the woods in tropical rainforests are removed for human interests in **petroleum** resources, mineral resources; developing **cash-crop plantation** and **subsistence farming**; hunting for ivory or fur from endangered animals as well. The disappearance of the rainforests gradually destroyed the habitat for numerous species. The carnivores on top of the food pyramids suffer first due to the shortage of food resources. Species counting on niche surviving requirements are also particularly **vulnerable** in such circumstances. Habitat destruction broke biotic **integrity** and led to genetic disorders.

As everything in the ecosystem is so closely associated together, the destruction of these habitats affects not just the natural species living there but the entire environment. As rainforests contribute significantly to stabilizing global climate, the increasing deterioration of deforestation can lead to frequent **droughts**, forest fires and greenhouse gas emissions in the globe. Human beings should reflect on our modern development and maintain a healthy ecosystem.

Part
1

Part
2

Part
3

Part
4

Part
5

Part
6

Part
7

中文翻譯

瀕臨絕種的動物－熱帶雨林篇

　　每個物種在生態系統中都有其位置，儘管狩獵是件殘酷的活動，**獵食者**和**獵物**都是維繫系統不可或缺的角色。然而，由於人類擴張領土，越來越多物種**瀕臨絕種**，滅絕的速度在過去兩個世紀內尤其**增快**。

　　所有物種都必須仰賴棲息地以生存，然而，人類團體為了滿足自己的需求而佔領自然棲息地。舉例來說，人類為了奪取**石油**原料、礦物資源，發展**經濟型作物**、**自給農業**，為了象牙或皮草貿易獵取瀕危動物，而砍伐熱帶雨林的樹木。雨林的消失逐漸縮減大量物種的棲息地，而食物鏈金字塔頂端的肉食動物尤其因為食物來源短缺而首當其衝，仰賴特殊生存條件的物種也在這種情況下特別**容易受影響**。棲息地的破壞減少生態**完整性**，並導致物種基因失調。

　　由於整個生態系統是如此息息相關，這些棲息地的破壞不只影響到當地的自然物種，更影響到整體環境。由於雨林在維持全球氣候扮演舉足輕重的功能，不斷增加的森林砍伐也導致全球越來越多的**乾旱**、森林大火和溫室氣體排放量。人類應該反省我們的現代發展，維持一個健全的生態系統。

重點字彙

1. **predator**（*n.*）掠食者；**prey**（*n.*）獵物、犧牲者

   The predatory hides behind the rock, waiting for the prey to get closer.
   掠食者躲在岩石後方，等待獵物靠近。

2. **verge**（*n.*）邊緣；邊界

   He dares his best friend to stand on the verge of the cliff.
   他激他的死黨去站到懸崖邊緣上。

3. **extinct**（*adj.*）滅絕、熄滅；**extinction**（*n.*）滅絕；消滅

   Failed to trace any evidence of living leopard cats, scientists are afraid that they might already be extinct.
   找不到任何石虎活動的證據，科學家恐怕牠們已經滅絕了。

4. **accelerate**（*v.*）加速；增加

   Despite being a frequent traveler, she never gets used to the scary moments when the plane accelerat towards the air.
   儘管很常旅行，她從來沒辦法適應飛機加速飛往空中的可怕時刻。

5. **cashcrop**（*n.*）經濟型作物

He inherited the farm and transformed the field to grow cash crops.

他繼承了這座農場，把田地轉型為改種經濟型作物。

6. **subsistence**（*n.*）自給、生計

The island is too small to grow subsistence crops, so it relies mostly on imported food.

這座島小到無法種植自給作物，主要仰賴進口食物。

7. **ivory**（*n.*）象牙

Celebrities stood up for the campaign calling to end the ivory trade.

名人紛紛替這個計劃挺身而出，呼籲停止象牙貿易。

8. **vulnerable**（*adj.*）脆弱的；容易受傷害

He has been in this vulnerable status since losing his job last year.

自從去年失業之後，他就陷入非常脆弱容易受驚的狀態。

9. **integrity**（*n.*）完整性；健全性

Studies show that family integrity plays a crucial part of a child's mental development.

研究指出家庭健全性對孩子的心理發展扮演重要的角色。

iBT 新托福字彙閱讀應試技巧

Part 1

Part 2

Part 3

Part 4

Part 5

Part 6

Part 7

Question 1: Which of the following is a false description for the concept of food chains?

(A) Animals use digestion system to absorb the food they eat.

(B) Respiration process helps animals to produce the energy they need.

(C) Decomposers help returning all the energy back to the soil.

(D) Most of the food chains do not have more than six levels.

解析 文中提到消費者需行消化作用來吸收他們攝取的食物,因此選項 (A) 是正確的;而呼吸作用讓動物將營養轉換為所需的能量,因此選項 (B) 也正確;大部分的食物鏈不超過六階,選項 (D) 正確,而這是因為每一階之間的攝取過程都會造成能量流失,最後就算分解者能將能量釋放回土壤中,也不可能是循環最初的完整能量,因此答案為 (C)。

Question 2: A petrol company decided to eliminate a large rainforest for the oil collection, which of the following species would be hit the first?

(A) Kapok trees   (B) Bengal tigers

(C) Fungi   (D) Boar

解析 石油公司決定為了採集石油而砍伐一座雨林，由於文中提到，首當其衝的一定是食物鏈頂端的肉食動物。選項 (A) 木棉樹為綠色植物，是生產者；(C) 菌類植物是分解者；(D) 野豬為雜食動物，不完全仰賴肉食食物來源，因此較能適應環境變化，因此答案為 (B) 孟加拉虎。

Part 1

Part 2

Part 3

Part 4

Part 5

Part 6

Part 7

Question 3: What is the process used by Primary Consumers to turn nutrition to energy they need?

(A) Photosynthesis
(B) Digestion
(C) Respiration
(D) Inspiration

解析 根據文章表示 "They absorb the nutrition through digestion then use respiration to produce the energy needed.",一級消費者消化吸收營養,並行呼吸作用產生需要的能量。因此答案為 (C) 呼吸作用,並非選項 (A) 光合作用、(B) 消化,或 (D) 靈感。

Unit **22**

22.1

Literature

Literature is one of the most lasting forms of human civilization. Written words provide the best record of people's thoughts in artistic languages. Sometime the language used in literature can be slightly different from that in **oral** usages. Its two main categories are **fiction** and **nonfiction**.

Nonfictional literature range from **narrative** nonfictions, **biography**, **autobiography**, history to **essays** and other informational text records of actual, real-life subjects. Narrative nonfiction works present facts in story-telling tones. Essays express the authors' personal points of views on specific themes and are mostly used in academic purposes. Both biography and autobiography are used to tell the history of a person's life but the former is narrative, told by someone else while the latter is done by the person himself/herself.

Fictional literature is diverse in content including **poetry**, dramas, fairy tales, mythologies, folklores, fables and novels as well as fantasy, science fiction, horror stories, legends, mysteries,

Unit 22

Part
1

Part
2

Part
3

Part
4

Part
5

Part
6

Part
7

etc. Mythologies are stories that associate historical events or natural phenomena with gods. Folklores are stories passed down by words of mouths. Fables are stories that use supernatural things such as talking animals delivering important morals. Although being written mostly on the basis of imaginary things, fictions always expand readers' minds to see more possibilities.

中文翻譯

文學

文學是人類文明中最雋永的表現之一，書寫文字以優美的語言記錄下來人們的思路。有時文學用語會和**口語**用法有些不同。主要可分為兩個種類：**虛構**和**非虛構**文學。

非虛構文學記錄真實事物的主題，從**敘事性**非虛構文學、**傳記**、**自傳**、歷史，到**論說文**以及其他記錄性的文字作品。非虛構文學以說故事的口吻呈現出真實的事物。論說文表達出作者對於特定主題的個人意見，通常用於學術用途。傳記和自傳都是講述個人生平，但前者為他人所寫，而後者為主角本人所撰。

虛構文學的內容非常多元，包括**詩詞**、戲劇、童話、神話、民俗傳說、寓言故事，以及奇幻小說、科幻小說、恐怖小說、傳奇小說、推理小說等。神話是將歷史事件或自然現象聯想到神的故事。民俗傳說是口耳相傳的故事。寓言故事用超自然事物，如會說話的動物，來講述重要的倫理道德。雖然大多建構在想像的事物上，虛構文學卻總把讀者的思維帶往更多可能性。

 重點字彙

1. **oral**（*adj.*）口語的、口述的

The tribe preserves the culture of oral history.
部落保留著口述歷史的文化。

延伸字彙

● fiction 小說：虛構的；nonfiction 非小說類文學；非虛構的
The independent publisher publishes fictional as well as nonfictional books.
這間獨立出版社同時出版虛構小說和非小說類的書籍。

2. **narrative**（*n.*）敘事文、記敘的；故事

The director is known for telling powerful stories through plain narratives.
這位導演擅長以平白的敘述方式傳達強烈的故事。

3. **essay**（*n.*）論說文

延伸字彙

● thesis / dissertation 論文

① The newspaper invites a politic critic to write an essay on the recent scandal.

報社邀請一位政治評論家替最近的醜聞撰寫一篇論述文。

② She barely left her study during the last stage of polishing her PhD dissertation.

修改博士論文的最後階段期間，她待在書房裡幾乎是足不出戶。

4. **biography**（*n.*）傳記；**autobiography**（*n.*）自傳

① The president hired a ghost writer for his biography.

總統雇了一位幽靈寫手來寫他的傳記。

② The senior ballerina refuses to write autography claiming that she is still expecting a lot in the future.

資深芭蕾舞者拒絕寫自傳，她對未來仍有許多期許。

5. **poem**（*n.*）詩；**poetry**（*n.*）詩（總稱）；**poet**（*n.*）詩人

① The student secretly formed a Dead Poets Society.

學生祕密的組成一個死詩人社團。

② The lovers write dozens of poems with each other.

這對情侶互相寫給對方幾十首詩。

③ The library has a wide collection of Chinese classic poetry.

這座圖書館有非常豐富的中國古典詩集。

Part 1
Part 2
Part 3
Part 4
Part 5
Part 6
Part 7

Literature Adaption in Film Industry

Literature adaptions in other media such as **animations**, stage plays or video games give new faces to the original stories. One of the most commonly modified versions are films. Movies allow the audience to see vivid images of the characters from the books and build the whole picture of stories on the big screen.

However, films also changed the way people digest stories. Since movies give audience instant **audio** and **visual** satisfactions, people lost the patience for long **soliloquies** or conversations. Moreover, people gradually lost the ability to think, make references and create a new based on their own imaginations. This also affects the way writers **compose** their books with shorter length and stuff lots of **stimulating** actions. Since the audience are used to the sudden **repositions** in space and time of the big screen, writer also put fewer words and details among the **transitions** of characters, locations and time periods in the stories.

How many people are there who still bother to study ancient Chinese language and the Tang Dynasty tales when the movie *The Assassin* already did the job for the audience? Since it only takes a few hours to watch *The Lord Of The Rings* movie series, do people still have the patience to read the original books? These are the questions we should reflect on in the ever changing world of entertainment.

Part
1

Part
2

Part
3

Part
4

Part
5

Part
6

Part
7

中文翻譯

改編文學作品的電影

　　文學作品在其他媒介的改編如動畫、舞台劇或電玩遊戲，都給原作全新的面貌，而其中以電影的改編最為突出。電影讓觀眾能夠看到書中的角色以活生生的影像出現，並在大銀幕上看到故事的全貌。

　　然而，電影也改變人們消化故事的方法。由於電影給予觀眾**聽覺**和**視覺的**即時享受，人們失去對冗長**獨白**或對話的耐心。人們甚至逐漸失去思考、聯想、用自己的想像力創造出新版本的能力。這也影響作家**撰書**的方式，用較短的篇幅寫書，塞進大量**刺激的**情節。由於觀眾已經習慣在大銀幕上看到時空的瞬間**變化**，作者也在故事中用較少文字解釋角色、位置和時間的**轉換**。

　　電影《刺客聶隱娘》都已經替觀眾做完功課了，有多少人還願意為了讀唐朝故事而研習文言文？只要花幾個小時就能看完《魔戒》全系列電影，人們還有耐心讀完原著嗎？在瞬息萬變的娛樂世界中，這些是我們應該反省的問題。

重點字彙

1. **animation**（*n.*）卡通、動畫；生氣、活力

The cartoon studio creates cute and lively animations.
這個卡通工作室出品可愛又有活力的動畫作品。

2. **vivid**（*adj.*）鮮明的；生動的、逼真的

She still vividly remembers that family tragedy 20 years ago.
她仍然鮮明地記得二十年前的那場家庭悲劇。

3. **audio**（*adj.*）聽覺的；**visual**（*adj.*）視覺的

① She spends all her savings on music collection and audio system.
她把存款都花在音樂和音響設備上。
② The red dress gives her a very strong visual impact on the meeting.
這件紅洋裝讓她在開會時有非常搶眼的視覺效果。

4. **soliloquy**（*n.*）獨白

The movie starts and ends with the same soliloquy.
這部電影的開頭和結尾都用同一段獨白。

5. **compose**（*v.*）寫作、作詩、作曲；構圖；組成；
   composer（*n.*）作曲家

   ① The sophisticated thesis is very well composed.
   這篇文章編排的非常精密。
   ② She is a very productive composer.
   她是個非常多產的作曲家。

6. **transition**（*n.*）過渡；過渡期

   After this messy transition, we will have a proper office.
   過了這段亂七八糟的過渡期，我們就會有正式的辦公室了。

7. **stimulate**（*v.*）刺激、使興奮；促使作用

   The surprising guest of the conference stimulated the press's
   interests.
   記者會的驚喜來賓引起了媒體的興趣。

8. **reposition**（*n.*）改變位置；放回；（外科）復位術

   The slight reposition on the layout made a huge difference on
   the appearance.
   版面稍微調一下位置整體觀感就差很多。

Part 1
Part 2
Part 3
Part 4
Part 5
Part 6
Part 7

iBT 新托福字彙閱讀應試技巧

Question 1: The first book Tom read was the story of the rabbit and the turtle which tells him never underestimate the weakest competitor. How should the story be classified?

(A) Mythology

(B) Horror

(C) Folklore

(D) Fable

> 解析　龜兔賽跑的故事寓意為不要低估最弱的對手，因此答案為(D) 寓言，以超自然的故事教育道德倫理。選項 (A) 為神話故事，(B) 為恐怖故事，(C) 為民俗故事。

Question 2: Judy received a request to write a book about the life of a successful entrepreneur. What category should the book be in?

(A) Autograpy

(B) Autobiography

(C) Biography

(D) Essay

Part
1

Part
2

Part
3

Part
4

Part
5

Part
6

Part
7

解析 由於撰寫者並非主角本人，因此茱蒂所要寫的書為成功企業家的傳記，答案為 (C) 傳記。選項(A)為親筆簽名，(B) 為由主角自己所寫的自傳，(D) 為論說文。

Question 3: Les Misérables is a French novel written by Victor Hugo and have been adapted to various forms. Which of the following is not its adaption?

(A) Les Misérables(musical)

(B) Les Misérables(movie)

(C) Les Misérables(novel, English version)

(D) Les Misérables(cartoon)

解析 悲慘世界為雨果的著作，原文為法文，被改編為選項 (A) 音樂劇、選項 (B) 電影、選項 (D) 卡通，但翻譯書通常都會盡量忠於原文，並不會因為翻成另一種語言而改編內容，因此答案為 (C) 英文版本。

Unit **23**

23.1 **Track 45**

Political Systems in the World

Politics is one of the most complex and fascinating subjects in human civilization. Five most common political systems are **Republic**, **Democracy**, **Monarchy**, **Communism** and **Dictatorship**.

Republic states are countries ruled by governments that are not based on **heritage** or authoritarian governance. Most of the Republic states are **democratic** countries. Such countries can be either crowned, single-party, democratic, capitalist, **federal**, **parliamentary** system or mixed.

Democracy is the system that allows people to participate in the states' decision making process through voting. Direct Democracy gives every citizen equal rights to participate directly in the governing process while in Representative Democracy, citizens elect representatives to make the law.

Monarchy is the head of a state who **inherits** the crown by carrying the royal blood line. The person ought to stay in the leading position until the **abdication** of the power or until the death. Absolute Monarchies have the ultimate say over every matter in the states. Constitutional Monarchies' power is limited by the states' **constitutions**. In Constitutional Monarchy, a Monarchy's rule is often assisted by **cabinet** members led by the Prime Minister.

Communism countries are often dominated by authoritarian governments. The states often practice planned economy in which the authorities have full control over the distribution of the resources. In some cases, citizens are required to take assigned jobs to support the states' development.

A **Dictator** is an individual who make decisions for the country with no restriction from constitutions or parliaments and often possesses great military power to **enforce** state policies. Elections under such system usually show the evidence of false democracy as the dictator is the only candidate.

中文翻譯

世界上的政治體系

政治是人類文明中最複雜也最迷人的主題之一。五大最常見的政治體系為**共和制**、**民主制**、**君主制**、**共產制**和**獨裁制**。

　　共和制國家由非**世襲**也非專制的政府領導，大部分的共和體都是**民主**國家，可能是君主共和、單一政黨制、民主、資本主義、**聯邦**制、**議會**制或綜合制度。

　　民主是讓人們透過投票參與國家決策程序的系統。直接民主賦予每一個公民直接參與管理程序的平等權利，而在代議民主制下，公民選出代議士制定法律。

　　君主是因皇家血統而繼承皇位的國家領導人，除非**退位**讓出大權，否則此人應居領導位置直至死亡。絕對君主制擁有國家所有事物的終極大權，而君主立憲制底下，君主的權力則被國家**憲法**限制。君主的統治，通常有以首相為主的**內閣**成員協助。

　　共產國家通常都是由極權專制政府統治，為了執行計畫經濟，當局有絕對權力控制資源分配，某些情況下，人民還會被要求接下指定工作以支援國家發展。

　　獨裁者能單獨在沒有憲法或國會的限制下為國家做決策，並且通常握有軍事大權以**強制施行**政策。在這種制度下，選舉通常都是偽民主，因為唯一的候選人就是獨裁者本人。

重點字彙

1. **Republic**（*n.*）共和國

   People overthrew the royal family and established the Republic.

   人們推翻皇室家族，建立共和國。

2. **federal**（*adj.*）聯邦制、聯邦政府

   Same sex marriage is finally approved by the Federal Government of the United States in 2015.

   同性婚姻終於在 2015 年在美國被聯邦政府通過。

3. **democracy**（*n.*）民主；民主國家；
   democratic（*adj.*）民主的

   The democracy did not come easily in this former authoritarian country.

   這個過去曾為極權國家的民主得來極其不易。

4. **monarchy**（*n.*）君主政治；君主國

   The monarchy has nothing more than the title in governing the state.

   君主在治理國家上，除了頭銜外沒什麼實權。

5. **dictator**（*n.*）獨裁者；**dictatorship**（*n.*）獨裁政權

The history textbook covers the fact that the former president was a dictator.

歷史課本隱瞞前總統曾是獨裁者的事實。

6. **parliament**（*n.*）議會、國會

The student activists occupied the parliament and started a major protest.

學生社運者佔領國會，開始一場大型抗議。

7. **cabinet**（*n.*）櫥櫃；密室；內閣

① The head of state ordered a cabinet meeting in response to the latest terrorist attack.

國家領導人因應最新恐怖攻擊，召開內閣會議。

② He stores the best of his wine collections in the small cabinet.

他把最珍藏的酒儲藏在一個小櫥櫃裡。

8. **heritage**（*n.*）遺產；世襲；**inherit**（*v.*）繼承

① The farm is a heritage he inherited from his grandfather.

這座農場是他繼承自祖父的遺產。

② The bookstore at the corner is a cultural heritage of the small town.

轉角的書店是小鎮的文化遺產。

9. **abdicate**（*v.*）放棄權利、退位

The violent king refused to abdicate and was eventually sentenced to death after the people's revolution.

暴虐的國王拒絕退位，最終在人民革命後被判死刑。

10. **constitution**（*n.*）憲法

Scholars call for constitutional modification to fit in the modern society's needs.

學者呼籲修憲以符合今日社會的需求。

11. **communism**（*n.*）共產主義；共產主義社會

The family has a huge generation gap between the parents from the Communism times and the children born after Republic.

在共產時代的父母和共和國之後出生的孩子之間，家裡有著巨大的代溝。

12. **enforce**（*v.*）執行；強制

The army has been deployed to the capital to enforce the anti-terror actions.

軍隊派駐到首都以執行反恐行動。

Part 1
Part 2
Part 3
Part 4
Part 5
Part 6
Part 7

23.2

Law

Law is a system of rules made by **legislature** composed by **legislators** to regulate the public's norms and behaviors. Law can be divided into two main areas: civil law and criminal law. In most of the countries, constitutions provide fundamental principles to run the states or the governmental institutions.

Criminal law regulates social conduct and delimit the punishments of acts that might be threatening, harmful or endangering social order. Punishments vary from countries. Jail sentences and fines are commonly used worldwide. Other comparatively extreme means such as **whipping**, **caning** and even **stoning** tend to be prohibited in most of the developed countries.

Civil law deals with **lawsuits** among rights and obligations of individuals and corporations. Civil law includes contract law, property law, trust law, tort law, etc. The term "Civil law" can also be referred to as the legal system used in European Continent with codified core principles. Continental law system contrasts with Common law derived from England and its Commonwealth states. In Common law system, court decisions are made based on precedential authority from judge-made decisional law.

Above all the other regulations, a constitution is a set of fundamental principles or established **precedents** for a country. It can be a set of legal documents or one single comprehensive document which is called a **codified** constitution. A constitution aims to regulate the relationship between institutions in the state including but not limited to the **executive, legislature** and the **judiciary**.

中文翻譯

法律

　　法律是由**立法者**組成的**立法機構**所制定之規範系統，藉以管理行為。法律可以分為兩大範疇：民法和刑法。在大多數國家中，憲法提供國家和政府機關根本性的準則。

　　刑法規範社會行為，並陳述具威脅性、傷害性或危害社會秩序會遭到的刑罰。每個國家都有不同刑罰，監禁和罰款在全球都相當通用，其他較極端的手段如**鞭刑**、**藤條責罰**甚至**石刑**，大多數先進國家則傾向禁止。

　　民法處理個人、法人團體的權利義務以及**訴訟**。民法包含契約法、財產法、信託法、侵權法等等。Civil law 一詞也指源自歐陸的法系，由成文核心原則組成。與大陸法系對應的是從英格蘭及其屬地的普通法系。在普通法系下，法庭依據過去法官的判決前例作出決策。

在所有其他規範之上，憲法是由一系列基礎原則或國家的**既定前例**組成的**規範**。這可以是一組法律文件組成，或是單一綜合文件，稱為成文憲法。憲法旨在規範國家機關，包括但不限於**行政**、**立法**和**司法機關**之間的關係。

 重點字彙

1. **legislator**（*n.*）立法者、立法委員；
   legislature（*n.*）立法機關

   ① The legislators from the ruling part voted to object the new rule.

   執政黨的立法委員投票反對新法。

   ② The legislature is often manipulated by lobbyists.

   立法機關時常受到說客的操縱。

2. **whip**（*v.*）鞭撻；（蛋、奶油）攪打；煽動；
   whipping（*n.*）鞭刑

   ① It's better to make the whipped cream two hours in advance to cool completely in the fridge.

   最好在兩個小時前就打發鮮奶油，才能在冰箱裡擺涼。

   ② Though rich and modernized, the state still practice physical punishments including whipping.

   雖然富有又現代化，此國仍施行體罰，包括鞭刑。

3. **cane**（*n.*）藤條；用藤條打；**caning**（*n.*）鞭刑（用藤條）

Caning is still a practicing corporal punishment used in Singapore.
鞭刑是在新加坡依然施行的體罰。

4. **stoning**（*n.*）石刑

Stoning is a barbarian practice that should be forbid completely in 21th century world.
石刑這麼野蠻的行為應該在 21 世紀的世界被徹底禁止。

5. **lawsuit**（*n.*）訴訟

Dozens of families filed a lawsuit together against the baby formula company.
數十個家庭共同對嬰兒奶粉公司提出訴訟。

6. **precedent**（*n.*）先例；（法律）判例

It takes longer for the judge to make a decision since there was no precedent of such cases in the past.
由於過去並沒有類似先例，法官花了比平常更久的時間才做出裁決。

7. **codify**（*n.*）編成法典、法規

The Constitution was codified by the founders of the state.
憲法是由建國者所編成的。

iBT 新托福字彙閱讀應試技巧

Question 1: Katrina's country does not have a king or queen but the president holds supreme power over the state. She and her family run a shoe factory. The state ordered the family to provide shoes for the military usage. What is the most likely form of the country?

(A) Absolute monarchy
(B) Capitalist republic
(C) Democratic federal
(D) Dictator communism

解析　此國沒有國王或女王，因此不會是選項 (A) 絕對君主。國家有權向私人產業指定生產用品，因此不可能是 (B) 資本主義共和國。總統握有至高無上的權力，因此選項 (C) 民主聯邦也不符合。答案為 (D) 獨裁共產制。

Question 2: What does "precedential authority" mean in the statement "Court decisions are made based on precedential authority from judge-made decisional law"?

(A) Legal principles set by the authorities.

(B) Judge decisions made in the past.

(C) The political authority held by the president.

(D) The legal power for judges to make decision.

解析 判決先例指的是過去的法庭判決，因此答案為 (B) 法官在過去所裁定的判決。選項 (A) 為官方制定的法定原則，(C) 為總統握有的政治職權，(D) 為法官裁判的法律職權。

Unit 24

24.1

 Track 47

Feminism

Feminism is the ideology of having equal rights among all genders. After centuries of fighting and campaigning, women finally have fairer conditions now than before. However, there is still a long way to go until all genders can reach the **ultimate** equality.

Women are often oppressed by men in this mainly **patriarchy** world. Children's names follow father-side surnames. While boys are encouraged to develop a wide range of interests, girls have little access to education. In some societies, women are not allowed to have their own possessions and even are considered properties of their male **custodians**.

Western feminism campaigns started in the 19th century when activists in the UK and in the US requested equal contract, marriage, parenting and property rights for women. By the end of the 19th century, feminists focused on political, sexual, **reproductive** and economic rights.

Currently, there are still numerous countries in which women still have been restricted or no rights to vote or receive education. Even in the relatively gender-equalized states, women still need to struggle for equal wage and fight against any sort of sexual violence including sexual materialization, **harassment** and **abuse**. Women ought to have control over their own bodies to enjoy sex freely and have rights for birth control and **abortion**. In short, women deserve rights and opportunities just the same as men do.

中文翻譯

女性主義

女性主義是倡導所有性別皆享平等權益的意識形態。在數世紀的抗爭和行動後，現在的女人總算可以有比起以前公平一些的待遇。然而，要達到**終極**平等，還有很長一段路要走。

女人在這個以**父系制度**為主的世界裡，時常被男人壓制。孩子要從父姓；男生被鼓勵發展各式各樣的興趣，但女生卻不太有機會受教育。在某些社會中，女人不但不能擁有自己的財物，反而被視為男性監護人的財產。

西方女性主義活動起於十九世紀，英國和美國的行動運動家替女性要求平等的契約權、婚姻權、子女監護權和財產權。到了十九世紀末，女性主義者專注於政治、性慾、**生殖**和經濟權力。

目前為止，仍有許多國家對女性的投票和教育權處處受限，甚至完全禁止。就算是在相對來說性別比較平等的國家，女性仍須奮力爭取薪資平等，以及對抗任何型態的性別暴力包括性別**物化**、**性騷擾**和**性侵害**。女性理當有權控制自己的身體，自由的享受性愛，並有避孕和**墮胎**等權利。簡而言之，女性理該享有和男性一樣的權利和機會。

重點字彙

1. **ultimate**（*adj.*）最終的、極限的；根本的

   Facing the company's financial crisis, the CEO's ultimate decision was to shut down the factory and moved the manufacture line abroad.面對公司的財務危機，執行長最終決定關閉工廠，把生產線移到國外。

2. **patriarchy**（*n.*）父權制；宗族制度；
   matriarchy（*n.*）母權制；母系社會

   ① Children following father-side surname is a typical characteristic of patriarchy societies.
   孩子從父姓是父系社會的典型特徵。
   ② This mountain tribe is a rare matriarchy ruled by a female chief. 這個山上的部落是個罕見的母系社會，由女性酋長統治。

3. **custodian**（*n.*）監護人

   The teacher requires students to write down their custodians' contact details. 老師要求學生寫下監護人的聯絡資料。

4. **verbal**（*adj.*）言詞的、口語的

   ① The poem demonstrates an excellent example of describing non-verbal sounds with words.

這首詩是用文字形容非言語的聲音的絕佳典範。

② Though incredibly intelligent, he always struggles to express himself with the poor verbal communication skills. 儘管聰明的不得了，他彆扭的口語表達能力卻總是教他難以表達自我。

5. **harass**（*v.*）騷擾；使煩擾

The foreign soldiers are accused of harassing local children near their military camp.
那些外國士兵被控在營區附近騷擾當地兒童。

6. **abuse**（*v.*）濫用；虐待

① The area is shadowed by the prevalent drug abuse.
那個地區壟罩在藥物濫用的陰影底下。

② The comedian grew up in a child-abuse family but found his way of living healthy and positively. 那個喜劇演員出身自虐待兒童的家庭，但自己找到健康又樂觀的人生。

7. **reproduce**（*v.*）繁殖、生殖；複製、重現；
reproductive（*adj.*）生殖的

① The street artist reproduced Mona Lisa with sand.
街頭藝術家用沙畫重現蒙娜麗莎。

② The scientists were shocked by the single cell reproducing itself into massive amount.
科學家被單一細胞自我大量繁殖給震懾到了。

—————— 24.2 ——————

Sexism and Racism behind *The Suffragettes* Movie

While it became a popular debate to support female rights around the world, feminism seems to be white women's thing in the media. White feminism is considered feminism **discourses** that ignore women of color, women with disabilities, and transsexual women. Women with colors also stand up to fight for equal rights but haven't received as much attention from the media. Even so, there are still brave women standing up to make their voices heard. For example, Pakistani activist Malala Yousafzai won the Nobel Peace Prize in 2014 for fighting for girls' education rights. Iranian women post photos on social media revealing their hair to protest that the forced wearing of a **hijab**. While such cases are encouraging, the inequality still exists as the UN **ambassador**, Emma Watson, once admitted that her privilege for being White and thus she hoped to help other women to have the same opportunities as she does.

The movie *The Suffragettes* released in October, 2015 received mass attention for the story about women fighting for the right to vote in Britain. The film is praised for celebrating the history

Part 1
Part 2
Part 3
Part 4
Part 5
Part 6
Part 7

of empowering women. But the film is also criticized for casting only White actresses. The majority of Suffragettes were white women at that time but the non-White members should not be **dismissed** in the society. In fact, groups of Asian women and Black women used to make contributions in the UK movements. The film received outraged comments about the fashionable photos with the leading actresses wearing white t-shirt bearing **slogan** "I'd rather be a **rebel** than a slave". Quoted from female activist Emmeline Pankhurst's speech in 1913, the line voiced by White women sounds rather **ironic** to Black audience today.

中文翻譯

電影《女權之聲：無懼年代》背後的性別主義與種族歧視

　　當支持女性權益在全球討論得沸沸揚揚之際，女性主義在媒體上似乎是件白人女性的事情。種種忽略有色人種女性、殘疾女性和跨性別女性的論述被視為白人女性主義。有色人種女性也有站出來爭取平等權益，但卻沒有在媒體上獲得同樣的注意。儘管如此，仍有勇敢的女性站出來表達自己的想法。舉例來說，巴基斯坦運動家馬拉拉因為爭取女孩受教權，獲得 2014 年的諾貝爾和平獎肯定。伊朗女性也在社群網站分享露出頭髮的照片，抗議強迫穿戴**穆斯林頭巾**的規定。但，雖然這些例子令人振奮，不平等依然存在，聯合國**大使**艾瑪華特森都承認身為白人而享的特權，因此她希望幫助其他女性得到和她一樣的機會。

　　2015 年十月發行的電影《女權之聲：無懼年代》，因為重現女性在英國爭取投票權的故事而備受矚目。這部電影因為頌揚解放自主權的女性歷史而受肯定，但也因為演員清一色是白人而遭到批評。當時婦女選舉權運動團體的成員，的確大多數為白種婦女，但有色人種不應該**被淡忘**在歷史洪流中。事實上，在當時的英國運動中，的確有很多亞洲婦女團體和黑人婦女團體貢獻良多。這部電影更因一張充滿時尚感的照片而收到許多盛怒的回應，照片中擔任主角的女演員個個身穿標語「我寧可當反抗者，也不要當奴隸」的白色上衣。這句話節錄自女權運動者艾蜜莉・潘克斯特於 1913 的演講，在今日的黑人觀眾看來**格外諷刺**。

 重點字彙

1. **suffrage**（*n.*）投票權

   The government decided to open youth suffrage for people over 17 to vote in this particular referendum.
   政府決定開放青年投票權，滿十七歲就能參與這次公投。

2. **discourse**（*n.*）論述；論文

   The new version of history textbook triggered a massive discourse on social media.
   新版歷史課本引發社群網站上熱烈的論戰。

3. **hijab**（*n.*）穆斯林婦女所戴頭巾

The women are busy helping each other to decorate hijabs with glamorous jewelries for the wedding.

女孩子為了婚禮，忙著幫彼此在頭巾上妝點華麗的珠寶。

4. **ambassador**（*n.*）大使；代表

She was elected to be the international student ambassador and would be responsible for organizing social events.

她獲選為國際學生代表，將負責籌辦聯誼活動。

5. **slogan**（*n.*）口號、標語

The copywriter is famous for creating catching slogans.

這個廣告文案編寫人出了名的會寫響亮的標語。

6. **rebel**（*n.*）反抗者；**rebellion**（*n.*）造反、叛亂；反抗

① People suffer from the conflict between government and the rebel.

人民夾在政府和反抗軍的衝突中，苦不堪言。

② The teacher told the parents to be more relaxed to the teenage rebellion of their daughter.

老師叫家長對待女兒的青春叛逆期行為放輕鬆一點。

Part 1

Part 2

Part 3

Part 4

Part 5

Part 6

Part 7

延伸字彙

同義字 ▶ unruly, wayward, willful

Tom can't bear his wayward and difficult brother.

湯姆無法忍受他任性又難相處的弟弟。

反義字 ▶ amenable, compliant, conformable, docile, obedient
　　　　　submissive

He's an amenable person.

他為人和善。

7. **dismiss**（*v.*）打發、不多想；解散；開除

① The director found the long-dismissed history deserved to be shown on the big screen.

導演認為那段被長期忽略的歷史值得搬上大銀幕。

② The teacher dismissed the class after announcing details of the end-of-term assignment.

老師在公布期末作業的細節後，讓大家下課。

8. **irony**（*n.*）反諷、諷刺；**ironic**（*adj.*）諷刺的

① The crowd was upset of the obvious irony in his tone.

眾人對他語氣中明顯的反諷感到相當不悅。

② The actor who played the faithful husband ironically got divorced for having an affair with a top model.

扮演那個專情丈夫的演員，很諷刺的因為和名模外遇而離婚。

iBT 新托福字彙閱讀應試技巧

Question 1: What does "patriarchy world" mean in the article?

(A) A world with levels of hierarchy.

(B) A world that rule by male political leaders.

(C) A world formed by close family structure.

(D) A world in which the father or eldest male is head of the family and descent is reckoned through the male line.

> **解析** 雖然"patriarchy world"廣義有宗族制度的意思，但在本文中是指父系社會，因此答案非選項 (A) 的階級制度社會，非選項 (B) 的男性領袖統治世界，也非選項 (B) 的緊密家庭結構社會，答案為 (D) 由父親或年長男性作為一家之主，並認定男性後裔傳承嫡系的社會。

Part 1

Part 2

Part 3

Part 4

Part 5

Part 6

Part 7

Question 2: What does the article suggest "ultimate equality" to be?

(A) All women should have the right to vote.

(B) All women should have access to education.

(C) All women should have the right to possess their own properties.

(D) All women should have all the rights that men own.

解析 文中第一段提到離「終極平等」還有很長一段路要走，而末段列舉出現今社會仍在追求的女性權益，因此，(A) 投票權，(B) 受教權，(C) 財產權，以上皆為平等權益包含的範疇，但真正的平等為文末最後結尾，也就是答案 (D) 男性擁有的權力，女性都應該享受。

Question 3: Which of the following did not receive positive feedback from the public?

(A) Malala Yousafzai's girls' education movement.

(B) Emma Watson admitting being privileged as a White woman.

(C) The Suffragettes calling for female rebellions in their promotional photo shoot.

(D) Iranian women revealing their hair on social media.

解析　同樣都是替女性發聲，但得到不同的輿論反應，選項 (A) 的馬拉拉女孩受教權運動，選項 (B) 的艾瑪華特森承認白人特權身分，選項 (D) 的伊朗婦女在社群網站露出秀髮，以上三件都備受肯定。但選項 (D) 的電影宣傳照中，演員所穿的上衣標語雖是鼓勵女性起身反抗，卻也碰觸到黑人族群的敏感議題，因此答案為 (D)，宣傳照並沒有得到正面迴響。

Unit **25**

25.1 ———————— **Track 49**

Sustainable Energy

Energy is required in everything in our daily life. Some energy sources are exhaustible such as fossil fuel. Fossil fuel includes coal, petroleum and natural gas. They are mostly formed by **anaerobic decomposition** of buried dead organisms that contain high percentage of carbon. Although fossil fuel is continually being formed via natural processes, it is still considered non-sustainable since it takes millions of years and it is way too slow for human consumption.

Nowadays, with the ongoing process of technology evolution, people also need to develop **sustainable** energy to support the planet in the long-term vision. Solar technology use **photovoltaic(PV)** panels to **convert** sunlight into electricity. Wind farms use wind **turbines** to produce electric power. The land can also be utilized for agricultural or other purposes in the space between each turbine. **Geothermal** energy is the **thermal** energy created and stored within the Earth. Gaining the energy requires drilling into the ground and carrying the energy by heat-transfer fluid. **Hydropower** is derived from falling water or fast running water. Human societies have been using water power since ancient time with water wheels and **watermills**. Modern **dams** are used to drive water to run turbines and **generators**.

These sustainable energy sources last longer than non-sustainable ones. They also produce less emissions and lower the chance for the worsening of global warming. Considering human societies' long-term well-beings, this is the area worth investing in.

中文翻譯

永續能源

我們的日常生活中無處不需要能源，有些能源是會耗盡的，如化石燃料。化石燃料包括煤礦、石油和天然氣。它們大多為死去的有機體埋在地底**無氧分解的產物**，蘊含高比例的碳。雖然化石燃料持徐不斷在自然產生，但需耗時百萬年才能形成，跟人類的消耗速度比起來實在太慢了，因此不被視為永續發展的能源。

現在，科技研發的同時，人們也需要發展**永續**能源，以在長遠上支撐地球發展。太陽能科技用**太陽光電 (PV)**板將陽光**轉換**成電力。風力發電廠用**風車渦輪**產生電力，而風車之間的土地也可用作農業或其他用途。**地熱**能源在地球深處產生，並儲存在地底，要取得必須鑽入地底，從導熱的液體取得能量。**水力發電**是從瀑布或湍急水流轉換能量發電的。人類社會從古代就會用水車和**水輪**研磨工廠利用水力能源，現代**水壩**更用水驅動渦輪和**發電機**。

這些永續性的能源比非永續性的還要長久，而且排放較少，甚至零溫室效應氣體。考量人類的長久福祉，這是值得投資的領域。

重點字彙

1. **anaerobe**（*n.*）厭氧性生物；**anaerobic**（*adj.*）厭氧的

   Scientists discovered a new type of anaerobic bacteria deep inside the ocean. 科學家在海底找到一種新的厭氧細菌。

2. **decomposition**（*n.*）分解；腐爛

   Anthropologists evaluate the tomb's era by analyzing the state of decomposition of the body.

   人類學家分析遺體分解的狀態，藉以評估陵墓的時代。

3. **sustain**（*v.*）支撐、維持；
   sustainable（*adj.*）支撐的住的；永續發展的

   ① The single mother has to take two jobs to sustain her family.
   那個單親媽媽必須做兩份工作才能維持家計。
   ② They designed the farm into a self-sustainable ecosystem.
   他們把農場設計成能夠自給自足永續發展的生態圈。

4. **convert**（*v.*）轉換；皈依

   ① The online currency converter updates foreign exchange rates on a daily basis. 這個線上貨幣轉換器每天都會更新外幣匯率。
   ② He was born a Christian but decided to convert to Islamic belief when 20.

他一出生就是基督徒，但二十歲時決定改信伊斯蘭教。

5. **photovoltaic**（*n.*）太陽光電

The library is known for being a green building with photovoltaic roofing. 這座圖書館是知名的綠建築，配有太陽光電屋頂。

6. **hydropower**（*n.*）水力發電

The government should invest more on hydropower infrastructure such as dams and cut down the reliance on carbon-based energy sources.
政府應該在水壩等水力設施上投資更多，以減少對碳能源的依賴。

7. **turbine**（*n.*）渦輪、葉輪

The cotton mill was built by a river and uses the water power to drive the turbines. 這座棉花場建在河畔，用水力驅動渦輪。

8. **geothermal**（*adj.*）地熱的；
thermal（*adj.*）熱能的、保暖的

Iceland is a pioneer in geothermal energy development. Geothermal energy provides 70% of its energy needs.
冰島領先地熱能源發展，地熱能源佔了全國需求的七成。

25.2

Nuclear Power Plant Theme Park

Nuclear power is relatively efficient than thermal power using nuclear **fission** reactors to general electricity. Nuclear power also has less emissions that induce the global warming. However, the disposal of nuclear waste is a tricky matter. People concern about the hazardous **radioactivity** released from extractions of **uranium** and transuranic **actinides**. Currently these wastes are stored at individual reactor sites situated around the world. Some experts suggest building centralized underground **repository**. The other main controversy about this energy source is the risk of devastating nuclear accidents such as the Chernobyl disaster in 1986.

Rising number of countries nowadays pledge to phase out nuclear power such as Germany. In Germany, nuclear power used to provide 22% of national electricity supply until the Japan's Fukushima nuclear disaster shocked the world in 2011. Germany authority announced that all nuclear power plants would be closed by 2022. So far, 8 of the 17 operating reactors were permanently shut down in Germany, including one near Dusseldorf. Instead of having the plant abandoned, people had it transformed into a theme park with 40 attractions including a **merry-go-round**, a **roller coaster**, a **Ferris wheel**. There are also a museum, restaurants, hotels, etc. The cooling tower was turned into a thrilling indoors **swing ride** inside and an outdoors climbing wall on the outside. Since the power plant has never been put in use, the whole complex is free of radiation. The theme park symbolizes a great example of offering people a safer, healthier and happier way of living.

中文翻譯

核能發電主題園區

核能發電利用核**分裂**反應產生電力,比火力發電更有效率,又不會排放溫室效應氣體。然而,如何處置核廢料卻是個棘手的問題。人們擔憂**鈾礦萃取物**和超鈾輻射元素的危險**輻射線**,這些廢料目前儲藏在世界各地的不同核能反應場,有些專家建議興建中央化的地底**貯藏處**。這種能源的另一個爭議就是毀滅性的核災風險,例如 1986 年的車諾比核災。

現在有越來越多國家宣示淘汰核能,例如德國。德國的核能發電過去曾供應全國 22% 的電,直到 2011 年的日本福島核災震驚全球。德國當局宣布將在 2022 年關閉所有的核能發電廠。目前為止,德國的 17 座核電廠中已有八座永久關閉,包括杜塞道夫附近的一座。與其將之廢棄,人們反將其改造為主題公園,內有四十多樣設施包括**旋轉木馬**、**雲霄飛車**、**摩天輪**,還有博物館、餐廳和旅館等。冷卻塔內部變成刺激的**旋轉飛椅**,

外面是攀岩牆。由於這座發電廠從未啟用，整體設施完全零輻射線。這座主題公園代表了一個新典範，提供人們更安全、更健康而且更快樂的生活方式。

 重點字彙

1. **fission**（*n.*）分裂；分裂生殖法；核分裂；
   uranium（*n.*）鈾；**actinide**（*n.*）輻射線元素

   Uranium fission can provide efficient energy power but also create actinides.

   鈾分裂可以有效提供能量，但也產生輻射線元素。

2. **hazardous**（*adj.*）有害的、危險的

   Though highly paid, he still decided to quit since the job was hazardous to his health.

   雖然薪水很高，但他還是決定辭職了，那份工作太過危害健康了。

3. **radioactive**（*adj.*）放射性的；
   radioactivity（*n./v*）放射性、輻射線

   Local residents protest against the storage of radioactive waste on the island.

   當地居民抗議反對把放射性廢料儲存在島上。

4. **repository**（*n.*）容器、貯藏處

The museum owns a large repository storing precious historical manuscripts.

博物館有一個大型倉儲，存有許多珍貴的歷史手稿。

5. **Merry-go-round**（*n.*）旋轉木馬

Taking a ride on Merry-go-round was the dream when she was a little girl.

搭乘旋轉木馬是她小時候的夢想。

6. **roller coaster**（*n.*）雲霄飛車

Children under 10 are not allowed on the roller coaster.

十歲以下的兒童不能上雲霄飛車。

Part 1

Part 2

Part 3

Part 4

Part 5

Part 6

Part 7

iBT 新托福字彙閱讀應試技巧

Question 1: Which of the following description does not match the right equipment?

(A) Solar energy and panels

(B) Fossil fuel and reactors

(C) Wind energy and turbines

(D) Water power and turbines

解析 不同能源需不同設備，選項 (A) 太陽能以光板轉換能源，選項 (C) 風力發電利用扇輪，選項 (D) 水力發電以渦輪，但化石燃料是燃燒以轉換能源，核能發電才需反應爐，因此答案為 (D) 化石燃料和反應爐。

Part
1

Part
2

Part
3

Part
4

Part
5

Part
6

Part
7

Question 2: Which of the following does not describe nuclear power?

(A) Nuclear energy is more efficient than coal energy sources.

(B) Nuclear power is opposed for making air pollution.

(C) Nuclear waste is hard to process.

(D) Nuclear plants concern people for their security.

解析 關於核能的描述,選項 (A) 核能比煤礦能源有效率,選項 (C) 核廢料很難處哩,選項 (D) 人們擔憂核能發電廠的安全性,以上皆為正確,但是核能發電並不會造成廢氣,因此答案為 (B) 核能發電並不會造成空氣汙染。

Unit 26

—————————— 26.1 —————————— Track 51

Arts and Politics

Art is powerful. Artists can use paintings, **sculptures** and even their own bodies to express themselves. Art works can reflect social-political **controversies**. Sometime art works can even be used as a force to lead social changes. Like activists and dissidents, artists could also be practicing their works under risks of being threatened by the authorities.

In the 1930s, German artists faced severe oppression from the Hitler's **Nazi** rule. As the authorities find the art works politically **subversive**, they put the **Modernism** and the **Expressionism** artists and art schools as targets of scrutiny. Paintings were burnt, confiscated or sold abroad in auctions. Art schools were closed, including the famous **Bauhaus**. Creating art works was strictly **forbidden**. Many artists were jailed and tortured. Some artists managed to keep **sketches** secretly but they did so under a great risk of losing their normal lives.

Art **Intervention** is using the artworks to interact with the audience, the space and even the public, the environment in attempt to change existing conditions. For instance, occupying a river island and recording the shrinking of its size to raise

awareness of environmental protection. Some artists may use more extreme actions to **provoke** debates such as sabotaging public installations or interacting with people on the streets. The fields they focus on could be anything from **climate changes**, animal rights, anti-war, **gender equality**, **racism**, etc.

Part
1

Part
2

Part
3

Part
4

Part
5

中文翻譯

藝術與政治

　　藝術的力量很強大。藝術家可以用繪畫、**雕塑**等方式，甚至使用他們的身體表達理念。藝術作品可以反映社會、政治**爭議**問題。有時藝術甚至可以成為引領社會變革。就像社運人士或異議人士，藝術家也有可能在當權者的壓迫下，必須冒險創作。

　　在 1930 年代中，德國藝術家遭受希特勒的**納粹**政權嚴重的壓迫。由於政府認為這些藝術作品有政治**破壞**之嫌，他們將矛頭對準**現代主義**以及**表現主義**的畫家和學院。畫作被燒毀，或沒收以拍賣出國。藝術學院被迫關閉，包括鼎鼎有名的**包豪斯學校**。藝術創作被嚴厲**禁止**。許多畫家被關押入牢，甚至嚴刑折磨。有些藝術家想方設法把**草圖**藏起來，但私藏畫作是必須冒很大風險的。

　　藝術**介入**以作品與觀眾、空間甚至大眾、環境的互動，達到改變既定狀態的企圖。例如，佔領河島並記錄面積的縮小，以喚醒對於環境保護的**認知**。有些藝術家會使用較極端的行動以**刺激**論辯，例如**毀壞**公共建設或在街上與民眾互動。他們的藝術可以涉獵各種領域，包括氣候變遷、動物權益、反戰、性別平等、種族歧視，等等。

Part
6

Part
7

重點字彙

1. **sculpture**（*n.*）雕刻品、雕像；**statue**（*n.*）雕像

   The Accademia Gallery, Florence, has a mass collection of sculptures, including Michelangelo's statue of David.

   佛羅倫斯的學院美術館，館藏豐富的雕刻品，包括米開朗基羅的大衛雕像。

2. **controversy**（*n.*）爭議

   The University was criticized for the controversy over accepting the donation from arm dealers.

   大學因為接受軍火商捐助的爭議而備受批評。

3. **Nazi**（*n.*）納粹黨、納粹主義

   Nazi history placed a heavy shadow on Germany's younger generations.

   納粹的歷史在德國的年輕一輩身上是沉重的陰影。

4. **subversive**（*adj.*）破壞性的；破壞份子

   The public is confused of the charge on the activists for being subversive.

   民眾對於社運人士被控為破壞份子感到相當不解。

5. **Bauhaus**（*n.*）包豪斯（德國建築與設計學派）

6. **modernism**（*n.*）現代主義；
   expressionism（*n.*）表現主義

   Expressionism was a modernism movement presenting the world from the subjective perspective to evoke moods or ideas.

   表現主義是一種現代主義的潮流，從主觀角度表現世界，喚醒情緒或想法。

7. **forbid**（*v.*）禁止；**forbidden**（*adj.*）禁止的

   ① She forbids her husband to gamble on football games.
   　她禁止丈夫在足球賽下注賭博。
   ② Smoking is strictly forbidden in this aircraft.
   　這架飛機上嚴厲禁止吸菸。

8. **sketch**（*n.*）速寫、素描；概略、草圖

   The painters made dozens of sketches before starting to paint on the canvas.

   畫家先做了幾十個草圖，才開始在畫布上作畫。

Part
1

Part
2

Part
3

Part
4

Part
5

Part
6

Part
7

9. **intervene**（*v.*）介入、干涉

The president expresses strongly that their domestic issues are not for other countries to intervene.

總統強烈聲明本國事務不應有外國介入。

10. **aware**（*adj.*）認知、知道；
awareness（*n.*）體認、認知、察覺

① Travellers have to be aware of the beauty and the risks of traveling alone before heading towards their journeys.

旅者在踏上旅程前，必須知道一個人旅行的美好以及風險。

② Despite their concerns about the young man's awareness of the complexity of running a business, he made an excellent CEO of the company.

儘管他們擔心這個年輕人不明白經營企業背後有多複雜，他還是成為了非常出色的公司執行長。

11. **provoke**（*v.*）挑釁、激怒、煽動

① The candidate's racism speech provoked numerous criticisms.

候選人的種族歧視言論激怒了大量的批評浪潮。

② The old man blames the young daughter for dressing too provoking.

老人怪年輕女兒穿的太露。

12. **racism**（*n.*）種族歧視

The candidate's racist implicating statement provoked a storm of protest from the colored people.

候選人暗示種族歧視的言論激怒有色人種抗議的怒吼。

13. **climate change**（*n.*）氣候變遷

The severe climate changes led to a series of devastating disasters in the past few years.

劇烈的氣候變遷在過去幾年帶來一系列毀滅性的災難。

14. **global warming**（*n.*）氣候暖化

The shrinking of the North Pole is a warning sign of global warming.

北極面積的縮小是氣候暖化的警號。

15. **gender equality** 性別平等；**transgender** 跨性別；**homosexual** 同性戀的；**heterosexual** 異性戀的

Part
1

Part
2

Part
3

Part
4

Part
5

Part
6

Part
7

26.2

 Track 52

Installation Art

Installation Art is widely used in **Contemporary** Art. The work can be built by anything from chairs, cushions, bed, books to buses or ship, etc. Since the objects can be found simply from everyone's daily life, the scenes often seem relatively **approachable** to the public and hit the audience's hearts even stronger.

For instance, a group of artists put sofa and books on anti-homeless **spikes** to **mock** the Social Cleansing Movement in London. The Movement has been criticized for forcing poor people out of London City by raising the housing prices, cutting the number of council houses and putting stainless steel spikes benches in the parks, doorways and edges around buildings to prevent people to rest on. The artists turned one **hostile** corner full of spikes into a cozy reading space by using simple objects. The installation received a great outcome from people resting on the sofa, reading the books and starting to reflect on the council's **homeless** policy.

One of the most controversial pieces of works was "Fountain" by Marcel Duchamp in 1917. The artist simply **rotated** a urinal, signed it and presented it to the exhibition. "Fountain" made a huge scandal at that time and opened a revolutionary page in the 20th century art. The original work is lost but a **replica** authorized by Duchamp is now in Tate's collection.

Part
1

Part
2

Part
3

Part
4

Part
5

Part
6

Part
7

中文翻譯

裝置藝術

　　裝置藝術相當廣泛被用在**當代**藝術中。作品可以用任何東西做成，小至椅子、抱枕、床、書，大到公車或船等等。因為每個人日常生活中都有這些東西，作品的意境就更容易**被**大眾**接受**，並對觀眾的心靈造成更大的衝擊。

　　舉例來說，有一群藝術家在反制流浪漢的**鉚釘**上放置沙發和書，藉以**嘲弄**倫敦的社會階級淨化運動。這個運動因為逼迫窮人遷出倫敦市而被強烈批評，他們提高房價，大砍社會住宅數量，還在公園椅子，或大樓的門口以及周圍空間，布置許多不鏽鋼鉚釘，以此防止人們在上面休息。藝術家把一個因為尖釘而**充滿敵意**的角落，用簡單的物件，改造成舒適的閱讀空間。這個作品反應甚佳，許多人在沙發上休息，翻閱書籍，並開始反思市政廳的**流浪漢**政策。

　　最具爭議性的作品之一，是Marcel Duchamp在1917年的Fountain。藝術家只是把一個尿斗**反轉**過來，簽名，就交去展覽了。Fountain在當時是相當大的醜聞，也開啟了二十世紀藝術極具革命性的一頁。原始作品已經遺失了，不過Duchamp認可的**複製品**現仍收藏在泰特現代藝術館。

重點字彙

1. **installation art**（*n.*）裝置藝術

   The coffin that can be dissembled into a sofa and a teapot is a piece of installation art representing life and death.

   這個可以拆解為沙發和茶几的棺材，是一件象徵生與死的裝置藝術作品。

2. **contemporary**（*adj.*）當代的

   She started her dancing career as a ballerina but found her passion in contemporary dancing in her late 20s.

   她的舞者生涯從芭蕾舞伶發跡，但在快三十歲時發現真正熱愛的是當代舞。

3. **approach**（*v.*）接近、靠近；聯絡；
   approachable（*adj.*）可接近的、易親近的

   ① The GPS showed that we were approaching the destination but we just couldn't find the restaurant!

   GPS 顯示出我們正接近終點中，但我們就是找不到那間餐廳！

   ② The fans found it disappointing that the singer doesn't seem as approachable as described on the news.

   粉絲很失望的發現，這位歌手並不如新聞上描述的那麼親民。

4. **spike**（*n.*）牆頭釘、大釘、釘鞋；釘牢、重挫

The military base is circled with spiked wall to prevent invasion.

軍事基地周圍有釘滿大釘的圍牆圍住，以防止入侵。

5. **mock**（*v.*）嘲笑、模仿

The stand-up comedian is known for mocking the politicians.

這個脫口秀演員以模仿政治人物為名。

6. **hostile**（*adj.*）充滿敵意的、不友善的

The manager's picky and arrogant attitude makes the office a hostile environment to work in.

經理既挑剔又傲慢的態度，讓整間辦公室充滿不友善的工作環境。

7. **homeless**（*adj.* / *n.*）無家可歸的；無家可歸的人

The charity provides free food for homeless people every weekend in the park.

慈善團體每個周末都在公園提供街友免費餐點。

8. **rotate**（*v.*）旋轉、轉動；輪流

They share the work by rotating cleaning tasks in the flat every week. 他們以每周輪流打掃公寓的方式共同分攤工作。

iBT 新托福字彙閱讀應試技巧

Question 1: Which of the following was least likely to happen to German artists during the Nazi's rule?

(A) Imprisoned

(B) Flee to America

(C) Ordered to make a portrait for Hitler

(D) House arrest

解析　表現主義畫家在納粹統治時期備受壓迫，由於被懷疑有破壞之嫌，藝術家可能被 (A) 監禁、(D) 軟禁，某些藝術家 (B) 潛逃出國，例如到美國。當局禁止藝術家作畫，因此他們不太有可能會被要求替希特勒畫像，因此答案為 (C)。

Question 2: Which of the following schools of artists are the main targets of Nazi's oppression? (Multiple choices)

(A) Modernism

(B) Impressionism

(C) Expressionism

(D) Realism

(E) Surrealism

解析 根據內文表示 "they targeted on the Modernism and the Expressionism artists and art schools",納粹當局壓迫的主要對象為現代主義與表現主義學派的藝術家,因此選 (A) 現代主義和 (C) 表現主義,而非 (B) 印象派、(D) 寫實主義或 (E) 超現實畫派。

Question 3: Why did artists create a reading space on the street of London?

(A) To raise awareness of younger generation's lack of reading

(B) To promote their new book

(C) To protest against chain bookshops

(D) To protest against the Council

解析 藝術家在倫敦街頭創造閱讀空間,主因並非 (A) 鼓勵年輕人看書、(B) 替新書宣傳或 (C) 抗議連鎖書店,而是 (D) 抗議市政府的反街友政策。

Part
1

Part
2

Part
3

Part
4

Part
5

Part
6

Part
7

Unit 27

27.1

 Track 53

Architecture Styles

After thousands years of innovation, architecture means more than a shelter in human civilization. The art of architecture can reflect living conditions, religions and history.

Buildings in warm and humid climate have large opening windows and tall **ceilings** to allow better air circulaiton. Shades, such as roof **eaves** in Chinese temples, extending from the edge of the house help keep the walls from getting wet when raining. In cold places, rooms tend to be smaller to keep the warmth. Many cultures share similar **underfloor** heating traditions such as Korea, Alaska and Iran. **Fireplaces** are even taken as a heart of home where decorations reflect the cultural taste of the household.

Religion is also a key factor influencing architecture styles. Gothic architecture is influenced by Christianity significantly and flourished during the **medieval times**. Gothic cathedrals and abbeys emphasize light and verticality; pointing towers, clustered **columns**, flying **buttress** and stained glass designed with biblical stories to express the belief of Christianity. A mosque is the center of Muslim community around the world. **Mosques** provide places for **worshippers** to worship and also play a key role in Islamic education. Most of the mosques share common features such as elaborate **domes**. In order to accommodate as many worshippers as possible, prayer halls rarely have furniture other than prayer mats. Mosques use Islamic **calligraphy** to write **Quranic verses** and decorate. However, any usage of Allah's image is forbidden as it is considered **blasphemous**.

中文翻譯

建築風格

數千年的發展下來,建築在人類文明上扮演不只是遮蔽物的意義。建築的藝術可以反映生活條件、信仰和歷史。

溫暖潮濕氣候下的建築物,用大而開放的窗戶和挑高**天花板**促進空氣流通,屋子旁邊突出的遮蔽物幫助排雨,如中式廟宇的**屋簷**。在寒冷地區,房間通常較小,藉以保暖。很多文化都有用**地板下**的暖氣系統保暖的傳統,例如韓國、阿拉斯加和伊朗。**火爐**更被視為家的中心,其裝飾則反映出家庭的文化涵養。

宗教也是影響建築風格的重要元素。哥德式建築深受基督教影響,在**中古時代**蓬勃發展。哥德式的大教堂和修道院強調**垂直性**和光線,用尖塔、大量的**圓柱**、飛**拱壁**,以及設計有聖經故事的彩色玻璃,來表達基督教信仰。**清真寺**是世界各地穆斯林社區的中心，提供**禮拜**的場所，也扮演伊斯蘭教育重要的角色。大部分的清真寺都有共同的特色，例如精美壯麗的**圓形屋頂**。為了盡可能容納多一些人來禮拜禱告，禮拜堂除了禱告用的地毯之外，幾乎沒有其他家具。清真寺用伊斯蘭書法裝飾牆面，也藉此寫出**古蘭經經文**。然而，將阿拉形象化是不被允許的，因為這被視為**褻瀆神明**。

 重點字彙

1. **ceiling**（*n.*）天花板

The artist spent five weeks finishing the painting on the ceiling for the cathedral.
藝術家費時五周才完成大教堂天花板的畫作。

2. **eaves**（*n.*）屋簷

The roof eaves of the temple are decorated with dragons and birds from Chinese legends.
廟宇的屋簷以中國傳說中的龍和鳥作裝飾。

3. **fireplace**（*n.*）壁爐

Children always sit around the fireplace waiting for the granny to tell stories.

小孩子總是圍著火爐坐著，等著老奶奶講故事。

4. **gothic**（*adj.*）哥德式

The actor will play a vampire in a Gothic romance movie.

這位演員接下來會在哥德式愛情電影中扮演吸血鬼。

5. **medieval times**（*n.*）中古世紀

Most of the buildings in the old town are left from the medieval times.

古城裡大部分的建築都是中古世紀留下來的。

6. **vertical**（*adj.*）垂直的；縱向的

The group of rock-climbers is planning to challenge the vertical cliff on the western side of the mountain.

那群攀岩愛好者計畫挑戰山西側的垂直懸崖。

Part 1
Part 2
Part 3
Part 4
Part 5
Part 6
Part 7

7. **column**（*n.*）柱子；欄位；專欄；縱隊

① Stay closer to the columns usually can keep you safe in an earthquake.

地震時靠近柱子通常可以保障安全。

② Please fill in the form and sign on this column.

請填好表格，並在此欄簽名。

8. **buttress**（*n.*）拱壁

The church is known for the solid stone massive buttresses with statues of the saints.

教堂有著知名的大型石造拱壁與聖人雕像。

9. **mosque**（*n.*）清真寺、回教寺院

The mosque was attacked by a group of far right people.

清真寺被一群極右派的民眾攻擊。

10. **worship**（*v.*）禮拜儀式、敬神；崇仰

The aboriginal people living here worship the spirits of the mountain.

這裡的原住民崇仰山中聖靈。

11. **dome**（*n.*）圓屋頂；蒼穹

The golden dome of the mosque shines under sunshine.

清真寺的黃金圓頂在陽光下閃閃發光。

12. **calligraphy**（*n.*）書法

The council invites a calligraphy master to write a set of Spring Festival couplets.

市政府邀請一位書法大師寫一對春聯。

13. **Quran**（*n.*）古蘭經

Anyone who has read Quran would know that Islam does not promote violence.

任何讀過古蘭經的人都會知道，伊斯蘭教並不鼓吹暴力。

14. **verse**（*n.*）詩、韻文；經文

She transcribed Buddhism verses for her deceased family.

她為逝去的家人抄錄佛教經文。

15. **blasphemy**（*n.*）褻瀆、不敬；
blasphemous（*adj.*）褻瀆神的

Entering this holy room with weapons is a blasphemy.

帶著武器進入神聖的殿堂是對神不敬。

Part 1

Part 2

Part 3

Part 4

Part 5

Part 6

Part 7

---- 27.2 ----   **Track 54**

Perfect Mixture of Christian and Muslim Culture - Alcázar of Seville

The Real Alcázar of Seville is a royal palace in Seville, Spain. The palace was originally built by Moorish Muslim kings and later the Christian kings added some Western parts and some designs inspired by Jewish influence. The combination of Muslim, Christian and Jewish characteristics made the Palace a cultural melting pot.

Visitors should enter the palace from Lion Gate, the entrance with an **emblem** of a crowned lion holding a cross. The Arab style **courtyard** of the Maidens with a rectangular pool and a fountain standing central and surrounded by sunken trees has a legend of virgin tributes presented by the Christian kingdom to the Moors. **Lavish** reception rooms are decorated with bright **geometric** designs, **interweaving** patterns and delicate **latticework**; each pattern bear its features. Next, you will step into a complete different type of culture starting from a Catholic chapel. The Christian parts of the Palace are decorated with some of the earliest paintings and **tapestries** of maps from the Colonial era.

Leaving the overwhelming Palace, there is the mind-blowing

gardens waiting for you. Fruit trees, **fragrant** flowers and **runnels**, ponds take every soul to wonders. Even till now, the Real Alcázar is still chosen by the royal family as the official residence in Seville. The inspirational designs also attract numerous movies to film in the Palace.

Part 1

Part 2

Part 3

Part 4

Part 5

Part 6

Part 7

中文翻譯

基督教與回教文化的完美結合——阿爾卡薩皇宮

阿爾卡薩皇宮是西班牙塞爾維亞的皇家宮殿。皇宮最早由摩爾人的穆斯林國王所建，之後由基督教國王加入許多西式建築，並有許多受猶太人影響的設計。穆斯林、基督教和猶太結合在一起，造就了皇宮這棟文化大熔爐。

遊客應從獅子門進入皇宮，入口有著一個戴冠持十字架的獅子**圖騰**。阿拉伯風格的少女**中庭**有座長方形的水池，中間為噴泉，四周種下陷的樹木，傳說中，基督教王國曾在此將處女進貢給摩爾人。**奢華的**接待室每一間都以不同的**幾何**造型、**交織**圖樣和精美的**格紋設計**。接下來，你會走進截然不同的文化中，從天主教的禮拜堂開始。皇宮的基督教區域裝飾有許多早期畫作，並有許多從殖民時代流傳下來的壁毯地圖掛在牆上。

離開震撼人心的宮殿之後，引人入勝的花園在外頭等著你。果樹、**香味四溢**的花朵和**流水**、池塘把每個人都帶入美好的奇幻境界。直到如今，阿爾卡薩宮仍是皇室在塞爾維亞的官方居所。靈感無限的設計更是吸引多部電影到此拍攝。

重點字彙

1. **emblem**（*n.*）象徵、標誌；徽章、圖案

   You can see the emblem of lily everywhere in Florence.

   你在佛羅倫斯各處都能看的到百合花的標誌。

2. **courtyard**（*n.*）庭院、天井

   The courtyard is the center of the mansion with a well in the middle.

   這庭院是整棟宅院最重要的地方，中間還有一口井。

3. **fountain**（*n.*）噴泉；泉水

   Every tourist came to the fountain to make the wish of returning to Rome in the future.

   每個觀光客都會到噴泉許願，希望未來可以回到羅馬。

4. **tribute**（*n.*）貢品；貢獻；勒索的財物

   The tea is a tribute from a nearby kingdom.

   這茶是鄰近王國的貢品。

5. **lavish**（*adj.*）奢華的、慷慨的；浪費的

   The old man frowned at his son's lavish apartment.

   老人家一看到兒子奢華的公寓就皺眉頭。

6. **geometry**（*n.*）幾何學；
geometric（*adj.*）幾何學的；幾何圖案的

This interior designer is an expert in simple yet modern geometric designs.

這位裝潢設計師是個擅長簡約摩登幾何設計的專家。

7. **interweave**（*v.*）交織、混雜；
interweaving（*adj.*）交織混雜的

She prefers wearing dresses with interweaving patterns.

她喜歡穿交織圖樣的洋裝。

8. **latticework**（*n.*）格子

The high-end fashion brand released the latest series of latticework hang bags.

高級時尚品牌發表了最新系列的格紋手提包。

9. **chapel**（*n.*）禮拜堂；教堂

She was baptized in the chapel in her neighborhood when she was born.

她出生就在社區的教堂受洗了。

iBT 新托福字彙閱讀應試技巧

Question 1: Which of the following feature does not suit warm and humid climate?

(A) Big windows

(B) Small rooms

(C) Tall ceilings

(D) Roof eaves

解析 溫暖多雨的環境中，建築的要點在於通風和排水，選項 (A) 大窗戶、選項 (C) 挑高天花板，以及選項 (D) 屋簷都有助於空氣流通和排雨，因此答案為選項 (B)，房間小的話適合保暖，較常見於寒冷地區。

Question 2: What do Islamic believers use for their worships?

(A) Chairs

(B) Benches

(C) Cushions

(D) Rugs

解析 伊斯蘭教的禮拜堂裡除了地毯之外，通常沒有任何其他家具，因此信徒做禮拜時不會是用選項 (A) 椅子、選項 (B) 長椅、選項 (C) 軟墊，答案為 (D) 地毯。

Question 3: Which of the following words can fill in the blank of the sentence, "Visitors should enter the palace from Lion Gate, the entrance with a/an _____ of a crowned lion holding a cross."?

(A) Statue

(B) Symbol

(C) Monument

(D) Portrait

解析 本文中此處為 Emblem，意為徽章、圖案。並不是選項 (A) 雕像、也不是選項 (C) 紀念碑，而選項 (D) 通常只限於人物肖像。因此答案為 (B) 象徵、符號。

Part 1

Part 2

Part 3

Part 4

Part 5

Part 6

Part 7

Unit 28

28.1

Definition of Art

What is Art? Should it be decided exclusively by the **elites**? Does one have to study in art schools to be an artist?

Art is in general agreed as something **aesthetic** with meanings. The problem is that beauty itself is very subjective. Say, the beauty standard reflected in Classical Art was pale skin and round belly since they implied wealth. Centuries later, the beauty standard in the modern society now encourages women to be slim and tanned with athletic skin tone. In term of the meanings, art has been affected largely by politics and religions throughout history. For instance, art was once only allowed for one purpose – to praise God. It was until the **Renaissance** Period that artists started to focus on people, which led to the beginning of **Humanism**.

As the world progressed through time, the access to knowledge became no longer exclusive for specific groups of people. Nowadays everyone can run exhibitions to showcase their ideas. Artists no longer are obliged to spending years in art schools. Art works are no longer restricted in paintings and sculptures. It could be any kind of **visual art**, digital art, installation art, **performance art**, **behavior art**, etc. The style could be abstract art, concept art, **cubism** and so on.

中文翻譯

藝術的定義

　　藝術是什麼？它只能交由**菁英人士**所決定嗎？是不是一定得讀過藝術學院才能成為藝術家？

　　普遍來說，藝術是某種**具有美感**而且富有意義的東西。問題是，美，本身就十分主觀。以審美觀來說，古典藝術中反映出美女的標準都是暗示財富的蒼白皮膚和圓滾滾的肚皮。好幾世紀以後，現在社會的審美觀鼓勵女性要有纖瘦的身材，以及曬得像運動員一樣健康的膚色。以意義來說，綜觀歷史，藝術總是受到政治和宗教的影響。舉例來說，藝術一度只被允許有一個目的——讚美主。直到**文藝復興**時期，藝術家才開始把注意力放在人的身上，也就引領了**人文主義**的開啟。

　　隨著時間而進步，取得知識的權利也不再只屬於特定族群。現在任何人都可以辦展覽展現他們的想法，藝術家不再被要求在藝術學校進修多年，作品也不再局限於繪畫或雕塑，可以是任何形式的**視覺藝術**、數位藝術、裝置藝術、**表演藝術**、**行為藝術**等等。風格也可以為抽象藝術、概念藝術、**立體派**等等。

重點字彙

1. **elite**（*n.*）菁英、菁英份子

   Only the most intellectual elites can entre that University.
   只有最聰明的菁英分子能進入那所大學。

2. **aesthetic**（*adj.*）美學、審美觀；美的、美學的、具有審美眼光的

   Figure skating is an aesthetic sport that requires athletics to be sensitive in the movement as well as in the music.
   花式溜冰是項美學運動，運動員必須對動作和音樂都十分敏感。

3. **subject/subjective**（*n./adj.*）主題、題材；主觀的；**object/objective**（*n./adj.*）物體、對象；客觀的

   As every news station has its subjective background, audience should watch and read news from as many types of media as possible to get a more objective idea of the facts.
   由於每間新聞台都有其主觀背景，觀眾應該從越多種不同媒體來源觀看以及閱讀，以得到與事實較接近的看法。

4. **renaissance**（*n.*）復興、新生；文藝復興時期

   Florence was the birth place of the Renaissance Period during the Medici Family's rule.
   佛羅倫斯在梅迪奇家族的統治下孕育出了文藝復興時期。

5. **humanism**（*n.*）人文主義；人道主義、人本主義

The refugee crisis in Europe became a difficult test for humanism. 歐洲的難民危機成為測驗人道主義的難題。

6. **visual art**（*n.*）視覺藝術

The audience was stunned by the 3D effect of this piece of visual art. 觀眾被這幅視覺藝術的立體效果給驚呆了。

7. **performance art**（*n.*）表演藝術

The artist invited the contemporary dance group to compose a piece of performance art.
藝術家邀請當代舞蹈團與他共譜這件表演藝術作品。

8. **behavior art**（*n.*）行為藝術

The artist is recruiting a volunteer to join her new behavior art work by sharing a meal in the art gallery.
藝術家徵求一位志願者加入他在藝術館裡進餐的行為藝術作品。

9. **cubism**（*n.*）立體派

Picasso was a master of Cubism. Some of his paintings were very unrealistic but powerful. 畢卡索是立體派大師，他的作品有些看起來並不切實際，但充滿力量。

28.2

Fauvism

"Un Donatello parmi les fauves", said a critic which means "among the wild animals" in French. Surprisingly, the art benefitted from this unfriendly comment. This **ironic** line gave the style a new name, **Fauvism**.

Fauvism began in the early 20th century. A small group of modern artists in France took some skills from Impressionism and were inspired by Post-Impressionist painters including Vincent van Gogh and Paul Gauguin, creating a stronger style with even **bolder** colors. The group was led by Henri Matisse. The artists shocked the society with wild brush works and **strident** colors. For the first time, color was given an independent role projecting moods and structures in the paintings rather than just playing its descriptive purposes. They simplified and flattened the structure of the paintings and **saturated** colors to make each and every element play its own role. The effect is strong and **unified**.

Fauvism encouraged artists to respond to nature in their paintings. They believed that individual expression tends to be more meaningful when it is compared with academic theories.

Though only existing for a very short period, Fauvism became an important **precursor** to Cubism and Expressionism as well as other modes of abstraction later on.

Part
1

Part
2

Part
3

Part
4

Part
5

Part
6

Part
7

中文翻譯

野獸派

　　一位評論家說：「一群野獸（法文：Un Donatello parmi les fauves）」出乎意料的是，這麼不友善的評價居然幫了藝術一把，這句**諷刺的**話讓此風格因而得名：**野獸派**。

　　野獸派起始於二十世紀初，一小群法國現代藝術家用一些印象畫派的技巧，受到後印象畫派的梵谷、高更等人啟發，將**大膽的**用色推向更極致。這個團體遊馬提斯領導。畫家以大膽的筆觸和**刺眼的**顏色，震撼當時的社會。史無前例的，色彩被賦予獨立的角色，在畫中影射情緒和架構，而不再只是做描述性的功能。他們簡化並扁平化畫的架構，使每種顏色都**極度飽和**，讓每一個元素都有自己的角色，這營造出非常強烈而**一致的**效果。

　　野獸派鼓勵畫家在畫中做出對大自然的回應，他們相信表達每個人的情感比學術理論更有意義。雖然只存在短短一段時間，野獸派仍舊成為影響立體派、表現主義和其他日後出現的抽象畫派的**始祖**。

 重點字彙

1. **ironic**（*adj.*）諷刺的、挖苦的

   The lecturer is notorious for giving students low grads and ironic comments.

   這個講師是惡名昭彰的給分低又會挖苦學生。

2. **fauvism**（*n.*）野獸派

   The Joy of Life was one of Henri Matisse's master pieces displaying the style of Fauvism.

   生命的喜悅是馬蒂斯的代表作之一，畫中展示出野獸派的風格。

3. **bold**　（*adj.*）大膽的；（字體）粗體

   The manager finds his proposal bold but not very practical.

   經理認為他的提案非常大膽但不切實際。

4. **strident**（*adj.*）刺耳的、刺眼的

   The way he cleaned the window made an extremely strident sound.

   他清洗窗戶的方式弄出好刺耳的聲音

5. **saturate**（*v.*）滲透；使飽和

His lecture makes everyone totally saturated with love and passion towards art.

他的演講讓每個人都完全沉浸在藝術的愛與熱情當中。

6. **unify**（*v.*）成為一體；統一、聯合

These smaller opposite parties agreed to unify against the ruling party.

這些較小的反對黨同意聯合一起對抗執政黨。

7. **precursor**（*n.*）先驅、前兆

Coco Chanel was the precursor to take male suit's elements into female clothes.

可可香奈兒是第一位把男性西裝元素帶入女性服飾的先驅。

Part 1

Part 2

Part 3

Part 4

Part 5

Part 6

Part 7

iBT 新托福字彙閱讀應試技巧

Question 1: What do the chubby female figures with pale skin in Classical Art imply?

(A) Fortune

(B) Healthy

(C) Illness

(D) Racism

解析 文中提到古典藝術中的審美觀提到，畫中以女性蒼白的皮膚和圓潤的身材，透露出財富。因此答案為 (A) 財富。

Question 2: Who was the leading artist of Fauvism?

(A) Vincent van Gogh

(B) Henri Matisse

(C) Paul Gauguin

(D) Pablo Picasso

解析 野獸派的代表藝術家為(B) 馬蒂斯。(A) 梵谷和 (C) 高更為後印象派畫家，(D) 畢卡索為立體派的畫家。

Question 3: What would be least likely for a Renaissance artist to do?

(A) Study at an art school

(B) Paint portraits for people

(C) Make a sculpture for the church

(D) Invite people to interact with the art work

解析　文藝復興時代的藝術家大多仍接受正規學院訓練，也會替人繪製畫像，這時人文主義興起，但教會依然有影響力，因此藝術家仍會替教會服務，但邀請人群與作品互動是現代才開始的創作方式，當時並不時興。

Unit 29

29.1

 Track 57

Music

Music is a form of art using sound and silence to create different **melodies**. Music can be soft or loud, light or heavy, cheerful or melancholic, delightful or violent.

Human voices are the most natural form of music. Apart from that, the basic classification for other instruments is wind, strings and **percussion**. The sound of wind instruments comes by **vibrating** the air in the **resonator** through the **mouthpiece**. Stringed instruments produce sound from vibrating strings. Percussion instruments have the oldest history among all instruments, following human voices. Percussion instruments need to be **rubbed**, **scrapped** or **struck** by hands or beaters. Other instruments include keyboard and electronic instruments.

From Classical music including symphonies and operas to folk songs, Jazz, Rock and Roll and different indigenous music around the world, music enthusiasts now have a wide range of music types to appreciate. Other types of music also emerge from digital development such as electronic **dance music** and **heavy metal** music. Like other forms of art, the affection for music is also very subjective. The same song can make some people burst out tears of joy while others judge it as annoying noise. Music serves more than just for pleasure. Music can soothe people's mind, heal emotional traumas and even boost public **morale**.

Part
1

Part
2

Part
3

Part
4

Part
5

Part
6

Part
7

中文翻譯

音樂

　　音樂是一門利用聲音和寧靜組合創造出不同**旋律**的藝術。音樂可以柔和或喧囂、輕柔或沉重、快樂或悲傷、賞心悅目或暴力十足。

　　人類嗓音是最自然的音樂型態，除此之外，其他樂器的基本分類包括管樂、弦樂和**打擊樂**。管樂器需要樂手從**吹嘴**吹氣，**振動共鳴箱**的空氣。弦樂器以振動弦發出聲音。打擊樂器是僅次於人類嗓音，歷史最古老的樂器，需要用手或打擊器或**刮**、或**擦**、或**敲擊**。其他樂器包括鍵盤樂器和電子樂器。

　　從交響樂、歌劇等古典樂，到民歌、爵士樂、搖滾樂，以及世界各地的原住民音樂，現在的音樂愛好者有非常多的音樂選擇可欣賞。其他音樂類型也隨數位發展衍生出來，例如電子**舞曲**和**重金屬**音樂。就像其他類型的藝術，音樂也是非常主觀的，同一首歌可能讓某些人喜極而泣，其他人卻評為惱人的噪音。音樂的功能不只好聽而已，也能緩和心境、療育情感創傷，甚至鼓舞**士氣**。

 重點字彙

1. **melody**（*n.*）旋律、曲調

   Adele's latest single is so popular that everyone can sing the melody.

   艾黛兒的最新單曲紅到每個人都唱得出旋律。

2. **wind**（*n.*）管樂；**strings**（*n.*）弦樂；
   percussion（*n.*）打擊樂器；敲擊、震動

   She is the first female conductor ever hired by this big jazz band leading 30 musicians specialized in wind, strings and percussion instruments.

   她是這個爵士樂團請過的第一個女性指揮，領導三十位集管、弦、打擊樂翹楚的音樂家。

3. **mouthpiece**（*n.*）樂器吹口；電話話筒；代言人

   She cleans the mouthpiece of her clarinet every day after practices.

   她每天練習完都會清洗單簧管的吹嘴。

4. **vibrate**（*v.*）振動；情感共鳴

   He leans on the rail and senses the vibration of the train approaching.

   他靠在鐵軌上，感覺到火車接近中的振動。

5. **resonate**（*v.*）共鳴；共振；**resonator**（*n.*）共鳴器

The soprano opens her mouth to maximize the resonator.

女高音張開嘴巴以將共鳴腔擴到最大。

6. **rub**（*v.*）擦、摩擦

The first step of making roast chicken is rubbing salt all over the bird.

做烤全雞的第一步是把整隻雞都用鹽抹過。

7. **scrape**（*v.*）刮、擦；擦傷；湊合過日子

She scrapped her leg when climbing over the wall.

她爬過牆的時候擦傷了腳。

8. **strike**（*v.*）打擊、敲擊；感動……；罷工

① The union of bus drivers announced a strike on next Monday.

公車司機工會宣布下周一罷工。

② He was stunned by her striking feature.

他驚豔於她立體的五官。

——————— 29.2 ———————

Music Therapy

Music Therapy is the prescribed use of a qualified therapist to change the psychological, physical, **cognitive**, or social functioning of individuals with health problems such as high blood pressure, speech impediments and various mental disorders. This treatment is particularly helpful for children with special needs since they are diagnosed as having **autism**, ADHD (attention deficit and **hyperactivity** disorder) and **epilepsy**.

Music Therapy can benefit health in many different ways. It can help patients improve oral communication skills, practice physical balance and heal stress and pain. Medical researches proved that music is healthy for the mind when it stimulates brain waves. Strong and fast **rhythms** make people alert. Slow and harmony melodies help people relax and **meditate**.

Therapists need to **assess** the patients before each treatment to understand the strengths and needs of each individual. Suitable practices can thus be tailored. The therapy can be done by listening to music, singing with music, **improvising** or even creating music. Sometime music therapist may encourage patients to move with the music. The treatment can be conducted individually or in a group activity such as discussing music with other members together.

中文翻譯

音樂治療

音樂治療是一種有系統有規定的療法,藉由改善心理、生理**認知**或社交功能等層面,治療病患的高血壓、口吃和各種精神疾病等健康問題。這種療法尤其對特殊兒童有幫助,包括**自閉症**兒童、過動兒和**癲癇症**兒童。

音樂治療對健康多有助益。它可以幫助病人改善口語表達能力、練習肢體平衡,以及治療壓力和痛苦。醫學研究證明音樂可透過刺激大腦電波,使心智更健康。強烈、快速的**節奏**使人警覺;緩慢、和諧的曲調則幫助人們放鬆和**冥想**。

在療程之前,治療師得**評估**病患,了解每個人的能力和需求,才能客製化適合的療法。療程可以是聆聽音樂、跟著音樂哼唱、即興創作甚至創作音樂。有時音樂治療師會鼓勵病患跟著音樂動起來。治療可以是個別病人分開進行,或團體活動讓病人跟彼此討論音樂。

重點字彙

1. **prescribe**（*v.*）開藥方；指定、規定；
   prescription（*n.*）處方；命令、指示、法規

   Please follow the prescription and don't change the dose without consulting the doctor.

   請照著處方服用，沒有問過醫生就不要亂改劑量。

2. **cognitive**（*adj.*）認知的；**cognition**（*n.*）認知

   She was so terrified that she started to show inconsistent cognitions.

   她嚇到開始露出認知不一致的症狀。

3. **impediment**（*n.*）口吃；障礙

   The king suffered impediment for ages until he met the life-changing speech therapist.

   國王曾多年受口吃所苦，直到他遇見改變他一生的言語治療師。

   延伸字彙　deterrent, drag, embarrassment, obstruction

4. **autism**（*n.*）自閉症

   The parents never gave up searching for the best therapist for their autistic son.

   這對父母從不放棄替自閉症兒子找最好的治療師。

5. **hyperactivity**（*n.*）過動、活動亢奮

The society should stop forcing hyperactive children with early medication.

社會應該停止逼迫過動兒太早服藥。

6. **epilepsy**（*n.*）癲癇

Epilepsy response dogs can give warning when someone has or is going to have a seizure.

癲癇照護狗可以在人發作或快要發作時發出警告。

7. **assess**（*v.*）衡量、評估

Every student is required to fill in the teaching assessment form at the end of the semester.

學期末，每個學生都被要求填寫教師衡量表。

8. **improve**（*v.*）改善、提升；**improvise**（*v.*）即興創作

① The working condition has been improved significantly with the new management structure.

新的管理結構上路後，工作環境大幅改善。

② The best man improvised a poem for the new weds on their wedding.

伴郎在婚禮上替新人即興作了一首詩。

9. **rhythm**（*n.*）節奏、韻律

The family loves music so much that even the new born baby can dance in the crib with the rhythm.

這家人愛音樂到連新生兒在嬰兒床裡都會跟著韻律舞動。

10. **meditate**（*v.*）沉思、考慮；冥想

No matter how busy he is, he always finds time to meditate 30 minutes every day.

不管有多忙，他每天都會找時間冥想三十分鐘。

 iBT 新托福字彙閱讀應試技巧

Question 1: Which of the following is match instruments incorrectly with the classification?

(A) Piano > String instrument

(B) Saxophone > Wind instrument

(C) Tambourine > Percussion instrument

(D) Accordion > Keyboard instrument

解析 以上樂器和分類的配對中，選項 (B) 薩克斯風是管樂器，選項 (C) 鈴鼓是打擊樂器，選項 (D) 手風琴是鍵盤樂器，因此答案是選項 (A) 鋼琴，鋼琴通常歸類在鍵盤樂器下，就算不論鍵盤樂而以單純琴弦論起，鋼琴的原理為敲擊琴弦發聲，比較接近打擊樂器。

Question 2: According to "This treatment is particularly helpful for children with special needs". What does it mean for having "special needs"?

(A) Spoiled children who have special requirements for their diet

(B) Naughty children that adults need to put extra attention on

(C) Vulnerable children relying on special medical care

(D) Talented children who can't live without music

> 解析 文中「這種療法尤其對特殊兒童有幫助」，所謂特殊是在於某些兒童比較脆弱，有特殊醫療需求，並不是選項 (A) 寵壞到會挑食，也不是選項 (B) 調皮到大人需要特別看管，更不是選項 (D) 天分高到離不開音樂，因此，答案為 (C) 依賴特殊醫療照護的脆弱兒童。

Question 3: Which of the following does not describe music therapy correctly?

(A) It is a customized practice   (B) It is a one to one treatment

(C) It can help meditation   (D) It can improve speech fluency

> 解析 關於音樂治療的描述，由於診前都要先做評估設計，因此選項 (A) 客製化療法是正確的；緩慢、和諧的曲調則幫助人們放鬆和冥想，因此選項 (C) 可以幫助冥想也無誤；而音樂治療的確可以幫助克服口吃，改善講話流暢度，因此選項 (D) 也正確。但是療法可能是治療師和病人一對一，也可能是病人團體活動，因此答案為 (B)，音樂治療並不限於醫病一對一。

Learn Smart! 057

iBT 新托福學術字彙「勝」經：必背精華版（附 MP3）

作　　　者	楊佳瑜
發 行 人	周瑞德
執行總監	齊心瑀
企劃編輯	饒美君
校　　　對	編輯部
封面構成	高鍾琪

內頁構成	華漢電腦排版有限公司
印　　　製	大亞彩色印刷製版股份有限公司
初　　　版	2016 年 04 月
定　　　價	新台幣 420 元
出　　　版	倍斯特出版事業有限公司
電　　　話	(02) 2351-2007
傳　　　真	(02) 2351-0887
地　　　址	100 台北市中正區福州街 1 號 10 樓之 2
E - m a i l	best.books.service@gmail.com
網　　　址	www.bestbookstw.com

港澳地區總經銷	泛華發行代理有限公司
地　　　址	香港新界將軍澳工業邨駿昌街 7 號 2 樓
電　　　話	(852) 2798-2323
傳　　　真	(852) 2796-5471

國家圖書館出版品預行編目資料

iBT 新托福學術字彙「勝」經 : 必背精華版
/ 楊佳瑜著. -- 初版. -- 臺北市 : 倍斯
特, 2016.04　面 ;　公分. --（Learn
smart! ; 57）
ISBN 978-986-92855-0-6(平裝附光碟片)
1. 托福考試 2. 詞彙
805.1894　　　　　　　　　105003631